The Source

Sarah Sultoon

ORENDA
BOOKS

Orenda Books
16 Carson Road
West Dulwich
London SE21 8HU
www.orendabooks.co.uk

First published in the United Kingdom by Orenda Books, 2021
Copyright © Sarah Sultoon, 2021

Sarah Sultoon has asserted her moral right to be identified as the author of this
work in accordance with the Copyright, Designs and Patents Act, 1988.

A catalogue record for this book is available from the British Library.

ISBN 978-1-913193-59-1
eISBN 978-1-913193-60-7

Typeset in Garamond by typesetter.org.uk

Printed and bound by CPI Group (UK) Ltd, Croydon CR0 4YY

For sales and distribution, please contact info@orendabooks.co.uk

tension, and the further I got, the faster I was turning the pages because I just had to know EVERYTHING'
From Belgium with Booklove

'*The Source* left me angry at the abuse of power and the cover-up, devastated for the long-term effects on the victims' lives ... A remarkable debut from Sarah Sultoon and I can't wait to see what she comes up with next' Novel Deelights

WHAT THE READERS ARE SAYING...

'A hard-hitting and grim story but told in such a way that it's impossible to put down'

'A page-turning debut thriller, beautifully constructed and delivered. For a work of fiction, every word seems real'

'Brilliantly written, with a strong story. Unputdownable'

'One of those books that will have you sneaking off to read it at every available moment ... utterly gripping and wholly convincing'

'A compelling thriller that kept me on my toes until the end'

'I loved this book. Gripping from the first page'

'Her writing drew me in, dragged me under, and so did her characters'

'A fast-paced, intelligent and compelling look at a very difficult subject ... almost horrifically authentic'

'A remarkable debut'

The Source

ABOUT THE AUTHOR

Sarah Sultoon is a journalist and writer whose work as an international news executive at CNN has taken her all over the world, from the seats of power in both Westminster and Washington to the frontlines of Iraq and Afghanistan. She has extensive experience in conflict zones, winning three Peabody awards for her work on the war in Syria, an Emmy for her contribution to the coverage of Europe's migrant crisis in 2015, and a number of Royal Television Society gongs. As passionate about fiction as nonfiction, she recently completed a Masters of Studies in Creative Writing at the University of Cambridge, adding to an undergraduate language degree in French and Spanish, and Masters of Philosophy in History, Film and Television. When not reading or writing she can usually be found somewhere outside, either running, swimming or throwing a ball for her three children and dog while she imagines what might happen if...

Follow Sarah on Twitter: @SultoonSarah.

For Oli, Liora, Guy and Ben

Part One

Marie ~ London ~ 2006

There is a girl. She's standing, at ease, neat and tidy in forgettable grey. Only the clammy fists inside her pockets would give her away, but no one here is going to shake her hand. Next to her, a man. They're partners in this, negotiating shoulder-to-shoulder with the two men opposite.

The transaction is quick – in fact for them, it looks effortless. One production-line-new ride, velvet blush interior, cream finish. Delivery to be arranged in the coming week. No money changes hands, but there is no doubt an agreement is sealed: heads nodded, eyes met, the implications of any transgressions clear from the two brick-set suits casting shadows in the hallway, from the flies buzzing to death on the strip lights overhead.

They're inside a sprawling factory complex just outside the M25. No identifiable marks link it to anything, anywhere. In truth, they easily could just be buying a car.

Except there is a girl. And the girl is me. We've just bought another girl; young, unblemished, untouched and unknown. She's there too, the third shadow, the only one whose outline is trembling in the corridor. No one's looking at her, not even me. Only the camera hidden in my buttonhole that's recording the whole thing.

~~~

'Can we go through it again? Please? Just one last time...'

The window squeaks as I trace circles through the thick condensation. The car's hot with nerves, but there's no way I can open it. Even the trees are listening, rustling with judgement as they watch us sit and prepare to go inside the complex. These buildings look like they rolled off the factory line themselves, but there's nothing as regular inside.

'I've got it, OK?' Dominic sighs as he fidgets. 'It's a simple business deal. We're there to snap up hot property for sale. But the more we talk about it, the less it feels like it. I know this is your first undercover, but I'll be doing it in my sleep soon...'

'*I* won't though, will I? And you still look like you've never worn those before...'

I flick a bead of water at his battered cargo pants and shirt. He thinks I'm only here because his usual producer's black and this lot are racist. She's drilled me at least. That's why I can get away with being so lippy. That's what I tell myself, anyway.

'If I get it wrong then we're both sunk, aren't we? I know it's all we've been dreaming about but we have to do it for real this time...'

Dominic rolls his eyes, wiping the sweat off his neck before his faded collar stains. Sure, he's worn the same costume in plenty of war zones – if the state's news media isn't in service of its military then no one else would join up either, would they? But Dominic's far more comfortable in a dark suit, slithering around corridors of power – so slick he's almost invisible. It's easy to forget who you're talking to when he could be any number of people. Journalists eat double dealing, hidden agendas and ulterior motives for breakfast, lunch and dinner.

'Come on. For me if not for you. What's our answer if he can't guarantee she's still a virgin?' I draw myself another circle as I say it, glaring at the trees shaking their heads at me in the breeze. We're about to negotiate with people farming out underage girls for money. Of course we have to pretend to be like them. They'd never believe us otherwise.

'I told you, I'll handle it. You're not the one doing the talking, are you? You just concentrate on standing there looking surly ... Not too surly, mind. Throw in some smug too. Remember, you're the madame. There's always a madame ... think of yourself as the landlord, if it helps. The landlord of a swanky new flat that's going to make you a killing...'

I shiver reflexively as he scratches at his groin, fiddling with the tip of a tiny camera nestled almost invisibly in his fly.

'Christ ... a camera in my actual pants. Whose idea was this again? I do hope you put the cost of buying a new one in the budget. No other news crews will touch this fella when we're through. Hereafter it will no doubt be known as the ball-cam...'

'Because they won't search you down there. They wouldn't dare. Nothing would be worse than to be seen as doing something gay, even if it's dressed up as self-preservation. They'd shoot themselves first—'

'I say no deal,' Dominic interrupts suddenly, as if we're still talking about the girl we're going to buy. 'There's no other answer. That's what we agreed. It's business, isn't it? That's the only reason we're here. We agreed the goods would be production-line new...'

'Right,' I say, itching at the wires taped flat across my chest. My camera's anchored in my buttonhole because they won't search me there either. I'm well past my sell-by date. 'And what if she's not white? We're going to insist on getting a look at her, aren't we? They won't be able to lie about that.'

'I know, Marie. I know. No deal. Velvet blush interiors are what we agreed.' He plucks at the van's seat, hand slick against the leather. That's the giveaway, right there. As if anyone normal buys a car with velvet seats. I look away as his hand moves back to his groin.

'I'll never get away without it itching at some point. I suppose that'll play OK, won't it ... given the substance of this so-called deal?'

'Well, don't scratch too hard, will you? The camera's toast if you give yourself a stiffy.'

I feel a bit sick as we both laugh. I guess I'm finally getting the newsroom's gallows humour right. But the joke's over before we've even finished – his phone vibrates, shooting tremors through the whole seat.

'We're on,' Dominic mumbles, jamming a cap on to his head with one hand, thumbing the phone with the other. 'It's finally happening. And once it starts, it'll have to finish ... Are you sure you're ready? Marie?'

'Yes, I am. It's just business,' I say, trees nodding with me as we step out of the van, leaves pointing with the wind along the path to the complex gates. There's only one way to go from here.

~~~

Close up, they're not what I expected. The heavies in the corridor, fine, you'd worry if they didn't have muscle, but these two? The main man, the one we've been calling Xenon for all this time – with straight faces – he looks so neat he could be showroom-clean. If the doors next to them swung open to reveal a brand-new Jag, I wouldn't be surprised.

I let my vision blur, looking past them to the wall behind, that curious mix of brown and grey where it could settle on either. It's all a matter of perspective, I suppose. Like everything. Just because these men don't fit my mental picture, doesn't mean they're not the real deal.

My eyes snap back into focus as grunts move back and forth, Dominic sticking to the script. Almost there. Just needs a reference to money. I will myself not to shiver as a bead of sweat trickles down my ribcage, threatening the wires taped to my chest.

There's a sudden jolt as the door opens, framing two more men. I don't need to see Dominic's face to know it looks exactly like theirs. Taut and pale with badly disguised panic, lips pursed so all their questions stay in their eyebrows. The air in the room thickens, like there's smoke creeping in under the door.

'What's this?' Dominic's voice grates, just the right side of harsh. No longer in the corridor, the heavies stand like sentinels either side of our targets. Still the third shadow quivers in the hall.

'We have a last-minute bidder,' Xenon says, grinning. 'There's a lot of demand for rides like this. I'm sure you understand why we have to give everyone a fair go.'

Nobody moves. I don't dare breathe.

'No deal,' Dominic says, sharper edges this time. 'I didn't come here for an auction. It's what we agreed or bust.'

My neck prickles as the latecomers step into the room alongside us. On the face of it, there's now four of us opposite four of them but we all know it's about as equal as knives on butter.

'I'm not sure that's your wisest move,' Xenon replies from between his teeth. 'You won't find anything of this quality on the market elsewhere. I can assure you of that.'

'Well *I'm* yet to approve of its quality,' Dominic snaps, looking towards the corridor for the first time. 'What's to say you're not selling me a dud? Photos never tell the full story, do they? And who does a deal on a photo?'

Pop goes another fly on the light overhead as they eyeball each other. I can't help but flinch as Xenon takes half a slow step to one side, door opening behind him. And now there's nowhere to look other than straight at her, they'll know if we so much as blink.

I let my vision blur again, over the strands of hair bleached lank round her face, the still budding curves that give away her age, the jutting collarbones, the painted nails, the air of desperation and defeat already hanging like a cloak around her body. And the hands, pinning her in place, invisible to everyone but me.

'Careful there,' Dominic drawls. 'If the merchandise gets damaged then no one will buy it—'

'Ten thousand,' a voice interrupts. One of the interlopers; Scottish, curt and sharp. I swallow my sigh of relief as the door to the corridor slams. At least I don't have to look at her anymore. But Dominic, Dominic doesn't skip a beat.

'Eleven—'

'Twelve!'

I freeze as the heavies move in step, improbably lightly, towards the Scot and his lackey.

'You said your maximum was eleven,' Xenon barks at them. 'Lying, were you? There's no love for lies around here.'

I sneak a glance at Dominic, still staring straight ahead. If it wasn't for the muscle twitching in his jaw, he could be made of stone.

'Proof of funds, then. Come on...' Xenon's smile twists as he continues, and it was ugly enough to start with. 'That's if you've really got twelve to barter. And don't you be moving too quickly now...'

My eyes sting with the effort of keeping them straight ahead instead of on the scuffle erupting to my left. One of the heavies lumbers back over to Xenon shaking out a crumpled piece of paper. There's one dense, slow-motion second of squinting before an almost imperceptible nod back towards the muscle.

And then there's a scream.

I don't look, eyes burning into the blank wall. Howls become cries that become pleas as they fade down the corridor into sudden silence, door swinging shut.

I swallow again. The air feels solid, a mass in my throat, a sponge in my lungs. Xenon turns back to us, knuckles white around the ball of paper he's crumpled back into his fist.

'Eleven it is, as it turns out,' he says, another smile spreading immaculate white teeth across his face. For a moment I think he's going to hold out his hand as colour floods back into his fist, but Dominic does it first.

'Instructions will follow,' Xenon says as they shake, Dominic grunting further assent. Then all we've got to do is move one foot in front of the other, round corners and up steps until the gravel of the forecourt crunches under our feet. And only then can we walk with purpose, straight towards the iron gates in the distance, one-two, one-two, pasty spring sunlight catching in our eyes, wind like it's stroking our hair.

That's all we need to feel. Because we did it.

Carly ~ Warchester ~ 1996

'You need to do it before you leave the house,' Rach grumbles, sparking up another tab as we squat in the bushes lining the fence that separates school from Victory Field. 'Like first thing. When you get dressed. What's the point in doing it now? It's not like anyone in this playground is going to give us money for another inch of your skinny knees...'

'Well Timmy said Drina did it with him for a packet of fags,' I mumble, waistband bunching in my fists as I roll it over again.

'And since when do you want to make like Drina? Tesco legs – open all hours?'

She frowns at me, mouth puckered round her cigarette like a cat's arse.

'I don't...' I blush as I fiddle with my skirt. It's got to go shorter. Not even a whistle from the builders on the way in. Let alone any coins. 'I just wasn't thinking, that's all...'

'That's your problem,' Rach interrupts, snapping off a leaf to burn. 'You only think about useless shit. Numbers, puzzles, sums – give you a riddle and you're away with the fairies. But how's dreaming about any of that going to get us any real kicks in this dump?'

The leaf hisses, curling in on itself as her cigarette punches a perfect hole through its middle.

'I'll go the long way home,' I say, poking a finger back into my waistband to smooth out a wrinkle. My finger finds a hole. At least two other girls must have worn this skirt before I got hold of it.

'It's Friday, they'll all be out, trying to finish up early. I'll just walk round and round the block till I get us something. Then if you go home the other way...'

My finger traces the hip bone sharp below my skin.

'That's my girl,' Rach says, snapping off another juicy leaf, all popping veins and plastic green, shrivelling as she burns a perfect four-leaf clover into its middle.

I smile. Suddenly there are four-leaf clovers everywhere as she murders her way through the bush. I've looked for hours, days even, practically mown half of Essex, never once found my own tiny stem of luck. And now Rach has made me loads.

'What's so funny? I'm serious, Carls.' She takes a deep drag, before blowing a cone of smoke into my face. 'You can't go around forgetting about proper stuff. This is how we get ahead. We walk past the same blokes most of the time, all digging the same pointless holes ... Finally we get a new lot because another load more army wives have shown up – because of course what this town really needs is more houses that look the fucking same – and you forget to take advantage?'

'Give over,' I splutter, grabbing for the cigarette packet sticking out of her pocket as she dodges me. 'Is that how you got hold of this little lot, then? Or did you swipe them? Don't tell me you've finally been allowed back down the shop?'

I muddle with the leaves by my feet as I steal a look at my watch. Only two minutes left before the bell goes, but I don't rush, no way. Only Rach knows I actually like maths. The packet hits me in the cheek as she finally tosses it over.

'Doesn't matter, does it? The point is, I got them. You should count yourself lucky I'm sharing with you...'

I finger the plastic around the packet, tracing the letters with my thumb. *Smoking Kills*. Not if something else gets you first, it doesn't. There's another hiss as her lighter flares. I start to cough the minute the smoke hits my throat.

'And I don't know why I bother,' she sighs, bush hissing disapprovingly as she stabs holes in a new clump of leaves.

I blush as I try again. I wish I was fifteen like her. It can't be right that I can do sums better than I can smoke. This time I blow out almost straight away. She smirks as my eyes water.

'Your brother,' she says, jaw clicking as she pops out a perfect smoke ring. 'Is he staying with you tonight?'

'I don't know, do I?' I try not to cough. 'Like there's ever any pattern to when he shows. Since he moved to the barracks he may as well have moved to the moon, learned another language for all I know. We may as well be invisible...' I trail off, eyes still streaming.

At least when Jason was around I could pretend it wasn't just me who had to deal with Ma, Kayleigh and our slowly collapsing house, every day springing a new problem that nothing can fix. At least when he was around I could catch at the memories floating like bubbles on the wind, popping if I dared grab at them too long. When breakfast was Ricicles, when tea was egg and chips, when bedtime was warm, soapy and clean. When everything didn't taste of vodka, didn't smell of burning, or wasn't covered in ash.

'Well, wait up for me then later, OK?' Rach elbows me as she stands, shattering my pile of clovers as she grinds out her tab. 'And don't even try giving me any of that crap about Kayleigh. She'll be dead asleep, won't she? She couldn't climb out of her cot even if she wanted to, and it's not like you're going to be leaving her alone. Unless you're about to tell me your drunk old lady's got it together for once? They'll be good as gold in the house on their own, and they better be, since I've finally found us something else to do in this shithole town.'

I wince as I get up to follow her out, legs numb from crouching, tar still thick in my throat. Best just to remember the colours bubbles turn in the sun, when the light catches them just right.

Marie ~ London ~ 2006

'Slow it down,' Dominic hisses into his cuff as we walk, scratching a non-existent itch on his cheek. The trees nod again, whispering as they lift and fall in the breeze. He's right. They're still watching. Only when we reach the gates does Dominic step in front of me, edging through the side access out on to the shallow pavement fringing the access road back up to the motorway roaring in the distance. Only now can we start to move at a clip, breathing in time with our march along the pavement, van purring up alongside us like a giant, sleek cat. Finally I allow myself a little mental jig, just for a second, just as I climb inside behind him. It's not like anyone can see me, is it?

Dominic exhales, head hanging between his legs, hands strafing through his hair.

'It's over, sunshine. You made it. And you're alright.'

Jemima murmurs as she rests a hand on his shoulder. If the van's a cat then she's its kitten, coiled watchful in the corner. I feel her eyes on the side of my face as her gaze flicks between us, adrenaline coursing through me like an electrical current. It should have been her, Jemima Jonas, the jewel in Nine News's production crown, Crufts-level news pedigree, award-winning trophy cabinet. Except it was me. And she knows it.

'Slow down a sec,' Dominic says, leaning forward into the driver's seat. 'Bill!'

'No way, Dom,' Jemima says, pulling him back. 'We're not far enough...'

Dominic tangles with her, reaching over me to stick his head out of the window.

'No one can fucking see me, Jonas,' he shouts into the wind, closing his eyes, gale thumping our faces as the van speeds on to the motorway.

'Jesus wept,' he yells, bouncing back down between us, all punk hair and manic eyes. 'If all this TV shit doesn't work out then at least I know I could be a pimp. Hah!'

I roll up the windows, meeting Bill's eyes in the rear-view mirror. I don't have to see his whole face to know he's smiling. If I was him, I'd smile too. He wasn't inside.

'Good job, Marie,' Jemima says, flopping back into her seat. 'And if our resident drama queen over here hasn't had enough for one day, shall we see if we actually did the job first rather than congratulating ourselves just for not getting caught?'

'Here we go again,' drawls Dominic. 'Jemima Jonas, Nine News's heart of stone and balls of steel. I just bought myself an underage virgin, for Christ's sake. Every news network in the country will weep for days when this goes out, not to mention those useless suits over at the Met, and you're more interested in giving me grief? It got hairy in there, since you asked. But we're fine, thanks. Just dandy.'

'Hairy? Hairy how?' She snaps open the computer in her lap, stabbing at the keyboard.

'They brought in another pair,' I say, swallowing the heartbeat racing up my throat. 'I thought it was just to jack up our price but they barely let the auction run before belting them—'

'You what?' Dominic interrupts, eyes blazing at me. 'You think all that was just for kicks and giggles? There's teeth still scattered all over the corridor...'

'There wasn't a madame though, was there? Two men. You said it yourself. There's always a madame ... and if it was really about the money, they'd have let it roll a bit longer, surely...'

'They told you that, did they? In the many conversations you've had over the weeks, nay, months, that you've been meticulously developing contacts to get us here in the first place?'

My face burns, even though I'm sure I'm right. Who would do all that just for a measly extra thousand?

'Are you telling me there was a ruck? And you didn't hit the button?' Jemima smacks her laptop closed. 'Tell me, what was the point, what was the bloody point of all our exit planning, all those code words, secret signals, hours of senior-management debate over whether this was too dodgy to even attempt, if on your first sniff of trouble, you just ploughed on like you were bartering over who buys the next round? What do you suppose we would have done if you hadn't come out?'

'We're OK, though,' Dominic spits, balling one hand into a fist in the other. 'Really, we are. Don't you worry about us. We can take this one for the team—'

'Just shut up, Dom, OK? That was the deal, remember? We needed at least a signal that it was all going tits up. You said—'

'I know what I said.' He cuts her off with a volley of knuckle cracking. 'I let it roll. We let it roll. I know what I'm doing, and it worked. We're here, aren't we?'

I fill the car with roaring traffic as I edge down the window. No one's even mentioned the girl, the third shadow, flickering like a ghost in the corridor. Did I at least get a shot of her? Will one jerky frame even be enough? I don't ask though, since they don't seem to care. And then I might have to admit to myself it's the only shot I can remember.

'We'll have to make sure no top brass hear those bits then, won't we?' Jemima says, low under the thudding motorway. 'Of course, that's only if you got it all...'

'Are you alright, Marie?' I jump as Dominic prods me. 'You've gone green...'

'Sorry,' I say, flinching as Bill swerves. 'Don't worry, I never throw up. I just get a bit woozy...' I lean my cheek against the cool glass, cars scudding past in a blur. I wish I'd thought of pretending to be car sick before.

'Take it easy,' Dominic says, resting a hand on my shoulder. 'You did really well in there. Plenty of people, senior producers included, would have pissed themselves before we'd even got through the door.'

I let my head loll like I'm tired. And then I see it. The flicker of movement that's out of place. The purposeful glance of the passenger in the grey VW speeding alongside us.

Staying level with us in the nearside lane just a beat too long. Just enough to check he's got the right van.

'Bill,' I murmur, searching for his eyes in the mirror. 'Do you see that VW on the right?'

'Huh?' Jemima looks up from fiddling with her laptop.

'Stash it,' I say, looking straight ahead as if I haven't noticed a thing. 'The laptop. Quick. And duck, if you can. That car ... something's not right.'

I grip the seat as my adrenaline starts to run again. Of course they're following us. We knew they were pros. We wouldn't have bothered otherwise, would we? Dominic goes rigid next to me.

'There's something in it,' Bill says in a low voice. 'I'm pretty sure they've been tailing us since we got on the motorway. I'm not certain, but I think there could be two of them. There's another van's been sticking behind us since this one pulled out.'

'Shit,' Jemima says, crouching in the footwell. 'Why didn't we anticipate this?' I can almost hear her brain working as I stare into the mirror, frown lines deepening on Bill's forehead. The two cars tighten round us like a cell.

'OK, OK, OK. Where can we go? Where would we go, more to the point.' Jemima cracks her knuckles in her lap. 'Would we go back to work? Home? To the pub? Where would we go if we actually were large-scale criminal perverts and had just done this? Shall we go chuck our phones into the Thames?'

She snorts at herself. There's that gallows humour again. I still don't totally get it. I guess it's only funny to people who think they understand just because they bothered listening.

'Hang on, Jonas. Let me think...' Dominic grips his knees, breath whistling through his teeth.

'They either think we're police or press,' Jemima says to herself. 'Why would they tail us otherwise? They don't give a toss who they are selling to, so long as no one shops them, and so long as they get paid.'

'There are Travelodges all around the M25,' I say, forcing myself to keep staring straight ahead. 'We can just book a room, hole up there for the afternoon, check our tapes and transfer the video while we're at it. We can't afford to let them tail us back to the newsroom so we have to stop somewhere. And it's not unreasonable that we would be meeting others or bunking up somewhere before a flight or train out. The rooms will have safes, we can stash the gear, even leave it there overnight if we have to —'

'Overnight?' I flinch as Dominic interrupts. 'Are you out of your mind? It's taken us months to finally nail this story down and now you want to while away time on some paranoid hunch?'

'Can you put your ego away for a minute?' Jemima fires back at him. 'A few hours won't hurt, and besides, the sooner we stop, the sooner we can look at these tapes which, by the way, are worth nothing unless we can see and hear our beloved perverts—'

'Bill!' I cut them both off as the Travelodge logo whips past on the left.

'I've got you, love,' he says, the car to my right peeling away into the fast lane. 'And we've got company,' he says, exhaling softly. I don't dare turn to check, sudden quiet thrumming through my brain as the motorway falls away.

'This'll shake them off,' I mutter into my collar, checking my camera's still stuck fast inside my shirt. 'They can't afford to cause a scene in a public place. And that's if this is a genuine tail...'

'You'll have to meet us inside, Jonas,' Dominic interrupts, shrill with fury. 'If we're playing along then best we do it right. You were never here, after all...'

'I can assure you, Dominic,' she replies silkily, 'I have every intention of playing along. In fact, I've already made management aware of our new plan. They're fine with it, just in case you were worried about breaking with protocol. And just in case you were planning on calling it in yourself, as we've discussed ad nauseam...'

Their bickering fades out as the Travelodge tower rises up by the kerb, jaunty purple logo like fresh graffiti against the blank-white sky.

I shiver as I get out of the car, cold air slapping my face, batting at the third shadow still trembling in my mind.

Wake up, Marie.

Carly ~ Warchester ~ 1996

Ma's on the sofa, eyes closed, mouth open. At least a packet's worth of fags crowd the ashtray rising up and down on her belly, but, as usual, there's none left for swiping.

Kayleigh's standing, rattling the bars of her cot, so close it's almost in Ma's face. I clatter my keys on top of the telly squawking next to the front door. I know it wasn't always like this when I got home from school, but these days it feels like I'm walking into the same film every afternoon, the same second when someone pressed pause, the same fog of smoke in every corner. Just like yesterday, the week before, the month before, there go Kayleigh's screams again, bouncing off the walls, through my head and back again, opening up new cracks in any memory that's still left. I can't be cross with her though, how could I be? She doesn't know how hard I'm trying to remember how it used to be. She just had the bad luck to be born in the first place.

I leave the door open as I wade through the crap on the floor to rouse Ma. She sits up with a start, ashtray flipping over in her lap.

'She's hungry, Ma. It's gone five. How long's she been in there?' I straighten up, sniffing. I know without looking that Kayleigh hasn't been changed all day. 'Ma! What have you got in?'

But all she can do is blink at me before flopping back down on to the couch, finished before she's even started. I turn my back as I scoop Kayleigh out of her cot, overflowing nappy instantly soaking my shirt.

'We're better off outside,' I murmur as I strip her, squatting on the front step to turn on the outside tap, drowning her filthy clothes in a puddle, letting the breeze wash through the room behind us. And now she's cooing instead of crying, fresh air kissing her naked body, cooling down the rash all over her velvet legs.

'I'm sorry, love.' Ma sniffs in the background. 'I just closed my eyes for a moment...'

I don't turn around. What's the point? It's the same speech as yesterday, as every day. At least she's not slurring. She barely bothers to try then. Instead I pretend I'm wringing Ma's neck as I squeeze Kayleigh's tiny leggings out under the tap, kicking her bloated nappy over to the wall. She hoots as I flick water into her face, clapping her hands, tummy wobbling as she laughs. It's so swollen I can tell myself she's eating right, even though I know it's because she's not. And the tinkle of her giggles and rushing water makes it easier to forget I am washing my angel baby sister, again, from an outside tap on the pavement. It wasn't supposed to be like this. It wasn't for me, least I don't think it was. Why should it be for her?

'I did give her some lunch. Or was it breakfast? I gave her ... What did I give her? Now, I know I've got some beans in. She loves beans...'

I roll my eyes, tucking Kayleigh inside my jacket as we sit, damp, on the step. I wish the clouds would part for just a moment and let the sun dry her instead of my shitty school blazer. This is a blazer that's dried a thousand other wet and screaming kids already.

'Yes, I gave her cereal. That's it. So she's had some milk at least ... Now, let me see...'

There she goes again, trying and failing to get up. I listen to Kayleigh suck her thumb instead, moving her body into the watery sunshine lighting the puddle around us. Her eyelashes flutter on her cheek as she spreads her toes into the breeze. I rest my chin on her head, wondering if Ma ever did this for me, once upon a time. Before she started doing anything for any scrounger that told her she had a nice smile.

'OK my angel,' I murmur as the clouds roll across the sun. 'Let's get you some beans.' A whistle screeches through the air as I stand, a construction truck rattling suddenly past. I close the door on a volley of catcalls. No need to try and work it when Rach isn't around to check.

'Where are these beans, Ma?' I spy an open packet of nappies by Kayleigh's cot. Thank God it's not a rinse-and-repeat day. She'd be like a lump of plasticine if she was fed right, round marble eyes staring as I change her. The telly's bright colours take over the entertaining as I suddenly remember my own shirt is still full of wee.

'You know you can't leave her in her cot all day,' I snap, unbuttoning my shirt as Ma starts to sob softly on the sofa. 'Just sit outside on the step if you can't actually go anywhere. You can even crawl with her if you have to...'

I turn my back on her hacking and coughing as I take the two steps into the kitchen in my bra. Three cans of beans are lined up all new and shiny on the otherwise filthy counter.

'Where did these come from?'

I peer round the doorframe as Ma blows her nose into her T-shirt.

'Your brother came by,' she says, pleating the rim of her shirt between her fingers. 'He might even be back tonight, he said.' She looks up at me, blinking like she's the child. 'He ... he left a few things...' She gestures into the kitchen.

I yank open the fridge door to find unopened packets of cheese and ham gleaming on the shelf. A bag of apples, a loaf of bread, even yoghurts, all stupid smiley-face labels. Yoghurts! I glare at Ma as I crouch down next to Kayleigh, spooning as fast as she can swallow. If the telly weren't on I think she'd try and drink the stuff, she's so hungry. And as usual I find her battered baby cup under a pile of filth in her cot and need to rinse it over a similarly filthy pile of dishes in the sink. I stare through the porthole window at the blank wall of the block opposite as water splashes over my hands. All these army houses look exactly the same from the outside, lined up next to each other like they're the soldiers. But if anyone came inside this one by mistake they'd think they'd shown up on an enemy base.

I bang the cup against the counter before taking it out to Kayleigh, furious with Ma still heaped on the sofa, wrinkled and slumped like the pile of dirty washing that doesn't even hide the holes in the carpet. She looks so close to dead that I don't know how she can still be alive. If I stop and think about it, I reckon it started even before Kayleigh was born. She just stopped being capable, I guess. Too many scroungers will do that to you. The army thinks that paying out a dead soldier's pension is the least it can do. In the name of God and Country, all that shit. Actually that free money just loops a bullseye around some already pathetic widow's neck.

Cold air suddenly blasts back into the room as a key rattles in the lock and the door swings open. Too late, I remember I'm still basically naked from the waist up. I snatch up Kayleigh and cuddle her across my chest as I shiver in the shadow of my brother in the doorframe.

'A welcoming committee, I see,' Jason says. 'Is that your best underwear?'

The room darkens as he closes the door, uniform creaking as he steps towards me. All shiny boots and starchy collar, this dump makes him look like he's wearing a costume, especially since he's got a laundry bag folded under his arm, of all things. I step back and stumble as he reaches out to pet Kayleigh, paddling my arm with his fingers as he grabs my shoulder.

'Have you gone sick in the head now, too?' I shrug into his hand. 'Like you should even be looking. Freak.'

He plucks Kayleigh out of my arms, smirking as I duck and ferret around on the floor for something to cover myself.

'So you get your kicks these days from hawking cheese and ham to your own family? What happened? Did the army kick you out? Not good enough for active duty?' I gabble defensively as I pull on a T-shirt.

'There's no need for all that, is there, sis? If I was in the field, who'd sort you lot out?' He croons down at Kayleigh, tickling her chin. 'We can't help having a swot for a sister, can we?'

My cheeks burn.

'And you think you're not? Don't give me that crap about living to serve ... Folding clothes right, dressing right, even shaving right, like that's different from learning in school? Just because it's not in a classroom doesn't make you any less of a nerd...'

Kayleigh coos as he laughs.

'Fighting talk, Carls. It's times tables that make you really intelligent, is it?'

Something explodes inside me as Ma titters on the sofa. I'm suddenly so angry I can barely see, let alone breathe through the fog in this tiny room. Once, it smelled of wet, clean washing — didn't matter there wasn't room to move when it was all hung up, because it turned the place into the inside of a flower, I could even play between its petals. Sometimes it smelled of cooking – I could breathe in a full tummy's-worth before I got to eat it too. If I dig around enough I can even remember the smell of felt tips. Now it just stinks of regret and despair.

'What do you think you're fighting for, anyway? A bigger house, or a car? Some new pointless piece of metal to wear on your shirt? What's the prize? Which bit of the country do we get if you knock someone's block off? Like the army has ever done anything other than completely screw this family up.'

He rounds on me, Kayleigh yelping as he grips her tighter.

'Listen, little sister,' he hisses. 'Don't fuck with what you don't get. Stick to your playground – even though the army built that, along with everything else in this town. This whole country's built on the army, every country lucky enough to call itself one is. We're nothing without the military. You want to play by someone else's rules, have aliens call the shots instead? You get to sleep at night with people fighting for you, every second of every minute of every day, and you just haven't got a fucking clue, have you? Look around you.' He waves a meaty hand in the air, at the whole rotten jumble we're supposed to be grateful for. 'You should be proud. Even Rach gets it.'

He smiles as I start to cry. The killer blow. Because what I really care about is the fact that Rach saw him before I did. She's not his sister. And now Ma's weeping too; of course she is.

'Pack it in, would you?' I sniff as I snap at her. 'Like it's nothing to do with you that we lost all the money we ever had? The only useful thing you've ever done is knock up with a squaddie in the first place, and even he was a loser who got himself killed before he could give a proper shit. And now look at us. Where's all his danger money gone? All our insurance? That's what they called it, right?' I wipe my cheeks, reaching for Kayleigh as she bleats for me.

'I swear spongers must just hang around Warchester, waiting for people to die, waiting to take advantage of where the latest chunk of change has been dropped in exchange for some squaddie who lost his life in some other shit-hole that's worth nothing to anyone normal. If this town's built on the army, then the army's built on death. There's no easier place to go scrounging if you know that. And Rach wouldn't get anything unless it came with a free packet of fags. Which is obviously how you got her fawning all over you.'

I cuddle Kayleigh tighter as she snuffles into my shoulder.

'It's our duty, Carls,' he mumbles, bending to scoop piles of laundry into his bag. 'All of ours, especially the ones of us living here. That's what she gets. Fags or not, she's smart enough to get it. That's the real intelligence, right there. And you're the one that's the swot.'

He snorts as Ma snivels, weeping on and on and on.

'Like I don't understand duty,' I mumble into Kayleigh's head.

Jason slings the bag over his shoulder as he straightens up, looking from Ma to us and back.

'What else does she need?' He jerks his head at Kayleigh. 'And you? Come on, spit it out.'

'Well, Ma needs a lobotomy, so she remembers what life is supposed to be like around here – you know, breakfast, lunch and dinner, showers, cleaning and shopping – the shit that army wives pick up even if they've been left solo and pathetic because it's all in the name of empire, right? And Kayleigh, well, she could use some clean clothes, regular meals, a few toys and stories, some cuddles – everything we apparently got when we were little, before some war took over someplace and killed everyone. And I could do with going to school without wondering whether either of them are going to be dead too when I get back—'

The words are still in my throat as the door slams, shaking the walls but nowhere close to bringing them all down. I can hardly tell Jason what I really need, can I? He'd know if he hadn't left us behind. Just like that, here we are again, suspended in the same spot on the same film, in the same endless looping nightmare; nothing to do and nowhere to be except wait for him to come back, or someone to change the tape. And in this town, it's only war that ever really does that.

I cradle Kayleigh, untangling pale hairs from her chubby fingers as she swats at my head. At least Rach said she'd visit later. That's a level up from nothing I guess.

Marie ~ London ~ 2006

Dominic kicks off his shoes, flinging himself on the bed. He's either groaning or sighing – whichever it is, I wish I couldn't hear it. My legs tremble as I turn away from him, propping myself against the window.

'I forgot to get the Wi-Fi code,' I murmur, breath fogging the glass as I stare outside. The cars on the tarmac below look like abandoned toys. I itch to poke them with a finger, knock one over, start a commotion somewhere else.

'Good thing, too. Far too banal for a load of paedo kingpins, if anyone was honestly listening.' I turn to see him sitting up, all socks and overcoat. 'Didn't you bring the laptop?'

'No. I wasn't carrying it to start with so...'

He groans again, flopping back on to the quilt.

'We need to wait for Jonas anyway, don't we?' Just saying her name makes me prickle with relief. She won't be, can't be, more than a few more minutes. Then there'll be three of us in here.

'I suppose,' he mumbles, sitting up again as he fiddles with the camera in his fly. 'I'm taking this out now though. If only because I need a slash.'

I jump as there's a soft tap on the door, relief curdling to alarm. It's too soon for it to be Jemima.

Dominic straightens up, shoving wires back into his pants. 'Seriously? Even Jonas can't move that fast...' Now there's a chime, like whoever's outside forgot they could just ring the bell. 'Where in God's name are my shoes...' He stands, smoothing down his hair. Another chime, another curse as he shoves a foot into the wrong shoe.

'Maybe it's room service? Or housekeeping?'

I cough, trying to hide the note of panic. We didn't request any-thing special. Just a suite. We're here on business, we said. Like we've been saying all day.

'I don't recall asking for extra pillows when I demanded the penthouse, do you?'

The doorbell chimes again. Whoever it is knows we're in here else they'd give up.

'Do we have to answer it?' Dominic mumbles to himself. 'Wait...' He kicks off his shoes again. 'Take yours off too, can you? Rumple yourself up, mess up your hair ... Quick! At least make it look like we might have been interrupted...' He fades as I turn back to the window, willing that a car might explode below us, anything to change the course of the next few seconds.

'Yes?' Dominic's voice floats, somewhere behind me. I squint into the glass, inside of the room outlined back at me. He's up against the door.

'Sir?' The doorbell chimes again.

'Yes? Can I help you?' *Sir*. It can't be them. I lean my head on the glass. Suddenly my neck feels like even holding my head up might make it snap.

'If you could just—'

'Hang on, hang on...' he interrupts, reflection fidgeting and bus-tling behind the door. I sidestep along the wall, out of vision. There's a squeak as the door cracks open, a rustle of voices. Dominic's? And then another click. The window stares back at me, blank-white with early-spring sky.

'The Wi-Fi password...' Dominic hisses, exhaling all his tension into the room. 'They forgot to give it to us. Jesus wept ... he even apologised, since we're in one of their alleged SuperRooms ... Hah!'

I twist round to find him flat on the bed again, clutching a bottle of wine in one hand, slip of paper in the other. Now he won't even notice that I didn't rumple myself up.

'Why didn't he just call? Why come all the way upstairs?'

'Because he also wanted to give us this,' he says, sitting up, brandishing the bottle like a weapon. 'Gift, apparently. Hang on...' He squints at the tag round the neck. '"Congratulations". Congratulations? Marie, what the fuck are you doing?'

I'm at the door before I even realised I've moved, clicking the inside lock, latching the chain.

'It's on our purchase,' I say. 'Congratulations. We haven't sealed the deal yet, have we? They want us to know they're still watching...'

I grip the chain, so powerless and flimsy between my fingers that I can't stop the third shadow flashing back into my mind, nor the whispers needling in my ear. *Never get comfortable, never assume it's over.* And now I'm really flailing, as there's another tap on the door, Dominic's hand suddenly tangling over mine. It should be clammy and hot but it's cool and smooth and...

'It's Jonas, Marie, come on...'

I yank away my hand as I stumble backward, crashing into the bed. A click and suddenly Jemima's there, standing calm, composed, a giant oak in a storm. Except she's angry, mega-cross, eyes practically throwing sparks on the carpet.

'Champagne?' she hisses, head swivelling from me to Dominic. 'Are you serious? We haven't even checked the tapes yet and you're skinning us on expenses?'

Dominic wraps an arm around her, finger against his lips, yanking her away from the door and on to the bed beside me. Even though her eyes are still blazing, she lets him touch her like there's no world in which it could be a threat. I look away.

'Look,' he whispers, shoving the bottle into her lap. 'Congratulations, see? They're watching us ... Did anyone see you come in?'

Jemima whistles as she fingers the tag.

'Jonas? Did anyone see you or not?'

'No,' she mutters, turning the label over and over in her fingers. 'I ducked through the fire escape. It was already open. And now I know why...'

The bottle rolls forgotten to the floor as she thumbs through her phone, muttering into the receiver. Think we've been followed. No immediate danger. Will check in every five minutes until you get here. Yes, we're checking the video while we wait.

She hangs up, staring at the phone in her hands like it might burst into flames at any second. I shake my head as its screen flashes with acknowledgment. Unbelievable. Just like that, the newsroom machine's coming to bail us out. All it took was one shout. Just the one emergency call.

'How did you know?' Dominic looks like a ghost in front of me. 'All that from a bottle of fizzy? I don't understand...'

'It doesn't matter now,' Jemima mutters, pulling her laptop from the bag at her feet. 'All that matters now are the goods.'

I scurry back towards the window, unlacing the camera inside my shirt as Dominic fumbles in his pants. At least now we're back to business. Just like them.

'Try it again, come on. Just reboot the whole thing,' Dominic hisses from behind me. As I twist round, I see it – grainy but it's there. That's our main man and he's right there on Jemima's computer screen. I practically bound back across the room, camera cables dripping from my outstretched hand. The shot flickers, goes black and then flashes up again.

'It can't be...' Dominic mutters as he stabs at the keyboard, pulling out the camera cable and reattaching it. 'Hang on...'

Jemima slumps, pulling headphones out of her ears.

'That's him, isn't it?' I say, hopping from foot to foot as I peer down at the laptop. 'We're golden, aren't we? What's wrong?'

I jump as Dominic flings the camera on to the bed, trailing wires flicking up into our faces.

'There's no audio,' Jemima says, through her teeth. 'Here...' I stare at the earbud she passes up to me. 'And without audio, that's just some fat guy in a suit he thinks still fits him.'

I gaze at the midriff wobbling on the screen. I can tell you every last letter of what he's saying, but no one else, not even Dominic, would have a clue. And he was there. The shot goes dark again as Jemima switches his camera for mine.

'Ssshhh, would you?' She swats at Dominic pacing behind her.

'This has literally never happened to me before. Literally. Never.' We all jump as the floorboards creak under his feet. 'Was all of it brand-new? You said it was...'

'Really? A microphone has never failed before? Especially on a hidden camera? Particularly one stashed between a cock and balls?'

I hold my breath as a shot flashes up on screen again. This time it's my shot. And this time, you can actually see his face. I have to look away, the sky, white beyond the window, inviting as virgin snow. And then I am lost somewhere between a cascade of relief and a flood of disgust, batting away clumsy hugs and shushing yelps of victory, all the while with a voice in my ear promising a virgin ride, production-line new, the absolute best on the market. Yanking out my earbud, I listen transfixed as Jemima mutters rapid-fire instructions into her phone, mesmerised by the blue line on the computer screen confirming the successful transfer of our precious video file. Yes, they've got it, yes, they've checked it, yes, they'll download it immediately and save it in multiple places, yes, of course no one will accidentally use it and no, don't be absurd, we're not staying on the line for anything other than word that the network's security vans are ready and waiting for us outside.

I smile back as Jemima beams up at me.

'What now?' I push my cheeks higher, make my temples sting. Make it real. It almost is, if not for the shadow trembling behind the fat guy in a suit he thinks still fits.

'We go home,' she says, stuffing cables into her bag as she snaps the laptop shut.

I sway on my feet, face slumping like melting ice. Home. Whatever that means. The absolute last place that I want to go.

Carly ~ Warchester ~ 1996

I lie fully dressed on my bed in the dark, Kayleigh's soft snoring tickling my ear. I've been putting her down to sleep with me most nights lately, tucked in tight between my pillow and the wall. I love watching her little chest lifting up and down, her eyelids flickering with the glow stars on the ceiling as she dreams. When Ma named her I went nuts at first ... Kayleigh and Carly? As if another scrounger's baby wasn't bad enough, after he conned her out of all our money? Now though, I love it. Kayleigh and Carly. We're two halves of a whole, same blue eyes, same pale hair, that spooky colour somewhere between white and yellow that I've only ever seen on our heads. Even our star signs make a raggedy circle on the ceiling, her Aquarius pushing out to one side, lighting up my knackered old Libra stuck next to it. We match.

She stirs as the wind taps the blind against the half-open window, cool night air stroking our faces as I lean over to settle her. In that moment I can pretend the noise drifting in from the estate is a tinkly stream and not breaking glass. But then a handful of gravel hits my chin and I spot Rach, grinning up at me through the gap, white stripes of bare legs gleaming in the dark under her tiny school skirt.

Rearranging my pillow so Kayleigh can't roll, I head out, throwing the usual glare at Jason's empty old bed against the wall opposite. Downstairs, Ma is still heaped on the sofa where I left her, either asleep or dead. Another waste of space. Like pretty much everyone and everything else around here except Rach.

I hang around for just one more minute, hands still warm from

Kayleigh's little body. She's as safe as I can make her, I think, palms closing into fists as I push my way outside. I think I might suffocate if I stayed in here any longer.

'Hey girl. You alright? No dramas?' Rach hands me a cigarette as I close the door.

'No more than usual.' Freshly painted purple nails gleam as her lighter flares into my face. 'Wow, those look ace. How'd you manage that? Where are we going? If you tell me we're off to meet the usual lot again I'm going back inside...'

I rest myself against the door as I say it, making sure it's shut tight. She knows there's no way I want to go back in there. The smoke hits my throat and I cough straight away.

'I can't hardly take you anywhere if you're still doing that.' Rach's nails suddenly look like claws as she leans towards me. 'You need to breathe deeper ... pretend like it's a pipe, look...'

Perfect hoops of smoke fan out around my head into the night air as we walk away. I try again and splutter almost immediately.

'Carls. This is worse than having to teach you how to do your bra up by yourself...'

'It's totally different. How stupid is that? Having to do them up behind your back? This is like breathing poison air...'

'Well everyone who's anyone's breathing it,' she says, pulling me to a stop.

I fluff my hair into the breeze as I gaze up at her. I knew Libra would be an air sign before I even found out for sure, Aquarius too. I love the feeling of real air, on my face, in my lungs, rushing through my whole body. But Rach is an Aries, she doesn't care about any of that. It's just my bad luck she's a fire sign.

'So what's up with tonight?' I smile in spite of myself. At least Kayleigh and I can fly away together, when she grows up. Librans and Aquarians are meant to be.

'You have to promise you'll do what I tell you, OK? No whinging or squealing...'

'I always do, don't I? What else would I do otherwise?'

She frowns at my cigarette burning down to a finger of ash in my hand.

'Sorry,' I mumble as I look away. 'Turns out Jase was planning to show up today, but legged it almost as soon as he opened the door. Didn't help that Ma practically pissed herself. She can't hear Kayleigh screaming and starving from a centimetre next to her but she's all smiles for Jase. Doesn't matter how long he's been gone, or what he's done...'

I trail off as I look up to find her sweeping open her blazer, all mad grinning and drama, jigging from foot to foot. In the dark, I can't be sure...

'Poppers? No way ... Rach!' A row of mint new caps poke out of her bulging inside pocket. Real, box-fresh poppers.

'Where did you get those,' I whisper, fingertips brushing rough cotton as I stretch out towards them. 'Actual laughing gas instead of poison air...'

'Wouldn't you like to know,' she says, pulling me down the road. 'They're ours, that's all that matters. Just for us, just for me and you. And poppers aren't laughing gas, Carls, for fuck's sake. This isn't for kicks and giggles, we're not twatting about with a bunch of schoolkids anymore. But we need to go somewhere first, OK? I promised.'

I fall in step beside her, head spinning. 'Promised who? Don't tell me you and Drina actually made up?'

'As if. Forget about her. I said, didn't I? No more dicking about with that pathetic school lot. This is the real deal ... if we ever bloody get there, that is...'

She speeds up as she ducks off the road into Victory Field, any four-leaf clovers hiding in the grass turning to mush under our feet as we head towards a clump of bushes on the other side of the lawn, lining the tall fence between the edge of the barracks and the park. The curls of barbed wire on top are so sharp I can see them even in the moonlight.

'It's just through here,' she whispers over her shoulder as she pushes through a gap in the bushes near the edge of the fence. 'Come on, look lively, will you?'

She twists and turns through the brambles until she suddenly stops dead. It's so dark I don't realise till I step on the back of her heel.

'Hey,' she stutters as she stumbles, fluffing her hair. 'Are you...?'

'Private Adrian Thomas,' a voice says from somewhere up ahead in the dark. 'But you young ladies can call me Tommo.'

Young ladies? Rach titters as I peep from behind her at a tall, lanky shadow leaning against the fence.

'Hey, Tommo,' she says again, all squeaky, elbowing me as she fumbles for a tab.

'Hey yourself.'

I freeze as he steps towards us. Cap, uniform, boots, the lot. A real squaddie. Exactly like Jason, except he's pleased to see us. There's a click as her lighter flares.

'And who's this?'

Rach shoves me forward.

'Carly,' I say, squinting at the badge on his shirt, same as Jason's. He smiles as he looks down on me.

'Well hello there, Carly. You must be Corporal Gates' sister...'

'Yeah, she is,' Rach answers for me as my jaw drops. 'He said you'd meet us here...'

'For sure he did,' Tommo says, grinning. 'We're having a little party tonight. Would you girls like to come? We'll get you home before dawn, don't worry.'

'Jason told you to meet us?' I sound as foggy as I feel. Why would he do that?

'That's right,' he says, taking another step towards us. 'He thought you might enjoy yourselves. And we'd love to have you. Come on, it'll be fun.'

Rach grabs his hand almost as soon as he starts holding it out.

'He can't have...' I mumble as I stare at them, two tall, skinny shadows beaming at each other. 'I only just saw him and he didn't say anything...' A light flicks on in one of the windows in the distance.

'He wants you to come,' Tommo says, still staring at Rach. 'We all do. It won't be a party without a crowd, will it?'

'We do love a party,' she says, drawing her tab down to the filter before dropping it into the dirt and reaching for me.

'Hang on,' I say as her hand tightens around my arm. 'You mean we're going in there?' I jerk my head towards the barracks buildings crouched low beyond the fence.

'We're off duty,' he says, eyes twinkling as he looks at me. 'It's time to let our hair down. Not that any of us have got much to let down, mind you, regulations being what they are...'

Rach laughs like it's the funniest thing anyone's ever said. Shadow passes over us as a crow flies over the moon.

'I'm not allowed into the barracks,' I say, panic rising in my throat. 'None of us are, unless visiting's officially on. Not even Ma...'

I trail off as I remember. How Jason banned her from even walking past the main entrance. Like her gigantic Kayleigh-belly was proof to the whole of Warchester that some scrounger was about to leg it with all her army money. Like we ever really had a right to it in the first place. So what if I had a dad who was killed in action? He was gone before he even knew my name. He probably never remembered Jason's.

'Now I can tell you're a Gates,' he says, cocking his head. 'You know which rules are worth keeping. That's why your brother's going to make sergeant in record time. You're right, of course. Officially. But when off-duty calls, all bets are off. Being off-duty's as important as being on, if you ever want to be successful in combat.'

'She's up for it, aren't you, Carls?' Rach's grip tightens on my arm.

'Come on,' Tommo says, smiling. 'Be off-duty with us. No one does off-duty better than the army.'

'Good girl,' Rach hisses between her teeth, and I find myself nodding.

Maybe Jason does get it, I think, remembering him clearing the room of dirty laundry faster than I could blink, hating myself for imagining the bright and shiny fresh food all stacked up in the fridge. Maybe he just can't say so. It's not like I ever can either, is it? The right words don't come even when I try and get some out.

We follow as Tommo leads us along the edge of the fence to a small opening between the bars almost totally hidden by brambles. It's so tight I have to hold my breath to squeeze through. There's a low hiss as a small camera mounted on the top of a fence post swivels and points straight at us as we slip towards the inner fence.

'Don't worry about that,' Tommo says, guiding us through a side gate hidden within the bars. If he hadn't pushed on the right one no one would ever know it could open. 'It's been dead for months. Still looks but it can't see...'

We quickstep across a low-lit path to a door in the side of a low building. Tommo turns and smiles, holding his other hand out to me. Rach hasn't let go of him since we met.

'Let's get this party started,' she says as she steps towards him.

I find myself smiling too as his hand closes over mine. It's rough and warm, like Jason's. I suddenly want to believe he asked for us to come too. I want to believe it so badly, I feel faint.

Music, chatter, laughter, all drift into the air as the door opens, a peek into a world turning just how I think it should, except I lost whatever place I had in it sometime I can't even remember. Others would just hear noise, but to me it sounds like harmony – reasons to keep walking down the same messed-up streets day after day after day, because they might be finally taking you somewhere else.

What else could I do other than keep walking? There's less than nothing left if I turn around. Tommo keeps hold of my hand as I follow him inside.

Marie ~ London ~ 2006

My trainers thump the old canal path skirting this length of the Thames as I run, chasing my own shadow as it disappears and re-appears with every dim street light that scuds past. Filthy river water puddles in every cracked paving stone but I keep my balance, of course I do, feet skimming over obstacles I know better than my own footprints. I've cased this path's every hiding place, witnessed every fumble in the dark, crunched through every discarded needle, the lot. This path's skeleton is as familiar as mine; anyone tries anything with me here and I'll know before they do. Faster, faster ... the rush of blood in my ears and ache in my lungs crowding out every memory of the warehouse, every ripple of fear as I remember how close we came to getting caught. Fear gives way to the rush of adrenaline as my body pops its emergency tank, skidding as I turn to retrace every thump back along the path towards my flat, faster still, till there is nothing I could possibly think about other than my pounding ears, trembling legs, stinging ribs.

Only as I reach the low wall bordering the edge of my estate do I stop, bracing my hands on my hips as I gulp my heartbeat back down my throat, turning a slow circle on the spot to scan for any surprises. The canal path's one thing, but this estate can turn on a pin.

'Long one, was it?' Alfie, number seventy-five, grins as he shuffles past, through the main gate. I'm breathing so hard he doesn't expect an answer. That's another reason I do it. I hawk instead, hitting the ground with a smack.

'Delightful. And still jogging, I see?'

I look up with a start to find Julie, all overcoated-up, clacking along the pavement to lean on the wall beside me. Julie, her frizzy hair framing her head like it's a lightbulb. Never gets any longer, never gets any shorter, no matter how many months, even years, pass between our meets. Just gets curlier, like it's resisting growing any more. It's pretty clever, when you think about it.

'What are you doing here?' I hawk again rather than look her in the face.

'You've been missing your appointments. You know that though, right? So surely you know that I do too?'

There's nothing left in my throat to hawk so I kick at the ground instead.

'Haven't I been going long enough that we can finally drop all the talking? I've got nothing else to say…'

A bus accelerates past, into the silence between us.

'You know the deal, girl. It's a requirement. You can jog away all you like—'

'I was on a story,' I interrupt, looking up. Who jogs? I run, never jog. 'A big one, massive, actually. Proper undercover-bust stuff, we've been working on it for weeks. It will even be in the newspapers too, soon enough.'

'I'm sure it was,' she says, smiling. 'But it doesn't change the fact you need to show up, on time, on schedule, and talk. Or sit in silence if they decide that does the job. But you have to check in, you know that. And it's my job to make sure you do. It will always be my job to check in on you. I'm your sponsor for life, love. You couldn't get rid of me even if you wanted to.'

'Fine,' I say as I straighten up. 'Fine. I'll go next week, OK? Wouldn't miss it for the world. But it's a bit much for social services to send you to chase me, isn't it? All that banging on about no cash but you can pony halfway across the country to remind me to clock in?'

'That's the headline news at your network? The lack of funding for social services?'

She stares at me, those intense eyes that have always felt like they can see into my brain. I can never drop her stare no matter how hard I try.

'Sorry,' I say, trying to look at the frizz round her head instead. Of course it's not news. No one gives a toss about social services. I only know because Dominic rants about it.

'So how are you doing?' Julie asks me again.

'I said fine, didn't I?'

'You don't look fine. You look skinny, knackered ... haunted.'

'It's just the dark hair,' I say, pulling at the strands on my neck. 'Occupational hazard when your face looks like paper to start with. Can I go now? Or do we need to talk about the haircut as well? All I said was to cut it shorter but she may as well have shaved it off.'

'I'm not stopping you,' she says. 'But you're on a short leash, OK?'

'Always nice to see you,' I mumble over my shoulder, beating a path to the main entrance. I mean it, even though it sounds like I don't. And she knows it too.

Seven floors up, round two corners and I'm in, leaning against the closed door. I guess I'm lucky to get to live in one, but I'm never sure how I really feel about these flats. The doors are so solid, that along with their tiny windows, it's almost impossible to break and enter unless you're the size of a five-year-old. But it's also almost impossible to get out quickly. Nothing holds those doors open, not even both hands and a foot. It takes a whole body.

I slouch against the door for my quick mental circuit. The kettle's still plugged in under the only window, waterline where I last left it. The sofa watches and waits along the back wall. No cushions, just a tidy pile of pillows and blanket. Nothing on the table in front except a remote control, still lined up perfectly with the corner of the table opposite my small tub of a television. Yanking open the fridge, I collect up the usual: apple, unopened block of cheese, king-sized slab of chocolate from the neat stacks of identical items on the top shelf. As I walk the few steps to the sofa, I feel the trance sweep over me, soothing, like a chill breeze on a sticky day. I've done this so many times now that I could do it unconscious. It's the only form of control I know.

First, the cheese, unwrapping the waxed paper like it's the present I know it will be. Trainers up on to the table, I stretch, quiet dripping into my bones as grease coats the inside of my cheeks. Now for the chocolate and its sexy purple foil. Perfect oblongs, two chunks each, snap, snap, snap, fingers turning brown. The factory strip lights flash into my mind as the lamp on the balcony flickers. *Can I be assured it will drive well? I need to be assured no one has ever driven it before.* I rub at my head, sugar stinging my teeth as I flick on the telly, turning up the cymbals of the Nine News intro. From this angle, the presenters look perfect, all immaculate swirls of blush and hair. But I know that up close, all they look like is a pair of clowns, makeup and hairspray grease-paint thick. It's just the right type of grooming for these particular cameras.

The apple crunches in my ears, lumps catching in my throat as I swallow. I wonder what Dominic's doing now? Is he lying in the dark, staring at the ceiling, reliving everything we'd become in his head? Does he feel relieved, scared, or neither? Blank and empty, like there's nothing inside him anymore? My tummy gurgles. It's finally time, I think.

Standing, I reach for the empty bin in the corner, checking its liner is tightly wound around the wire rim before holding it between my legs to sit back down. My eyes travel the kinks of white plastic pooling at the bottom as I count slowly down from five. Mouth open, fingers in, and it takes less than thirty seconds to get it all out. I don't even need to cough.

And there it is, all tumbled into the bottom of the bag, a solid scream from my deepest insides. It's all out. Every last bit.

In one swift motion, I loosen the plastic liner, looping the end around my wrist. There's a rubbish chute at the end of the balcony, by the lift. Flushing's too good for this particular scream. I don't want it washed clean. Filth like this could only ever be buried intact.

There's a spring in my step as the door slams behind me.

Carly ~ Warchester ~ 1996

'What's your name?' The glass separating us from the woman in the cubicle makes her face look dirty.

I mumble back at her, distracted. There's a bowl of condoms on the other side of the glass next to her, separate bright plastic packets all jumbled together like sweets.

'CARLY,' Rachel shouts next to me. The clock ticking just above her head says we should totally be in maths. I rub my eyes.

'Knackered, are you?'

I elbow Rach as she smirks. I'll never admit it. This kind of tired is worth it. It means something other than staying up with Kayleigh because she's more teeth coming in, or figuring out which shop I haven't swiped milk from recently enough that I can get away with doing it again. Never mind wondering whether kids can eat spam from a tin.

'Take a seat,' she says, nodding at the plastic bucket chairs lined up on the wall behind us as she scribbles on the pad in front of her. I scowl as I catch the eyes of two other women leaning on a filing cabinet. One of them keeps nodding over at me as they carry on talking. As if she could possibly know our story.

'We'll call you,' the woman says, sharper, as she looks up to find me still standing there.

Rachel pulls me over to the chairs in the far corner. I pleat my skirt between my fingers as I sit. I don't know why we have to wait. We're the only ones in the room.

'How good was last night?' Rachel swings her legs, hands tucked under her thighs. 'And I forgot to tell you, Drina actually asked if she could come with us yesterday.'

I giggle, leaning back into my chair. Suddenly it's OK that maths is rolling by, somewhere else. There's no chance I'll end up like Ma if I can pull this off. Detention will be worth that at least. Like our nights at the garrison, where we're suddenly worth more than anything else could be, just for being ourselves. Pretty amazing, when you think about it. And all in two weeks.

'It might not be so bad,' I say. 'Matty might like her. He's always left out...'

'Are you serious?' Rachel's chair squeaks as she turns to look at me.

'Matty would leave you and Tommo alone if he had someone to go with.'

'Yeah, but Drina? She's literally never done one nice thing for us in her life. Like we're going to bring her to the barracks like we're just crashing a house party or something.' The pop and crack of her chewing gum echoes around the room. 'Besides. The squaddies won't touch her. It's too obvious she'd end up pushing a buggy round town in no time.'

'She's alright,' I say, looking up at the clock again. 'It would have already happened by now if it was going to. We might even do better out of it with her around.'

'What, like get more poppers? She's always got her own.'

'Not since Timmy left. I heard her slanging him in the bogs last week.'

Rachel laughs. 'We're not taking her for nothing,' she says. 'Ask Jase about Matty. Tommo thinks he likes boys...'

I glare at Rach. I hate it when she talks about Jason. He may have opened the barracks door but he should never have gone to live there in the first place. What's the point of having a real brother if we don't stick together? Why should it be me who does all Ma's jobs? He might not have needed to join up in the first place if he hadn't taken his eye off the ball when that sponger started hanging around. I fidget on my hands, I know what he'd say. He's the one fighting for us now. Good thing too else we'd have nothing. Like everyone else around here.

'Does Tommo know how much you fancy Jase?'

She goes all coy. 'I don't, since I met Tommo,' she says.

'"Since I met Tommo"? You're not bloody Cinderella, Rach,' I say. 'Sneaking a shag in the barracks is hardly sweeping you off your feet with a bunch of carnations is it?'

I smile as I wrap my arms round myself. We sound like actual grown-ups.

'What of it? You've done alright in the end, haven't you? We haven't been sat in the middle of a roundabout smoking other people's fag butts for ages now. Whose idea do you think that was, anyway? To build gardens in the middle of roundabouts as if people in this town are actually going to sit and enjoy the smell of petrol? They'd have been better off putting those dumb bottle banks in there. Somewhere to put all the empties. Like anyone in Warchester thinks about their rubbish—'

'Carly?' The door next to the cubicle opens to frame a woman peering over her glasses around the room.

'Be right back,' I shout over my shoulder to Rach as I follow the woman down the corridor and into a windowless side room. The door closes behind us without anyone having to push it. The woman makes a great show of shuffling papers, and opening and closing drawers in the tiny desk, before pushing her glasses back on her nose and looking at me.

'How can I help you today, Carly?' She looks like a woodpecker, I think.

'Well, Rach said I could get the pill from you,' I say, reading Wendy on her name badge. Wendy Woodpecker...

'The contraceptive pill, you mean? Or emergency contraception?'

'The pill, you know, the one I need to take every day.'

'I see ... And how old are you?'

I shift about in my seat.

'I'm afraid you will need to answer a few questions,' she says, blinking at me as she fiddles with the clipboard in her lap.

'Fourteen,' I lie, wondering what will happen if she has to check my medical records. Then I remember this is an army clinic. Jason probably sorted this out too.

'And you've started your periods?'

'Well, yeah...'

'When?'

'When I was twelve...'

'And do you have a regular sexual partner? A boyfriend?' She looks up.

'Sort of...' I flush. 'It's the same guy recently, if that's what you mean...' I trail off as she looks down at her notes.

'I'm asking because the pill won't protect you from sexually transmitted diseases,' she says, like I'm six, or younger, even. 'Have you been using condoms until now?'

'Yes,' I say, face burning.

She sits, waiting as if she thinks I'll say something else.

'And have you ever had unprotected sex?'

The upside down watch on her white coat ticks into the silence.

'Have you ever been tested for any sexually transmitted diseases, Carly? You might also have heard them described as STI's...'

I cough.

'Sexually transmitted diseases are very serious illnesses like gonorrhoea, syphilis—'

'And AIDS,' I interrupt, forcing myself to look at her. 'I know what they are. And I don't have them. I've always used condoms before. I know how to protect myself. I just want the pill now I've...'

'Yes, I see,' she says, looking down at her pad again.

'When did you first become sexually active?'

'Why does that matter?' I fidget in my seat, another clock ticking above her head. It's well into history now. We're so screwed. At least I hate history. Who cares about what happened ages ago? It hardly matters now, does it? Ma wasn't mental, once upon a time. Like that makes any difference now she's basically brain dead.

Wendy the Woodpecker blinks at me. 'And do your parents know you are sexually active?'

I laugh in spite of myself.

'I'm sure you're aware you're still a minor,' she says, six-year-old voice again. 'You're having underage sexual intercourse. Does your boyfriend know how old you are?'

'I know, alright?' I am suddenly uncomfortably hot, school blazer scratching like an itchy blanket. 'And I know what I'm doing. Can I have it or not?'

'I'll need to check your weight,' she says after a minute, motioning to the scales by the wall next to the desk. I stand, relieved to take off my jacket and shoes. 'And if you could just roll up your sleeve...'

I follow instructions, turning this way and that, nodding, grunting, even smiling, until finally the door opens, fresh air rushes in, she hands me a small slip of paper, a paper sack full of condoms and says 'don't forget to take it every day' even though I'm already halfway down the corridor.

Outside, I feel like the breeze is kissing my face.

'See?' Rach says. 'It'll be so much easier for us now...'

I walk faster, her babble fading out behind me. If we can just make it back during first break then it should be easy to sneak in without any drama.

Marie ~ London ~ 2006

I can tell, near enough, what time it is just by the light in the room. The balcony faces east, high enough that dawn always hits the little window over the sink, so I know exactly when it's OK to give up trying to get to sleep. I collect up the clothes I've laid out on the table before heading to the shower; in, quick lather, rinse and out.

Amazing they think this stuff actually smells like strawberries, I think while I dress, watching the soap settling back in the bottle resting on the shower dial. The only people who buy it have probably never eaten any. I always used to think it smelled like candyfloss.

Brush through the hair, blot of powder, bit of chapstick, done. *Marie's ready*, I think.

Back at the sofa, I neaten everything up: one pillow, then another, then the blanket folded on top. I line the remote control against the corner of the table, make sure the square blanket and oblong pillow are perfectly parallel. *Pa-ra-llel.* There's another new journalist word. It used to mean lines, symmetry, maths. Now it means similarities, echoes, comparisons. How can we make this story more relevant, compelling, relatable? Marie, can you find a parallel example? I'm always the one who has to find the parallel example. They're not hard to find if you know where to look.

This early in the morning, the nine-minute train journey passes almost as soon as it's started. A quick click-clack along the road and I'm there, through the turnstiles and up the stairs into the newsroom, hanging up my coat and slipping into a seat at the end of the news desk like I've been doing this every day of my life, lullaby hum of computers washing through my head.

'Marie? Is that you? Good God...'

Blood rushes to my cheeks as I see Olivia Guy striding towards me from the far end of the newsroom. I'm barely on my feet before she pulls up in front of my desk, hand outstretched, billowy silk blouse, massive gold hoops swinging in her ears, jewellery everywhere, all bounce and swish and fanfare. I squirm, brushing non-existent crumbs off my trousers. She looks like she might even say 'Ta-Dah!' next.

'Marie ... my word,' she gabbles, breathy, eyes oversized and twinkling like her earrings. 'What on earth are you doing here? And this early? I told Jemima and Dominic to take it easy, at least for this morning...'

'I'd rather—' I blush harder as she wraps her warm, soft hands around one of mine. How come Olivia, the actual managing editor, suddenly knows my name?

'Come!' she interrupts, pulling me along behind her. 'Tea please, Gabe,' she barks to the assistant waiting outside her office, all glass panels in the back corner of the newsroom. 'And some breakfast ... What would you like? Bacon sandwiches? Pastries? Gosh ... both I think ... Just get us the full works,' she shouts over her shoulder, tossing her hair, Gabe disappearing in a blur to my left.

Before I know it, I'm on her fat purple sofa, the one reserved for the big guns, with her perched on the armchair opposite. Perky, plump and velvet, this is a sofa that thinks it's seen it all.

'You've contributed to a truly outstanding piece of journalism, Marie,' she says, leaning forward. 'Jemima explained your role in all this ... Absolutely remarkable. I was frankly astonished not to have met you before. You should be incredibly proud of yourself. I'm confident we can effect some real change with this. It will put the Met in a terribly uncomfortable position... As it should, of course...'

I try not to fidget as she smiles, tangling a hand in the necklace gleaming on her collarbone, all different shapes awkwardly locked together.

'It's quite an achievement for someone at your level to be involved in something like that. It's quite an achievement for any journalist...'

She keeps staring at me even as the door opens, and in chugs a trolley of steaming tea and paper bags. I swallow as my mouth waters. I can always eat at work. I shake my head as the door closes again, as if the trolley came in by itself. Lucky there are a few seconds of crackle and crunch to spare as Olivia settles back into her chair, waving a sandwich.

'So, tell me. Is this your first job in journalism? Did you have any experience before you came to us at Nine?'

I choke on a mouthful of tea as the door opens again. This time her head turns.

'Morning, Liv,' Dominic trills. 'Oh sorry, didn't mean...' He tails off as he spots me.

'Dominic! Join us!' Her baguette points towards me on the sofa. 'Didn't I tell you to lie in? Oh, never mind...'

I look into my mug as he sits down. Back to feeling like a fraud now he's here. He's the one who did all the real work. I just watched it happen. And we're both complicit until we do something about it.

'I was just getting to know Marie,' Olivia says as she pushes the bags of food forward again. 'Help yourself. Gabe got enough to feed the whole newsroom, as usual ... Honestly, the man is such a blunt instrument sometimes...'

Dominic snorts as he grabs a pastry.

'So talk me through it,' she says, eyes narrowing as she assesses us. 'What's your plan? You haven't rushed back to the Met to get their comment yet, have you? I know that's the part you always enjoy the most...'

I sip at my tea. The rhythm of the room feels familiar again. No need for Olivia to know any more about me than she already does. That my name's also on this story.

'Nope,' Dominic mumbles through a mouthful of croissant. 'But I will, today. Once you've approved my script.'

'No need to rush.' The sandwich waves again. 'We don't want to tip them off too early. Have you sent through a new version?'

'I made the initial changes, yes, but—'

'I think you're going to need to flesh out the victim's side a little more, for the script to really sing. For it to really make the impact it deserves.'

'Wait. It's not enough that we have actual sex traffickers on camera?'

I shrink into my blousy purple cushions. He'd be furious if he knew I could hear the croak in his voice. Here's a man who's also been up all night.

'Dominic,' she says, putting the untouched sandwich back on the table. 'You don't need me to tell you that's the smoking gun, alright. Of course it is. But think of the viewer. The viewer only sees a grainy shot of a random person ... It could be anyone. Where's the money shot? The one that makes the viewer sit up and listen, instead of zoning out or reaching for the remote? The one that really illuminates the gross perversion of power and control at play here? Settle down, settle down...'

She holds up a hand, silencing Dominic before he can start.

'I know we'll have to pixelate, but even so. Right now all the viewer sees, and hears, is a clipped negotiation about a car. You've said it yourself. These are professionals. They know how to talk without completely incriminating themselves. I know we've got more than enough to stand up what the conversation's actually about. Your journalism is first-rate, no question. But without hearing from a victim herself, a girl who has been through the terror of trafficking, the whole torrid story of being groomed, being sold, having to escape ... well, then the viewer is left with little but your dulcet tones lilting on top of a pile of text messages. I know what you saw, but, as it stands, the viewer misses out on that entirely.'

'Let me get this straight,' Dominic mutters, crunching a paper bag into his hand. 'Just so we're all on the same page. You're telling me you want full sex-slave technicolour? Another victim of sex trafficking? On tape by the end of today? Simple as that, is it? It's not enough that we're exposing a national trafficking ring?'

I squeeze my cup. I don't care if it burns. Even though I blurred it at the time, suddenly all I can see is every strand of bleached hair framing every cell of the girl's hollow face. The girl we couldn't get a clean shot of so we could show everyone else.

'Oh Dominic, I'm not sure I'd put it quite like that. But yes, I think it falls flat without someone other than you instructing the viewer on what these girls are going through. It misses the point entirely. We just hear you telling us, rather than showing us, what's going on. You don't need me to point out it's not as simple as a headline, do you? We have to compel people to watch, to re-member, and ideally to act ... not just read and crumple a few hours later.'

More silence. I swallow hard, tea burning a path down my throat. *Now. It's now, Marie! Don't prepare. Begin!* I cough, just to soften the ground.

'Olivia, I could have another go at the Salvation Army. We might have better luck with the branches outside London. They'll potentially be more interested in raising their profile than the ones here. If we can get a suburban branch of the Salvation Army some national exposure, for example...'

I don't even jump as Dominic bangs his hands on the table, howling.

'Do you think we haven't already tried? Olivia, are you honestly suggesting we hold this back because you think it merits hearing from the Salvation Army, of all the more absurd sentences I have ever uttered in my life? And lest you forget, I'm also supposed to be sealing this deal sometime soon with actual money, unless you want to watch me have my eyeballs removed with a spoon.'

'Hang on, Dominic,' she says, leaning forward for her sandwich, more weapon than conductor this time. 'There you go again, rushing seven steps ahead of where you need to be. Let me be quite clear on this. There is nothing of higher value to me than your and your crew's personal safety – as evidenced by assigning our entire logistics department to monitoring your movements and encrypting your communications for the duration of this project. Lest *you* forget, I've been reading all these messages too. I know exactly what your next step is supposed to be. I'm simply making suggestions to maximise this story's potential – as befits a project of this level of risk. Surely that's a shared goal? You know as well as I do that it's all too easy for the authorities to spin a distraction, especially when they've been humiliated. And Marie's made a very smart suggestion indeed...' I shiver as she nods at me, hooded eyes at odds with her approval.

'I'll crack on,' I say, brushing more non-existent crumbs off my trousers as I stand, edging past Dominic and out as fast as I can without running. Their bickering fades into the background as the newsroom's lullaby rises; the rustle of typing, the murmur of phones, the swish of newsprint.

I know Dominic can't have tried the Salvation Army. He can't speak its language.

Carly ~ Warchester ~ 1996

I sit up with a start in the dark, the front door closing below me, rattling the chain lock hanging on its frame. Jason? It can't ... but it must be? I pad over to the door in my socks, listening for any sound other than Kayleigh's soft snoring. Creeping out on to the landing, there's the unmistakable thud of boots moving around downstairs.

'Jase?' I whisper as I tiptoe down into the sitting room, blinking into the glare of the overhead strip light as I pull my skirt straight. I squint, irritated. There's a side lamp by the telly but the bulb went, I don't know, forever ago.

'You're awake,' he says from behind me. I turn to see him in full gear in the kitchen, fridge door propped open by a bulging shopping bag.

'Well, yeah...' I say, rubbing my eyes. 'What are you doing here? I was waiting up for Rach—'

'She won't be by tonight,' he says, cutting me off. Even the cartons of milk are standing to attention in the fridge door. 'Where's Ma?'

'In bed, for once,' I say, blinking as my eyes adjust. 'She even made it downstairs and back again today. I still had to feed Kayleigh though ... Wow, are those eggs?'

I stare, distracted, as he unpacks the rest of the bag. There used to be eggs when Kayleigh's dad was still around. And other stuff, like crisps and KitKats. I knew he'd snuck over whenever Ma told me to have an egg for breakfast. As if he hadn't bought them with her money! Jase doesn't answer, snapping the door closed as he crunches the bag into his other hand.

'Everything alright lately?'

'Alright? Like how? I've been at school if that's what you mean...'

'Does Kayleigh need anything new? Or you?' I flush as I spot a box of Tampax on the counter by the fridge. Oh God. I wish Ma could at least do the washing herself.

'I could do with some money ... Cash, I mean...' I say, staring at the floor. 'Only so I could get stuff for myself instead of waiting for you...'

'Have you got a winter coat as well as that?' He nods at my fraying school blazer. 'Or gloves? What's Kayleigh got?'

'You know we don't,' I say, rubbing the worn patches on my elbows. 'But it's not like Ma's going to take Kayleigh out anywhere.'

'Has she still got that rash?' I blink at him.

'Who? Kayleigh?'

'No, Ma,' he says, rolling his eyes.

'Yeah,' I say. 'She needs to see the doctor. Every morning I tell Ma to take her but—'

'I'll sort it out,' he says, cutting me off again.

'Where's Rach got to, then?'

His boots squeak as he turns away to the sink, flooding water over the pile of dirty dishes.

'And how come you're here so late? Jase?'

He ignores me, squirting soap into the basin. Actual soap, strawberry-red like slushy syrup. Forgetting myself, I walk the two steps into the kitchen and open the fridge door, emptying a whole packet of sliced ham into my mouth almost as soon as I've picked it up; thick, salty and delicious. This ham's the real thing, not our usual sweaty pink stuff. Gulping and chewing, I could be anywhere else in the world until the squeak of a tap closing reminds me we're still in our tiny, filthy kitchen, still neck deep in our tiny, filthy town.

'Are you ready?'

I jump, trying to swallow as I turn to look at him. Our eyes meet for just a moment. I can't be sure but think he might have been smiling.

'To go out, you mean? Pretty much,' I say, coughing. 'Can I have a drink?'

He passes me a cup from the sink.

'I'll take you in,' he says, wiping his hands on his trousers. 'Matty'll be pleased to see you.'

'Oh ... right,' I say, running a hand over my hair, still mussed up from lying next to Kayleigh. 'That'd be good. I was waiting for Rach. Tommo said you'd all be off-duty tonight...'

'I know,' he says, pushing past me. 'Look lively, will you?' The room is suddenly flooded with darkness as he flicks off the switch by the door.

Drizzle falls in a fine mist outside as we walk in step down the dark street. There's no moon between the rainclouds, and the busted street lamp two houses down means it's even darker. Jason keeps a step or so ahead of me, arms swinging by his sides like he's marching. I stuff my hands deeper into my pockets. The bush is slick with rain as we duck into Victory Field.

'So this is the way you go in too?'

He doesn't answer, his boots marking a path in the wet grass.

'Is Rach already there?' I jog a bit to keep up. 'Hey...'

'Forget about her,' he says, turning towards the track cutting across the middle of the fields, away from the barracks on the other side. 'You're with me, remember?'

'But isn't it across there?'

I jump as he stops suddenly, turning and glaring at me. In the dark, the only thing I can really see properly are the whites of his eyes.

'We're going in through a different unit. There's someone I want you to meet first, OK?'

I feel wetness seep into my socks through my shoes as I notice his hands clenching and unclenching by his sides.

'How come? I thought...'

'It worked out alright for you when you met Matty and Tommo, didn't it?'

'Well, yeah, but...'

'So come on, and you'll see them afterwards.'

I wiggle my toes as we start to walk again. Maybe I'll even get those proper thick boots with chunky soles and laces like everyone else soon. The park is so quiet that apart from the tap and scrape of our shoes on the path, I think I can hear the drizzle landing. On the far side of the field, another gate that looks like part of the fence until Jase pushes on it, two bars opening into a clump of tall grass. We pick our way to the edge of a low building and a single door at the end of a long row of closed windows. A small camera on the ledge above swivels towards us. He nods at it, before the door swings open in silence. It's been quiet and dark for so long now that I feel like a ghost.

Inside, the light is still low, walls glowing down a long, windowless corridor. Jase doesn't turn around but keeps walking until we draw up outside a door with a name plate. *Captain Robert Leigh Parish*, it says when I peer at it. *Forewarned is Forearmed*.

Jase turns and looks at me for a moment. 'Carls...' He hesitates. His eyes look funny; wet, even. 'Just do as you're told, OK? That's all anyone needs to do when they're in here.'

And before I can even ask why, the door opens inwards, Jason suddenly tall and stiff in a salute as if he's been standing like that the whole time. For there, framed low in the doorway, is half a man; a brick-set uniformed torso and head on top of two beefy stumps poking from a shiny silver wheelchair, eyes glittering up at us.

'Why, you must be Carly,' the head says, nodding. 'Jason's told me all about you.'

Marie ~ London ~ 2006

'Now? Really?' Dominic looks up from his slump in front of the bank of monitors blinking in one of the windowless edit suites opposite the news desk. His breakfast has barely gone down, crumbs falling off the hand rubbing his eyes. People stash themselves in here to hide as much as to edit, each sponge in the soundproof walls a vault of tears, fury, betrayals – you name it. Except these are sponges that never leak.

'Yes, now. We're on the clock, remember? A few hours in the Travelodge so we didn't get our heads kicked in was too much for you last time I looked and now you want to have a second breakfast?'

I smooth down the buttons of my coat, looking at the light reflecting up at me from my boots instead of at his stunned face.

'Oh come on, Marie. It's not even ten. How did you even get them to answer the phone?'

'Her name's Beata,' I say, squinting at my reflection. 'She's nineteen now. The Salvos got hold of her a couple of years ago. Romanian, came here where she was fifteen on the promise of a job, food, board ... all the usual patter. Then she was basically treated as a house servant with benefits...'

'Seriously? But I spent weeks...'

'I called a branch in Broxbourne. They jumped at it when I told them they'd get national exposure. But we need to get going now, unless you want to scratch your arse in traffic instead of in here.' I reach round the door for his coat hung on the peg on the back.

'I don't understand,' he says, blinking at the monitors like they might answer him instead. 'I gave the London lot my name, repeatedly. And I'm the one on the actual telly...'

I bat him with his coat.

'Broxbourne, you said? Like, where the zoo is?'

'Mary's waiting downstairs. Come on,' I say, dropping his coat over his head. 'She'll love hearing about the zoo. After all, she knows you're a big cat, doesn't she?'

'Broxbourne...' he mumbles as he stands. 'Of all places.' I finally look back at him as he buttons up. 'Does that zoo have the big five? I've yet to see a rhino in this country...'

We laugh together, just for a moment, as we walk down the stairs to the lobby. Except I know it's really because of Mary. He adores her – warzone camerawoman of legend.

'Why, if it's not Lady Mary ... Come here, you gorgeous old thing...'

Eyes twinkle at me from behind the set of glasses perched on Dominic's shoulder as he embraces her.

'Look at you, Mister Investigative!' Mary pulls away, holding Dominic by both arms. 'What's this suit and all ... You look like the head boy!'

'I was once, in fact, the head boy,' Dominic says, vamping on the spot. 'And you, my saint, my liege, look exactly as I left you all those weeks ago in Iraq ... except a bit cleaner... Ow!' Mary socks him on the arm as she smiles at me.

'Marie, is it? Oh dear ... this could get confusing...' She stretches out fingers the mustard-yellow of nicotine.

I shake her hand, staring. Her smile looks like it is coming from her whole face, fighting against the tight pull of grey hair in a long ponytail. Lucky, because if she wasn't smiling so hard she might look like a rat, her eyes deep in their lined sockets. I find myself wiping my hand before stuffing it back into my pocket as we walk outside, even though I like rats. They hang around when everyone else has long given up. We only see them when they're desperate.

'I only got home last week,' she says, hoisting her gear into the boot of the van waiting by the kerb. 'Try and get out of going again if you can, the place is a mess. The office is a dump, the hours are godawful and the stories ... Don't get me started. We never film anything original, we're just out with the military all the time – and they reckon combat operations are nearly over? I've seen it all before...'

She keeps ranting as she follows Dominic into the back of the car. I gabble our location to the driver as I climb into the passenger seat, trying not to miss any of their conversation. This is a tide of details I can just dissolve in for a while.

'...Honestly, Dom, it's impossible to do any real journalism other than follow the army around. The Brits and Americans are so overcommitted ... and for what? It's like they learned nothing from the first time around, except that they cut too hard and too fast after the bloody Cold War. If I never film another military operation it will be too soon. We never hear from civilians, we're barely allowed out of the armoured cars, and the best pictures I can ever come up with are roads exploding, yet again.' I feel her kick out on the floor behind me.

'What are we doing again, honey?' She leans forward into the gap between the seats.

'It's just an interview,' I say, trying not to turn my head as we pull into traffic. 'Sorry, it's just I get a bit nauseous if I don't look straight ahead...' *Nor-zee-us*. I still can't say it right. 'Her name's Beata. She's a victim of sex trafficking. The Salvation Army have set it up ... She wants to tell us her story, but I'm not sure she realises her face will be on camera yet. They know that's the plan but are more interested in the exposure they will get on national television.'

'Hey that's a good story!' I flush as I see Mary smile in the rear view mirror. 'And the network's committed to it? They will actually interrupt their blanket coverage of the West's magnanimous takeover in the Middle East?' I watch as her eyes roll.

'Yes, and the best part is we've also infiltrated a trafficking ring,' Dominic interrupts. 'It's taken us weeks. I even stashed a camera in my pants for some undercover filming.'

'In your pants? What were you filming, his dick?' I try to snigger too as Mary's smoke-hardened laugh echoes around the car.

'Well I knew I'd get frisked,' says Dominic. 'And that's one place those guys would never look. You wouldn't believe how slick their operation is. They are moving girls around the country like knock-off cars ... Tailed us out of there and everything.'

'Good grief. There's no need for warzone reporting if you can pull all that off. And what about you, honey? How long have you been at Nine?' I flinch as Mary squeezes my shoulder.

'Almost a year,' I say. 'I started just before the—'

'You've been an intern for an entire year? Damn, we're into child labour at the networks these days?'

'I'm an assistant producer, actually,' I say, indicator thumping over my heart. 'I got a staff job pretty quickly after the London bombings...'

'What?' Dominic interrupts. 'You're on staff? When did that happen?'

'A couple of months after the attacks. I was just lucky – my internship happened to coincide with a massive breaking news story and there weren't enough people to go around—'

'No-one ends up in Jonas's pocket because of luck rather than judgement!' Dominic barks from the back seat. He hasn't clocked that I can see him, questions written all over his frown.

'I knew her before, actually. We go back...'

'Back? Back how?'

'We met in the supermarket by the office. You know, the twenty-four-hour one. I used to work the night tills there.' I crack open my window just so some other noise fills the car.

'Eh? Are you having a laugh?'

'They didn't pay much at the *Deptford Gazette*,' I say, smoothing down my coat as rain spatters my lap. 'I was an apprentice on the copy desk and needed...' I trail off, blushing even harder as Dominic roars with laughter.

'What did she do, pick you up over a ready meal and a bag of Percy Pigs?'

'We got talking, didn't we? Her break was just when our shifts changed so I used to see her. I worked a couple of nights a week, whenever my shifts at the paper started late enough…'

'See her? What do you mean? Did you chat to everyone buying midnight munchies or just the ones who weren't drunk and disorderly?'

'She'd dropped her ID. I found it, and gave it back to her when she next came in.'

'And just like that, she gave you a job?'

'No, she gave me advice…'

'On how to break out of the *Deptford Gazette*?'

'Sort of, she…'

'Oh stop it, Dom,' Mary says before he can get going again. 'Countless times I've listened to you bang on about how working at a local paper is the best training you can get.'

'OK, OK, OK,' Dominic says. 'Marie knows I think the *Gazette* is actually pretty good. It's moonlighting with Jonas that I don't get. She's never been one for the local rag … well, not since she hit the big time, anyway. How did you get talking? The scoop on a fox stuck in the Dartford Tunnel?'

'Well there was a lot of cat-up-a-tree stuff,' I say, wiping raindrops from my forehead. 'But I also got to do some court reporting and—'

'Court reporting? Like what?'

'I got my first real start around the Damilola Taylor trials.'

Dominic whistles. 'Really?'

I close the window with a thump.

'The *Gazette* was his local paper. They were desperate. It was all we covered for a while.'

'Damilola Taylor…' Mary murmurs. 'Why do I know that name?'

'He was just a schoolboy. Stabbed to death in a stairwell on his way home when he was ten,' Dominic says. 'Black, obviously. So for a while the defence tried telling everyone he fell on a broken bottle...'

'I must have missed most of it after 9/11,' Mary says. 'Damilola? Where was he from?'

'Nigeria,' I say. 'Like Jemima...'

Dominic's snort echoes round the car.

'I should have known ... Jonas is such a soft touch.'

Mary's head wobbles in and out of the mirror as she shakes her head.

'Don't let this macho crap fool you, Marie,' she says. 'Dominic is as soft as they come.'

'Yes I'm all heart and no trousers,' Dominic trills. 'That's what the ladies say about me, at least.'

'Oh put a sock in it,' Mary says, meeting my eyes in the mirror. 'I once had the misfortune of working with a reporter – who shall remain nameless, I might add – that refused to dig on a trafficking investigation because, and I quote, "underage whores wouldn't get on pre-watershed and that's where the air time is". The nerve of that guy!'

I am thrust forward as Mary punches the back of my seat.

'After all these years it still makes me crazy. But this ... this story you guys have pulled together is really something. It's potentially game-changing, isn't it?'

'Oh, Lady Mary, you are making me blush,' Dominic says, grinning at me as he pushes her out of frame to squint at his reflection. 'But you're right, of course. As usual. This lot are literally hiding in plain sight while those losers in Organised Crime sit around whining about online privacy and who knows what other distractions—'

'Who we still need to speak to, don't we?' I interrupt. 'If we are going to have a cat in hell's chance of changing this game?'

I fight the urge to smile as Mary and Dominic look like I've smacked them both in the face.

'Easy, tiger,' Dominic says, raising an eyebrow. 'As much as I edify the local press, I don't believe the venerable *Deptford Gazette* will have availed you of a hotline to Scotland Yard.'

He turns to Mary. 'You've got nothing else on the clock after this, have you? We can swing past on the way back, save us going back out later. We'll get nothing on camera while they get their story straight but at least we can say we tried ... and tell Olivia we tried, more to the point, before she teaches me how to suck eggs again.'

'For you, anything,' Mary says, plastering her grin back on to her face.

I wonder what her real story is, hidden in all those lines round her eyes. No way they are all from laughing. Nothing is ever that funny.

'Give Jonas a heads-up, would you?' Dominic's eyes narrow at me in the mirror.

'Will do,' I say, pulling out my phone. 'I already told her about Beata.'

'I'm sure you did. But we'll need to get ahead on the editing while we sit on the M1 to give us any chance of making tonight's deadline.'

'So why don't you drop me off first on the way to the Yard? Between us we'll have it done by the time you get back. Unless you want to show Mary the zoo, that is...'

I bite back the start of a smile at his nod in the mirror, like it was all his idea in the first place. The road blurs and clears in front of me as Mary starts up another one of her stories, windscreen wipers brainlessly scraping perfect crests out of the driving rain.

Carly ~ Warchester ~ 1996

I stare down at the head, nodding and grinning up at me as if it's a wind-up doll. Jason's hands are at my back, nudging me forward, the full-beam overhead strip lights making my eyes water. After all the dark and shadow of our journey, I feel like I'm waking up in a dream. The door clicks closed behind us with a soft thunk.

'Sit, please, sit,' the head says, reversing and wheeling over to a desk in the far corner along the wall, a couple of chairs for normal people sticking out next to it. I shuffle forward, skirt riding even higher than it already is as I sit. The wall above the desk is lined with maps that I don't recognise, there are all sorts of papers and files everywhere, and there is a weird speaker with a flashing red light on top, which sounds like someone has pressed the wrong channel on telly. It's completely different to the squaddies' dorms. I guess that's what it is to be a captain – or half a captain, I suppose. I stuff my hands under my legs. I wish I hadn't rolled my skirt over so many times before we left.

'At ease.' The head jerks at Jason, still standing behind me.

I press my legs down on to my hands, looking round at the rest of the room. There is a flat bunk on the other wall, two pairs of boots lined up underneath it. Boots? For who?

'So, Carly...' The head beams at me, craggy face brown and lined. His eyes are almost hidden by a thick felt hat pulled low over his forehead. 'Thank you for coming in to see me this evening. After all, you must be tired ... It's a school night, isn't it?'

My skin prickles under my blazer. It's impossible not to stare now my head is at the same level as his. Up close, his neck is the same width as his face, sitting on top of a chest so deep that his uniform looks like it needs an extra pocket on the front. I watch as his thick hands clench his shiny wheelchair hubs. He must have been ten feet tall once, I think.

'Who are you?' The words leave my mouth before I can stop them, blush burning up my neck. 'What happened to your...'

'Legs?' The head smiles wider, teeth yellow in the strip light.

I nod, trying not to look down at the stumps, although I can see them twitching in the bottom of my eye.

'Apologies, sir,' Jason says, stiff in his seat, fixing a stare past the head at the wall.

'Goodness, young man,' the head says, eyes blazing at me. 'No need to apologise for your sister. They look a little alarming, don't they? Blown clean off, I'm afraid to say. I was unlucky not to retain my knees ... but lucky to preserve so many other necessary functions, and the support of the military, of course. We know this is a possibility in combat. We sacrifice ourselves for the good of others, and we are only ever proud of this.'

He peers closer at me, lips stretched around his teeth like he'd be laughing if someone wound him up again. I don't dare move or breathe. I wonder whether he will fall out if he leans too far forward. Even the weird speaker is quiet for a moment as we sit, frozen in position.

'I understand you know some of our finest young recruits, Carly,' he says after a moment. 'Block 16 is home to our elite intelligence unit – a breeding ground for some of the British military's finest warriors. They speak very highly of you.'

His eyes rake me up and down as heat spreads from my neck to my face.

'Come now, young lady. This is a matter of pride, too. It is important to us – it should, of course, be important to us all – that our fighters relax when they are off-duty. We ask so very much of them, after all. So very, very much...'

He cocks his head to the side as he pauses. Silence spreads

through the room again, until the box squawks in the corner. I stare at his legs, or where they are supposed to be. I can't help myself. Is this really what Jason thinks I should be proud of? When this happens to people. And for what?

'You see, Carly,' he continues, 'it is a tragic consequence of defending our country that some of us end up like this.' He gestures to his stumps, pointing towards me like weapons. 'And particularly now, of course. I ask you, has there ever been a more testing time for the British military? I expect Jason has told you all about the cuts we have had to contend with. Such challenges lie ahead ... such extreme challenges. But we will not be defeated ... Would you like some water?'

He wheels away from me as I nod, stealing a glance at Jason. If it wasn't for the muscle twitching in his cheek, he could be made of stone.

'Jase!' I whisper as, back to us, the head opens a small fridge next to the bunk on the other wall. The muscle starts to jerk like a spasm as he ignores me. I jump as the head appears at my other elbow, having wheeled almost a full circle back around us before I can so much as blink.

'Please, drink,' he says, hunching towards me to drop a bottle of water into my lap. It sits like a cold slug in the dip between my legs as he glides back round us up to the desk.

'Drink,' he commands, suddenly sharp. I fumble with the lid, hands slick from burrowing under my legs.

'That's better,' he says as I sip, cringing as a weird mineral aftertaste coats the inside of my cheeks. Who buys water in bottles when you can turn on the tap?

'Something you will learn, Carly, as you continue to visit with us, is the importance of following a direct order. The importance of doing what you are told, by your superiors, without fear, favour or question.'

I swallow again, even though there's nothing left in my mouth.

'Your brother here,' he says, frowning as the box crackles again, 'is one of our most promising recruits. Of course, he would be, being from such decorated, noble military stock...'

I sense Jason stiffening beside me.

'You see, Jason understands, instinctively and guilelessly, the importance of enabling the challenges we set before him—'

'So why did you bring me here, then?' I interrupt, suddenly electric with fury. Yet again, it's Jason who's the war hero, except I'm the one stopping Ma killing Kayleigh just by forgetting she's there one too many times.

The head swings round in surprise, sliding towards me with another creepy laugh-like grin.

'Spirited too, I see ... I like that. I'm not surprised, of course. I would expect nothing less from this particular family.'

I blink at him. His grin looks like it's been painted on.

'I understand you have a new baby sister too now, is that right? Little Kayleigh? Gosh, those early months can be so difficult, can't they...? So emotionally draining and tiring ... Now, let me assure you, Carly, we consider it our duty to ensure Jason is able to help provide for you and your sister, given your mother's, shall we say, struggles...'

He cocks his head to the side again as he stares back at me. My throat closes over.

'I'd like to make sure Jason can continue to do so,' he says. 'From what he tells me, it doesn't seem like your poor mother is going to be able to do so herself anytime soon. She is lucky to have another daughter as dutiful and intelligent as yourself.'

Now the head swims in front of me as tears prick at my eyes. Don't talk about Kayleigh, I think. Don't make this place about her.

'Let's suppose I see to it that Jason is able to provide whatever you need for your precious baby sister,' he says. 'And you, too, of course. We can't have you going without. And let's suppose that you bring along some other friends next time you visit the barracks ... Let's suppose they understand this privilege comes with a price, of course, not just anyone can associate with these levels of intelligence ... And let's suppose, therefore, you and Kayleigh are able to live comfortably, perhaps even help your Ma – that is what you call her, isn't it?'

I jump as Jason pulls himself into a salute again. In another world I might even laugh. He looks ridiculous, saluting at a blank wall, at least two feet taller than the half-man in the chair opposite. As ridiculous as the idea that I'll take orders from some random I've never met, that Jason will make me follow them, that Ma will keep on losing what's left of her mind just because some man who was never around in the first place ended up dead for some reason none of us could see, touch or feel. Let alone understand.

'Is something funny?'

I squirm. There's that weird grin again. It's not ridiculous now. It's nothing but real, and its meaning is unmistakable.

'I'm glad to have met you, Carly. A sense of humour will be as valuable as discipline, as we move forward with our ... arrangement, shall we say.'

I clear my throat, wiping my hands on my skirt.

'Can I go now?' I say, watching the half-man's knuckles whiten on his wheels.

'Of course,' he says, finally letting one side go to extend a hand towards me, suspended in the air as we stare at each other. No one has ever shaken my hand before. It reaches out to him as if operated by someone else. All I can think about is Kayleigh. Her velvet skin. Her hungry cries, her blistered legs, her torn, stinking blankets.

'You are here of your own free will, after all,' he says, grip swallowing mine like a glove. 'You can come and go as you please ... so long as our needs are met, of course.'

My knuckles start to crunch and roll together as his fingers tighten around my wrist.

Marie ~ London ~ 2006

'Nice job...' Jemima crows, pausing the tape just as Beata blinks. Even though the frame is frozen, I know her eyeballs are still twitching beneath her lids. People with her story can't close their eyes to their nightmares, even for a second. If this isn't a money shot I don't know what is.

'We've got more than enough colourful stuff to play with. You are absolutely sure she is game for being on camera? She understands what that means, right?'

'She's wearing a wig. Can't you tell?' I crunch my empty plastic cup into my fist as Jemima squints at the monitor. 'She's not afraid. And those are her words, not mine...'

Jemima ignores me, muttering to herself as she reads through the script in front of her.

'The government estimates there are some four thousand victims of human trafficking here in the UK ... Four thousand, is it?'

I nod, standing and stretching. These edit suites may as well be prison cells.

'But officials at the Natural Crime Agency told us that figure could be far higher...'

'National,' I interrupt. 'You mean the National Crime Agency.'

Jemima curses, stabbing her pencil at the papers on the desk.

'I'll get the coffees, shall I?' I say, slipping out into the newsroom before I hear any more, scurrying past the gaggle vamping around the water machine on my way to the kitchen. You have to be a regular on the pub circuit to join in with that lot. I keep my head down, speeding up as I round the corner. Finally this story is coming together, and it's going to land with more than just a splash.

'Aha, you're back!' I skid to a stop as Olivia's voice clangs off the tiles.

Of all the people to find in the kitchen. I look up to find her taking her phone out of the fridge like she's doing exactly what anyone would expect her to be doing. 'How is it all looking?'

'Pretty good, actually,' I say, steadying myself by putting a hand against the coffee machine as I try not to gawp at her. 'I think it's all the detail you wanted. Her name is Beata, she didn't even want us to blur her face. She came here on a promise when she was fifteen, and ended up as essentially a housemaid with benefits. She has definitely had a rough time, the whole nine yards...'

'Of that I have no doubt,' she says, frowning at the phone in her hand. 'These bloody things overheat so quickly...' The fridge hums to her as she puts it back in. 'I look forward to seeing the edit. It's her story we need to thread the whole piece together. That's how we make the viewer sit up and pay attention. That is how we make it as impactful as it deserves to be. It is really that simple, when you think about it. Take the viewer right to the heart of it.'

I nod vigorously as she stares at me. No one wants this more than me, not even Dominic. A frown crosses her forehead as she looks past me into the doorway.

'Sorry to interrupt,' Thomas says, brushing past me as he walks in. 'Do you have a quick second for me? I've been calling...'

I turn around, even though I know he doesn't mean me. Thomas Thorne has never so much as grunted at me before. Tall, lanky and pressed in a dark suit, he looks like an ironing board. Come to think of it, most of the wannabe reporters around here do. It is as if they think it won't matter that people can barely tell them apart, when in fact all they care about is just the opposite – making themselves the centre of attention.

'Yes, I'm sure you have,' Olivia snaps, forehead still creased as she pulls her phone back out of the fridge. 'Fire away...'

I try not to smile as he gapes at her. Maybe that's why she does the fridge thing. An instant delaying tactic. Everyone wants a piece of her, so she's got to have a few tricks.

'Come on, Thomas, spit it out...'

'My contact on Andromeda,' he says, after a moment. 'You know the one I told you about...? They want to meet, and it has to be now, ahead of the Met's official briefing later. It's obviously connected ... I'm sure I'm going to get us a scoop. So I wanted to check if I could...'

'Excuse me, what? An official briefing? On Operation Andromeda, no less? From the Metropolitan Police? Today? Was that scheduled? And if it was, exactly how is it that I wasn't told about it before now?'

Her frown fades to surprise as I have to prop myself up against the coffee machine. Andromeda. Just using the word, just saying it out loud, unlocks a door into the past for everyone in this country. The Met's botched investigation into sexual abuse in the military – the doubts that became reasonable, the charges that couldn't be proven, the scandal that will never die. The untouchable British Army, down but not out. It never could be, could it? What is a nation without an army? Or worse, an army without a nation? *We live to serve.* No one knows which came first.

I shiver as I remember, coffee machine pinging brainlessly behind me. But Thomas doesn't skip a beat, adjusting his already perfect collar.

'It seems it missed our diaries ... caught everyone on the hop. It's not just us, I called around to double check. But the Met assure me it has been planned for a while. Two pm sharp, apparently, at New Scotland Yard. They are offering it up live too – they've practically cleared the street for the broadcast trucks already...'

'That is extraordinary,' Olivia says, as icy as the phone in her hand. 'A press conference on a national disgrace missed our diaries? And exactly who have you had in charge of our diaries?

The camera pool? Blithely ignoring every scheduled live press conference so they don't have to be the ones to turn up and shoot it?'

'I know. I am sorry,' he says, only the squeak of his excessively
shiny shoes betraying the fact he's shifting from foot to foot. 'But
I've got less than an hour to make this meeting. My contact has
to slip away and get back again before the briefing starts...'

'Back up a moment, Thomas. Why is the Met reopening this
can of worms so publicly? And now, out of nowhere?'

'That's why I need to get going,' he says, now not even bother-
ing to disguise his tap dancing. 'Remember what I told you about
this contact? We can't talk by email or on the phone, it's too sensitive, so I've really got to motor...'

'Where is Dominic? Marie?' I start as Olivia barks at me.

I'm suddenly miles away on the copydesk in Deptford, sifting
through testimony that I already know backward, spell-checking
court reports, absorbing allegations usually too horrific to bear.
Charges amounting to a factory line of abuse, as military in its
efficiency as the organisation it lived to serve.

'He's already at the Yard, or on his way back,' I say, fumbling
for the phone in my pocket. 'He dropped me off first with the Salvation Army tapes so we could get on with the edit while he took
Mary with him to get a response from the Met...'

I trail off, the bottom dropping out of my stomach as horror
spreads across her face.

'Shit,' she says, licking her lips, eyes glittering, doll-perfect blush
giving way to pale sheen. 'Shit, shit, and double shit. This is going
bury us ... Dammit! All those institutionalised mistakes, all those
monstrous allegations. This press conference better be more than
just a squeak if it is going to change the record on Andromeda. And
we are damn well going to point it out loud and clear if it doesn't.
Heaven only knows what they've come up with this time...'

The insides of the fridge clatter and smash as she repeatedly
slams the door, cursing and screaming with every bang.

'Pray tell me why are you still standing here, Thomas? Go and get me the inside track, won't you? This isn't the local rag. Do I really need to tell you twice?'

She fades as I slump against the coffee machine, pinging and pinging and pinging behind me. As quick as that, our trafficking story is on ice? We're practically going to bury it ourselves. I'd click my fingers if they weren't already numb.

'And Marie! What are you waiting for? Last time I had the pleasure of renegotiating his contract, I do believe Dominic was still in the pay of this company as home affairs editor – who only knows why, mind you, if he can mismanage his relationship with the Met this catastrophically. Drop everything and get him back to the Yard immediately. And to this damn press conference!'

I catch my breath, all the questions straining to come tumbling out lodging into a plug in my throat, all the energy that had been fizzing round my body at the promise of a scoop now just buzzing away into the floor. Our precious trafficking tapes, every frame lacquered with tension, anticipation and elemental terror, just gamely stuck on pause, for who knows how long. And with every minute we do nothing, they get away with it. They keep getting away with it.

The third shadow sharpens, even as I dig fingers into my eyes, darkening as if she knows we're all about to betray her.

Carly ~ Warchester ~ 1996

'Jase!' I hiss at him as he walks ahead of me down the corridor, lumbering from foot to foot like he's an elephant. I reach forward, trying and failing to grab the arm swinging at his side. My hand is still frozen from my first ever handshake.

'Outside,' he hisses back at me as he speeds up. One-two, one-two, one-two. I take two steps to every one of his.

'What's to stop me screaming my head off?'

'Try it,' he warns under his breath, 'and I'll rip your tongue out of your mouth.'

I swallow hard, staring at the back of his neck as he keeps walking. It's as wide as his head. Same as the half-man, I think, but I'll never find my way out unless I follow him. I gulp as we finally step out into the night air, willing the breeze's kiss. Instead I just feel sick.

'OK,' I say, plucking at his elbow. 'Now can we talk? I've done everything you said.'

I watch that muscle twitch in his cheek as he stares down the path back out on to Victory Field. He starts to walk, slowly this time so I can fall in step beside him.

'You did good,' he says, looking straight ahead. 'I'm proud of you, OK? We'll be alright for the next while if you can keep that up.'

'Keep what up?'

He doesn't reply, just keeps walking in a straight line like he's a robot.

'Who was that weird guy?' I persist. 'How come he can still be in the army without any legs? Doesn't everyone need to be able to fight if they have to? Shoot, march, all that stuff?'

He snorts, speeding up again.

'Jase!' I shout, blinking at the tears pricking my eyes. 'Will you fucking stop and talk to me? It's alright for you, all banter and jokes in the barracks, hot dinners, hot showers, clean clothes...'

I have to stop for a moment, suddenly heaving with sobs.

'You don't know what it's like, finding Kayleigh burning in her own shit every time I come in from school. Finding nothing for breakfast unless you've decided it's worth coming by. Finding nothing hanging clean in the cupboard, only dirty clothes on the floor. Finding Ma exactly where I left her, day after day, night after night ... I may as well be invisible. Finding nothing to do except pretend I like smoking fags with Rach, when actually they make me want to puke. And the worst part is I can still remember when it wasn't like that, before that tosser told Ma whatever she needed to hear to hand over the keys to the fucking kingdom. Maybe I wouldn't care so much if it had always been like this, but now Kayleigh's here I have to, don't I? Someone has to, right? And only since we met Matty and Tommo and those guys does it feel like anyone has actually given a shit...'

I cough as I wipe my eyes. I can't believe I am finally crying. I know I've wanted to, in the half-light as Kayleigh dreams. But the tears never come, it's like they know what might happen if they do. I don't dare look up as the gravel path crunches, Jason walking back towards me.

'Finished?' A bright-white hanky appears in his hand, under my face. I blink at it. I don't think I have ever even seen a hanky apart from in a magic show. The material scratches my nose as I blow into it before looking up. His eyes are blank.

'Who was that guy?' I ask again, staring up at him. 'Do you know him? Like, properly know him? And where did this come from? We've barely even had tissues before. Is that how we've ended up with so much nice stuff recently? Because you've been helping him out?'

'He runs operations,' he says, after a minute. 'Top-level intelligence. I can't even tell you what, I don't even know the half of it myself. But those units are the most important of all, especially now. He makes things run tidy ... looks after people who have got injuries and that.'

'Injuries? Like no legs and arms?'

'Sort of,' he says, looking at the floor. 'The army owes them especially. We all owe them. I told you.'

'Looks after them? Like how?' I rub the hanky between my fingers. 'You can't seriously mean he's there to make sure cripples can still get themselves off?'

I jump as he yanks me back into the shadows of Victory Field.

'You will never use that word again,' he hisses as he leans towards me. 'They are soldiers. That is all any of us are. Everyone is a soldier, or at least they should be. We'd be nowhere without soldiers. We forget about the ones who are dead, but soldiers like him – they're living reminders of what we have to be grateful for. If you can't see it now, then you might as well be blind for the rest of your life.'

I let all my breath out as he turns to fiddle with the padlock on the gate. Is all this supposed to be OK just because these people have lost half their bodies?

'Rach might not do it for anyone else, you know,' I say after a moment. 'She really likes Tommo, and thinks he's really into her too...'

'She'll do it if you ask her. She gets it's part of our duty, she always has. And besides, it doesn't have to be her...' There's a click as the lock finally closes. 'We just have to get it done, one way or the other. We can't afford not to. Our family can't, and neither can the army.'

'Well it's not going to be me.' I force myself to look at him as he turns. 'I'm not going with one of those guys, soldiers or not. And actually, she'll do it if *you* ask her, not me. She told me if you were her brother, she would do whatever you said...'

'It has to be you,' he interrupts. I can see the whites of his eyes in the dark. 'I can't have anything to do with asking anyone. I told you, there's stuff I don't even know, and what I do know can't touch this. Not now. Not if we want all the stuff to continue.'

'What stuff? You mean like food and clothes? Money?'

'Think about Kayleigh,' he says, suddenly grabbing me by the arms. 'Ma can't look after her. She's useless, always will be now. We're the ones who have to—'

'We? All I do is think about Kayleigh!' I shout as I try to wriggle free. 'I'm the one who feeds her every night, who washes her, who finds a rag when we're out of nappies ... me. And now you are telling me I have to find someone to dish out blow jobs so we can keep eating?'

I feel tears streaming down my face again but I don't care anymore.

'What happened to all the army money we got? They can't just have handed the lot over when Pa died, there must be more. She said the army would look after us forever after what he did. Is it all because she got herself knocked up again? Is that it? Just because she let herself be ripped off by someone who had nothing to do with God and fucking country?'

I stop, breathing hard. I think I'm going to be sick. Drizzle starts to fall again, mingling with the water on my cheeks. Jason just stands there like dead tree trunk.

'You weren't there for that either, by the way,' I say, swallowing bile back down my throat. 'Already joined up and well out of our shit-hole. I had to handle that scrounger by myself. Just like Kayleigh is my responsibility. Mine.'

A sliver of moon pokes out as the clouds move over our heads. I jump as a crow flaps past my head, watching its black shadow arc into the sky.

'So that's it, is it?' I say, waiting for Jason to speak. 'Get Rach or Drina or whoever in to take care of business and we're all good? It's that simple?' I laugh, in spite of myself.

'You need to keep going to school,' he says.

'What has school got to do with anything?'

'It's over if social services start messing in our business. I mean it.'

'That lot? Are you having a laugh? Ma is way too much trouble for them. Last time they came over they practically ran back out again.'

'I'll know if people start asking questions,' he hisses, grabbing my arms again. 'This has to be neat and tidy, Carls.'

'Well why don't you do it, then? Freaks like that should take their kicks however they come.'

And with that my arms are finally free, except there's a hand around my neck, lifting me off the ground like I'm a kitten for the bucket. The air disappears as I start to panic, eyes bulging, ears ringing, heart thudding in my chest as the dark gets darker until everything is almost black...

Thump. I crumple to the ground as he drops me, rubbing my neck as he looms overhead, outline like a mountain against the moon, the highest mountain on earth.

'Get it done,' he says. 'And if you squeal, Ma is all you and Kayleigh will have left. This is bigger than all of us. The only way it can end is if we keep getting it done.'

I blink, cough, then throw up in the dirt next to me. Everything comes up. My heart, my guts, the lot. And by the time it's all out, he's gone.

Part Two

Marie ~ London ~ 2006

My hands slip as I brace myself inside the cubicle, shiny walls slick under my sweaty palms. Did Olivia even notice me legging it? Or that crowd at the water machine, as I bungled into the glass doors? Rage, confusion, disappointment, all coming at me like churning fog ... I could have been anywhere but the newsroom. Andromeda, back from the dead, back to torment us all yet again, right as I was about to haul myself, giddy and triumphant, over another rock on my own personal mountain. Presenting our trafficking story to the Met was always going to hurt. It's not like laminating institutional failures in technicolour is ever going to feel good, is it? But answering back with Andromeda, practically gift-wrapped in stinking corruption – it can't just be down to Dominic's middle finger in the eye?

My stomach churns as I gulp and swallow, forcing the lurch back down my throat, open toilet gaping up at me like a frozen, silent scream. *Not at work, never at work!* Quick snatch at mundane details – tuneless humming as someone peers into the mirror, click of lipstick, clack of face powder. A rustle and clunk to my left, the swish of a door to my right. The slow drip of a tap, the tinkle of a cistern, the hollow, shallow rattle of my breathing. Smear hands on trousers, pull out phone, type in the usual code, blue screen flashing back practically before I can blink. And with that, I'm back in the current, flushing the empty toilet as I leave, down the stairs, through the turnstile, out into the still-sheeting rain and into a cab before the shower can roll off my coat.

'Where are you?' Jemima shouts almost as soon as I've got the phone to my ear. 'Grinding the coffee beans yourself?'

'We've got a problem,' I say, pinching the phone between my head and shoulder to finish buttoning my coat. 'Olivia is climbing the walls. I bumped into Thomas buttering her up in the kitchen. The Met has convened a massive press conference out of nowhere this afternoon...'

'What? Wait ... where did you say you were? I thought...'

My heart sinks as newsroom clamour rises suddenly in the background, even over the thunder crashing across the darkening sky. That's her up and out of the edit suite, then. Months of work immortalised on tapes that no one may ever see. I spit into the puddles gathering in the gutter as I keep the passenger door open with my foot.

'It turns out none other than Thomas Thorne has a source on Operation Andromeda,' I say, blinking away Beata's spooked eyeballs. 'It must be a good one too, as it stopped Olivia in her tracks. I was there when he collared her to tell her about it. He's been tipped off before a massive press conference the Met has convened out of nowhere this afternoon. Completely unexpected, nothing in the planning diaries. It's taken everyone by surprise. She's convinced whatever they are about to say will bury our story from here to the moon, and if it doesn't, all she cares about for the foreseeable future is taking them down. She's sprung Thomas to chase whatever he's got. The cavalry are rolling out as we speak, and she wants Dominic to drop everything immediately...'

I hold the phone away from my ear for a moment as Jemima screams, swallowing acid back down my throat.

'Can you call him?' I say, coughing, no idea if she is even listening. 'I'm just outside holding us a cab, if you can hustle.'

'Get going if you've already got a ride,' she snaps. 'Fast as you can, you know the drill. Our cameras need to be in the best spot on the street outside, mark up the whole pavement if you have to, I don't care if you have to redecorate the entire street to do it. I'll be right behind you—'

Horns drown out whatever she says next as I slam the door, directing the cabbie. And no sooner do I pocket my phone than it starts up again. This time it's Dominic braying into my ear.

'What's Thomas got? He must have given something away ... Marie, are you there? Hello?'

'Hey. Where are you? Did you speak to Olivia?'

'Yes, of course I did – Christ, there is literally not enough air time in the world for me to list the ways in which I loathe that slithery posh git.'

'Dominic, listen to me. Where are you? Are you still at the Yard?'

'We're turning around now. Of course there wasn't any traffic when we left, and now it's fucking gridlock in the opposite direction. So what's Thomas got? Come on, Marie, what exactly did you hear him say?'

'I don't know. He hardly said anything, frankly. He just ambushed Olivia in the kitchen and told her that the Met was scrambling a press conference on Andromeda. And that he thought he might get an advance heads-up if she could let him off doing his actual job to go chase it down. It basically took him less than half a second to turn her head and get our trafficking story shanked into the long grass—'

'Operation Andromeda,' he interrupts, sighing, as if it's all we've been talking about the whole time. 'Andromeda, today of all days. At least we know we've really spooked them, if they're willing to publicly address arguably their worst shambles in history just to delay us showing them up, yet again, as completely incompetent.'

'Do you really think it's because of us? Because of trafficking? All the Met do is dodge questions on Andromeda, and suddenly now they can't wait to grab the mike?'

'I'd like to think so,' he replies as thunder growls across the sky. 'Of course I would, wouldn't you? But if Thomas, of all the prize dickheads, actually has a genuine source...'

'Well, we already know Thomas is full of it. This could easily just be another one of his distractions – trying to make it look like he's the one with the right sources, and not you. Like he's the one on top of everything. You've said it yourself a million times, he is totally self-serving. He's been after any beat for months, not just home affairs – anything, frankly, that would get him off shift work on the news desk. He'll have got wind of our trafficking scoop and started agitating every contact he's ever had.'

'What else did he say?' Even through the roar of the storm I can hear the cracks in Dominic's voice. 'I couldn't get anything out of Olivia but he must have told her what he thinks he's got. There is no way on God's green earth she would spring him on a hunch. She only plays dumb and coy when it suits her. And Thomas wouldn't know how to develop an investigative lead if it broke his perfect nose. It's a shame I'm apparently the only one who can see that. You would think by now—'

'How long will you be?' I interrupt, saliva running almost immediately as I point the cabbie to the pavement outside the coffee shop I spot on the corner of our next turn. One precious little pocket of time is all I'll need.

'We're going to swing by for Jonas, or try to at least. Thirty mins, tops. See you there, OK?'

He hangs up before I can say anything else, but I don't care as I'm already halfway inside Costa, relief turning to alarm almost immediately as I see how crowded it is. I have to stop myself pulling my soaking hood back over my head. Back and forth go instructions over hissing machines and clouds of steam, a black coffee and syrupy lump of something resembling cake in a paper bag appear in exchange for my last coins, and finally I reach a small table in the corner near the toilets; finally, I reach an oasis in the storm. The cake is in my stomach sloshing around in burning, bitter coffee, faster than I can drape my coat properly over the back of the chair.

I'm suddenly giddy with warmth, from the inside out, stretching out my legs, trousers hanging lighter around my calves as they start to dry, steam spurting and hissing in the background like the coffee machine is trying to speak, but no one's listening. As usual Julie drifts into my mind, like she knows what's coming, like she doesn't even have to read my mind to show up whenever I might be about to need my fix. And of course now it's Beata quivering in my head. Is she lying in the dark, staring at the ceiling, reliving everything she told us? Does she feel relieved or scared, or neither? Does she feel blank, empty, vacant? Like there's nothing inside her anymore?

The burn stabs again as I stand, pushing my way into the bathroom, slamming a cubicle door shut. It takes less than ten seconds for everything to come back out.

I spit as I flush, leaning against the toilet door with my phone in my clean hand. *Do you want coffee*, I type as I slump, heartbeat regulating with every gurgle of the cistern refilling in front of me. *I'm only round the corner.*

Carly ~ Warchester ~ 1997

I jump as the bedroom door creaks opens, face still inside the jumper I'm pulling on.

'Knock, can't you?'

Ma's leaning in the doorway as I poke my head out. Anyone watching might think I'm about to smile at her; she's actually standing up straight, wearing decent-looking clothes. She's even got an apron on, of all things, even if it's only to pretend she's not halfway through a bottle. But her getting better at pretending has just made everything more complicated instead. More questions to duck, more stupid games to play, as if the food and clothes that seem to appear just when we need them are because of her, not me. And all because staying sober and awake for more than an hour at a time is enough for social services to look the other way.

I try not to sneeze as I snort, bits of wool still inside my nose. I've wanted one of these fluffy jumpers forever, all jelly-baby bright, and now I can't stop sneezing whenever I wear it. I got it myself, by the way. Not her.

'Where are you off to?' She coughs into a hand, can't look at me.

'Out with Rach,' I say as I squint into the mirror on the wall. My face looks stripy from the fairy lights twinkling round the frame. Pretty, pretty. Like it should be.

'Where to?'

'What do you care?'

'I'm your mother, Carly, I have a right to know.'

'You have a right? Haven't we done enough pretending that you have a right to anything?'

She stares at the floor. Even she knows I don't have to answer to her now she's been incapable for so long. I push past to the better light in the bathroom, examining the chunky studs shining round the curve of my right ear in the tiny mirror above the sink. If it wasn't for the swelling round the top, my ear could be made of gold, but instead it looks diseased.

I frown at myself. I should never have let Rach get her hands on it. Like a job in Claire's Accessories makes her a professional. She's barely been out of school a month, and that's only because she's two years older than me.

'Please, Carly...' I spot Ma staring behind me. All hollow pale grey, she may as well be a hundred years old. I start brushing my teeth to drown her out.

'Ly-Ly?' A pudgy little hand swats at my leg.

Spitting toothpaste into the sink, I squat, cupping Kayleigh's face with my hand, running my thumb over the shiny hair-slides she's clipped all wonky into her downy fringe. They aren't from Ma either. It's only Rach who really knows what we both like.

'Ly-Ly stay,' she lisps, pulling fluff off my jumper. 'Ly-Ly see Lay-ly...'

I pull her to me, wondering if she can hear my heart thudding against her face. She snuffles into my front like a pig.

'Please, love,' Ma says, leaning on the doorframe, arms lolling against her sides like she's about to slither on to the floor. 'You're only fourteen...'

'You didn't give a shit when I was twelve,' I say, squeezing Kayleigh in my arms. 'You couldn't even look after your own baby. Do you think now she's made it to three you can give me chapter and verse? She's still here because of me, you useless old cow. Not you.'

'I know it hasn't been easy,' she says, sagging into the doorframe. 'I don't know what we would have done if Jason hadn't—'

'Jase? Seriously?' Kayleigh squawks as my arms tighten round her. 'Here we go again...' I have to drop Kayleigh as I straighten to round on Ma. She's too heavy for me to carry anymore. 'What would we have done if good old Sergeant Gates hadn't kept showing up with enough food and cash to get us through another pointless few days? You think it's all down to him? I suppose I should count us lucky that you're his actual mother because, hey, guess what happened the last time a loser showed up enough times with a big smile and box of fucking chocolates? Got enough brain cells left to remember how that turned out?'

I snort as I turn back to the mirror, reaching for a lipstick from a jumble on the windowsill. I know she'll have nothing to say to that. Violet-purple lips smack back at me as I blow a few kisses into the silence. At least now I've got new things too, the right stuff for a girl my age. Kayleigh too. It doesn't hurt as much when I remember how they were all taken away from me for no reason. We're hanging on now, and it's because of me. I know how to see us right.

'Lyyyyyyy...' Kayleigh tugs at the hem of my skirt above her head as she starts to cry. I click my lipstick shut, tucking it into my bra before untangling her hand.

'Sweet dreams, angel,' I say, pushing past Ma as I remember the Zippo I've left in our room. Digging around under my mattress, I finger the loops and curls of Carly carved into its silver front, a lighter with proper style. At least there are still some people who do things especially for me, I think, smiling as I tuck it into the other cup of my bra. I bang the door on Kayleigh's cries on my way out.

'Alright?' Rach looks up. She's leaning on the opposite wall. 'Hey, that jumper looks ace.'

I smooth the soft wool down over my front, like I'm stroking a cat. Her hair is scraped into a bun on top of her head, pulling her face tight. Smoke billows out of her nose as she looks down at me, a new blue gem twinkling from one nostril.

'Oooh. And that looks ace too,' I say, stroking my arm. It feels so good. I wish I never had to take this jumper off. 'Did you do it today?'

'Yesterday ... plenty of time to take advantage now I'm around all day. Do you want one too?' She jangles a huge bunch of keys in her pocket. 'They even let me keep these overnight now. So we can go back in whenever you like. See, I told you jacking school would be worth it. Mad, right? You turn sixteen and *bam*, suddenly everything you've been deciding for yourself for years doesn't matter to anyone else anymore. Even if there are people who don't like what you're doing they can't do a fucking thing about it. Guess you have to draw a line in the sand somewhere, right? You'll see, soon enough...'

I pinch my nose. 'Did it hurt?'

She snorts, twirling the keys around a finger as she starts to walk down the road.

'I can do it now. We've got time before getting Drina if you want. It's only half ten.'

I trot to keep up, rubbing my nose between my fingers.

'How do you do it? Is it with the ear gun? Do you just use that? Or is it different? Doesn't it need to be bigger?'

'There's a setting. You just change it.'

'What, like a ruler?'

'Ruler? What are you like?'

'Yeah, like a measurement or something.'

'It's like a nail gun, Carls. Not a fucking ruler.'

'But I mean the actual bit, you know, the needle or pin that makes the hole...'

She stops and turns. 'Do you want one or not?' The gem looks like a star with her head all high up in the night sky.

'Maybe not yet. Half of these are still infected...' I run my fingertip down the studs on the lip of my ear.

She leans down and squints at my ear, before flicking it with a finger.

'Hey!' I grab at my ear, squeezing into the pain shooting through it. 'What was that for?'

She grins. 'Toughen you up.'

I rub my ear, eyes smarting. 'I am tough.'

'That's not what I hear.'

'What? What do you mean?'

The whites of her eyes roll at me as she sticks another tab into her mouth, lighter sputtering like a broken-down car. I pass her my Zippo. Its big flare makes her nose stud flash blue.

'You need to learn to do it without poppers,' she says after a minute, blowing a cone of smoke into my face. 'It's easy after the first bit. And it's not like it ever lasts long, is it? Could be worse...'

Blood rushes to my cheeks. I look down into the dark, spots popping in my eyes from looking at my Zippo flame.

'We can't have it so they need to find poppers every time they want it backwards. We're on the clock, remember? You'll get used to it after a while ... Homos do it their whole life like that, don't they? Bite on your lip. Or on the grass, or sheet, whatever. Just grab something to chew on when you turn around.'

I sneeze as I drop my head into my jumper. Even I can't pretend anymore that I don't know the real reasons why we keep doing everything we are told, no matter what it is.

'Is that what tonight is about, then?' I say into the thick ribs of my neckline. I don't care if it makes me sneeze again. It's like a cat is stroking my cheek.

'Uh-huh,' Rach replies through her teeth. Suddenly my jumper feels itchy and hot.

'Let's just go. They'll let us in early, get it over with. Drina did good last week at least,' I say.

Rach starts to walk again. The night darkens round us as clouds roll over the moon.

Marie ~ London ~ 2006

'You beauty,' Dominic sighs, holding his umbrella over me as I hand him a takeaway cup. 'Were you in Costa? I got your message just as we ditched the cab so I stuck my head in to look for you. That said, I didn't look too hard. The queue was so long I almost lost the will to live just looking at it.'

He slurps as we huddle in the steady rain outside New Scotland Yard, sign revolving above our heads like it thinks it's a lighthouse.

'Why did it bother becoming New Scotland Yard?' I say, eyeing the sign mindlessly rotating over Mary, who's whisking round a patch of pavement with yellow hazard tape, planting her tripod square in the middle. 'Seems like it's been making the same mistakes for years.'

Dominic snorts as he sips. 'Very good. You should've waited for Jonas to arrive before unleashing that one. She'll be here soon enough.'

'I thought you guys were going to bring her?' I clutch the other coffee cooling in my hand.

'The traffic was appalling, and besides, I had to dodge Olivia. I'd already hung up so many times I could practically smell her on the war path. Surely anything to do with Andromeda should be considered as my territory, and mine alone? It's a police investigation. Unless I've misread my contract, I'm still in the pay of our esteemed state broadcaster as home affairs editor, so how is it that any Dick, Harry or Thomas can fuck around in all my leads? I just wish it wasn't all kicking off seconds before we were about to land another scoop.'

'That's the point, isn't it? That's what you think, anyway? They're trying to bury us...?' I trail off as he frowns.

'Indeed, Sherlock. Spin is to be expected, obviously. If Her Majesty's press can infiltrate and expose a grooming and trafficking ring, why can't Her Majesty's police force?' He vamps on the spot as he talks. 'I'd just never have expected a headline on Andromeda, of all cans of worms. And even an ego the size of mine can see a fractional possibility there's something else in it ... And if it turns out I've missed it...'

He pauses as a cab screeches up next to us, gushing water over the kerb. We step back as Jemima steps out, phone still cocked between her head and ear.

'...I understand,' she says into the phone, rolling her eyes at Dominic and nodding at me. 'I'll call you back shortly, OK? I've just met up with them.'

'Well?' Dominic stares at her as she smooths down the braids wound tight and immaculate against her head.

'Well, she knows you're upset. And she gets that none of us want to put the trafficking story on the shelf for long ... It's not as if she routinely sidelines scoops either. But she doesn't see why Thomas chasing a valid lead, especially on a national story like Andromeda, should be such a big deal—'

'Did she say what he's got?' I interrupt before Dominic can.

Jemima frowns at me as she unfolds an umbrella over her head. 'She wouldn't go there, so it must be good. I tried "but we're the senior investigative team" and no dice. She says she'll have a word about Thomas not giving us a courtesy heads-up that he was working something but gave me the whole "I didn't expect this from you, Jemima".'

'But what about our trafficking story?' I can't help myself, the third shadow trembling back into my head.

'She's as disappointed as we are—'

'Bollocks is she.' Dominic cuts her off. 'All she cares about, and all she's ever cared about, is owning the next headline. Why else would she let a chancer like Thomas out of the gate without so much as a by your leave? She's never given a toss about real investigations.'

'That's not true and you know it.' Jemima squares up to him. 'Don't lose it with us just because you haven't had the guts to lose it with her. This isn't all about you and your grudge.'

I jump as Dominic flings his cup on the pavement.

'If she thinks I'm working with toe-rag, in any way, shape or form—'

'It won't come to that. We'll get to his source before he even knows what he's got—'

'Why don't I go into the press conference,' I say, stopping them both mid-sentence. 'No one knows me in there, much less knows I worked on the trafficking story. If it really is all about redirecting the spotlight then they'll hardly take a question from either of you, will they?'

'Eh? Don't you start! You think it'll look anything other than ridiculous if Nine don't bother sending an actual correspondent into a national press conference on Operation Andromeda?' Dominic unbuttons his coat to finish looping a tie around his neck. 'And I will quit on the spot if Olivia even tries to put someone else in front of the camera instead.'

'Pack in it, would you?' Jemima says. 'You shouldn't go inside, and you know it. If you blaze in and make a giant performance of yourself because we're all pissed off our trafficking story has to wait, you won't get publicly blacklisted, but privately ... The shutters will come down, the lot. No one will tell you anything for a while. For them to be rushing the microphone out on Andromeda, they're either fighting like rats in a sack, or they really are going to change the record. And you need to be ready for that. It will be a far bigger deal than whatever we have on trafficking.'

'Why would I make it a performance? I'm perfectly capable of controlling myself.'

'I know you are,' Jemima murmurs, wringing his coat as she squeezes his arm. 'But I also know how deep it runs ... and how knackered you are. The last few weeks haven't exactly been lighthearted fare, have they? Making friends with people smugglers and all that…'

'Don't call it a grudge, OK?'

I stare at our pairs of feet on the wet street. Why does Dominic suddenly sound like a defeated child? I know that two and two and two make six, but for some reason, this is adding up all wrong.

'I'm sorry. I really am.' I watch Jemima's feet as she shifts her weight from one to the other as she replies. 'But you are better served working your leads, especially if Thomas is working whoever his are. Home affairs needs to own Andromeda. And Olivia won't forget about that little girl in the meantime. Or Beata. She told me to make sure you knew that. She'd have told you herself if you hadn't hung up.'

Now it's Dominic's foot nudging at the puddle. I look up to see him wipe an eye.

'Nice save,' Jemima mutters to me as he trudges down the street without another word, pulling his collar up around his neck. 'Let's go in, shall we? Won't hurt to be early.'

I barely hear her, staring as Dominic's back disappears into the shadow of the storm, past and present blurring with the rain, shadows crowding my head.

Carly ~ Warchester ~ 1997

'How long's she going to be?' I stare back at the receptionist through the glass. It must've been a busy morning – her condom fishbowl's already half empty.

'Just take a seat, Carly, would you?'

I square up to her as she pushes her glasses up her nose with her middle finger. I don't care whether she's really trying to give me the finger.

'Drop it, Carls,' Rach hisses, yanking me back from the glass and into a seat. 'Don't make this any worse than it already is.'

'Rachel Baines?'

A tall woman in a white coat clacks out of the door in front of us.

I snort as I look up. She looks like a pencil, all skinny in her white coat with her tiny head and silly black bun of hair.

'Could you come with me, please?'

'Eh? Why?' Rach asks. I watch out of the corner of my eye as she straightens, bracelets clattering against her plastic seat. She's basically a walking advert for Claire's now. As if anyone will think all that tacky jewellery is the real deal.

'It won't take a moment. This way, please.' The woman half turns towards the open door.

'I'm sorted. I'm just here with her...' Rach's hand flicks at me.

'That's fine. We know you are. If you could just come this way for a moment, please.'

No one speaks. The clock ticks brainlessly into the silence, like it always does.

'Who's asking?' Rach's chair scrapes as she fidgets.

'It's this way. If you could just come with us for a moment...'

She must be a robot, I think. A robot pencil. There's a curse, then another scrape before Rach's boots clump through the open door.

I pop my chewing gum in time with the clock, slouching back into my chair. My arm hurts where Rach grabbed it, just like the rest of me. Just enough that I can feel it in the background, making it impossible to ignore what we have to do practically every week these days. But I can't afford to think about that too much. There's no way out of this town other than with the army. Not for girls like us.

One minute passes, then two, then five. Pop, tick, pop.

'Carly? We're ready for you now.'

I look up to find the pencil standing in front of me again, bun nodding towards the door. At least I manage to turn my wince into a grin as I follow her down the corridor. From behind, she looks more like a starving penguin, feet and hands jerking about as she walks.

'Where're we going?' I call after her as we round a few new corners before she stops in front of a door with light streaming out underneath. There are never any windows in these cubicles.

'I'll be just outside,' she says into the room as she opens it.

I squint as sunlight pours into my face. Not only is there a window in here, but there's a blue coat instead of white on the woman waiting at the desk inside.

'You must be Carly,' she says, peering at me.

'Who are you?' The door closes behind me with a soft click. I turn and jump to see Rach sitting in a chair in the back corner. 'What are you doing in here?'

Her mouth looks all pursed up like she's smoking, except she's not. I twist back to the woman, who's pointing at a chair near the desk.

'Please, come sit down...'

Rach nods at me, pulling her mouth tighter around her invisible cigarette. Shuffling forward, I sit, forgetting not to wince.

'Carly, is it?' she smiles at me.

I sneak another look at Rach. She's picking at her nail polish, face still set.

'I'm Nurse Govern,' the woman says, nodding and smiling all over again. 'And how are you feeling today?'

'What?' I stare at her.

'How are you feeling today? Better?'

'Better?' I snort. 'What's going on? I just need—'

'We'll get to that. Rachel has explained.'

'Rach, what's she on about?' My head swivels between them.

'It's alright, girl...' Rach's face softens a bit. 'We'll get going in a minute, OK?'

I turn back to find the nurse with a clipboard in her lap.

'As I said, I'm Nurse Govern,' she says, 'and I work with social services. Between us, we visit all the clinics in the country. It's our job to make sure everyone who comes here is supported on their journey, no matter what has happened to bring them in. And you and Rachel have been visiting with us for a while now, haven't you, love?'

I freeze in my seat. She cocks her head as we stare at each other.

'Rachel's explained why you need the morning-after pill. It all sounds perfectly reasonable, so don't worry. We're here to help you...'

'What's this got to do with social services?' I stammer, Jason ringing through my head before I can block him out.

'You're fifteen, is that right, Carly?'

'Nearly,' I mumble, shuffling in my seat at I look past her to the opposite wall. There's a load of box files balanced on top of each other in big stacks that look like they're about to fall over.

'Well, I'm afraid I can't usually prescribe these without an adult present, but I think we can make an exception just this once, given that your sister's here with you.'

'Sister?' The question leaves my mouth before I can stop it.

'That's right,' she says. 'Isn't it?'

We all sit – still, like chess pieces.

'And given your sister is nearly seventeen, that puts us on the right side of the line, doesn't it?' Her pen hovers over her clipboard.

'Yeah,' I mutter into my shirt, shivering as I look down at my legs, white stumps poking out below the hem of my skirt. If I couldn't feel my feet I'd look like Captain Perv himself. I jump as the nurse's chair squeaks, on wheels too for some reason, even though she's still got her own legs.

'Would you roll up your sleeve for me? I'll just need to check your blood pressure.'

I shrug off my blazer and unbutton my cuff, staring at the little silver wheels on the bottom of her chair legs. She can't honestly believe Rach is my sister, can she? The machine on my arm hisses and sighs as she opens a drawer full of small, white cardboard boxes.

'You can put that back on now,' the nurse says, pointing at my blazer as she rests a box in her lap.

I look up at her as I finish doing up my buttons. She's just sitting there, waiting.

'Thanks,' I mumble, trying not to meet her eyes. 'Is that it, then? You'll give it to me?'

'Are you sure you feel well enough to take it? Your sister says you've had a nasty stomach bug. It's like the pill itself, it won't work if you throw it up. When's the last time you were sick?'

I stare past her at the files stacked against the wall, willing them to just crash over.

'Carly? Are you sure you're OK, love?'

I jump as she rests a hand on my leg. I can't speak, words thick and stuck in my mouth, tears pricking at my eyes as I hang my head. My stupid, useless throat. No one could put anything that far down without it making them sick, could they? Half the girls in school use their own fingers, for fuck's sake. So how am I supposed to manage other people's pieces?

'Not since yesterday morning,' Rach says. I don't dare look up. 'Right, Carls? She was awful sick but she's OK now.' Her chair scrapes as she fidgets.

'Could you give us a moment, Rachel? There's a chair down the corridor outside where you'll be comfortable.'

'She's alright, aren't you, Carls? Nothing you can say to her that you can't say to me—'

'It's just down the hall,' the nurse interrupts, hand squeezing my leg, somehow warm and cool at the same time. 'She'll be out in a moment, don't worry.'

I hold my breath, clock ticking into the silence before a particularly big scrape, then a slamming door. My leg stays warm even as the nurse takes away her hand.

'Would you like some water, Carly?'

I stare into my skirt as she moves the small white box from her lap into mine.

'You'll need to take one pill now and the other in twelve hours. You might feel a bit weepy and tender for a few days, but don't worry, that's all normal. And remember to take your regular pill as usual, you won't be protected otherwise.'

I reach for the box, turning it over and over in my fingers.

'I think you and I both know that Rachel isn't your sister, is she?'

I wrap both hands around the box before she can take it back.

'It's OK, love. I know you don't want to have a baby, do you? You're still a baby yourself...'

'No, I'm not.' I force myself to look up, staring at her hair rather than at her face. 'I take care of myself, take care of everyone.'

'It helps with our paperwork if we can say, and others can corroborate, that there was either an adult or family member present when prescribing these tablets to a minor,' she continues, as if I wasn't speaking too. 'But the truth is, we will give them out regardless if we think withholding them poses a greater risk to the patient. What do you think about all that?'

I blink at her hair.

'You're not in any trouble,' she tries again. 'Let me be very clear on that. You never told me Rachel was your sister. She didn't either, come to that. I put the words in her mouth, to make it simpler for me and for you. I know she's important to you. And I know it's as important to you that you take these pills.'

Somehow her eyes find mine, dark, never-ending, like the inside of a telescope.

'We're here to help you, love. Just remember that. If there's anything you'd like to tell me about your circumstances, or how you came to need this appointment ... You're not alone. You don't need to go through this on your own.'

'I'm not alone,' I croak, trying and failing to tear my eyes away. 'I've got Rach. She'll see me right. She looks after me, takes me everywhere. She's the one who brought me here.'

'Yes, we've seen you both many times before, haven't we?' Her eyes harden.

'I'm fine, OK? You don't need to worry about us.'

I flinch as she stands with me, uncurling to her full height as I hide away the box. When she was sitting down, she looked like she'd be smaller than me.

'I should be here for a few more morning clinics,' she says. 'You can come in and see me whenever you'd like. Nurse Govern...' She taps at the name badge by her upside-down watch. 'And there's no need to bring your sister next time. Not now we know each other.'

I can't help but turn back to look at her as I leave. She's still standing, watching me, lit up by the sun behind her.

~~~

Outside, I practically have to run to keep up with Rach, but bounce backwards as she suddenly spins round to glare at me.

'What?' I brush my hair out of my eyes, pulling my blazer

straight. 'We're sorted, aren't we?' Rach's laugh makes my tummy flip.

'You just don't get it, do you? Now we've got social services up our arses too because you can't keep it down!' She hawks at my feet. It looks like a snail, all plump and wobbly in the dirt.

'It's never been a problem before, has it? And if I take the pill in the morning instead of at night then there won't be any danger—'

'Of puking it up?' Her eyes blaze with her lighter as she pauses to spark a tab. 'It can't happen again, Carls. Like, ever. We've got to get this right, every time. Or else we're toast, we're proper fucked. We all are. We've been bringing the others in with us, remember?'

I notice red scratches running down her neck and around her collarbone as she looks away from me, wind blowing smoke back around her head as she exhales.

'It was just the once,' I mumble, scuffing over her snail with my wet shoe. 'Sometimes they push down so hard I think I might swallow them whole. It's not like it happens every time, is it? And if it ever does again, that nurse said I could come back whenever I wanted.'

'Oh yeah?' She rounds on me. 'And what else did you say to that good old nurse?'

'Nothing, I swear. I would never.' I rub my foot into the dirt again. 'Besides. Drina said I'd grow out of it.'

'For fuck's sake.' I jump as she shouts, stamping out her cigarette. 'What are you doing, talking to Drina about it? How many times do I have to tell you? We can't talk about this stuff, Carls. Ever! We show up, we do, we leave. Neat and tidy, that's the deal. It's bad enough we've had to blag you the morning-after pill ... the last thing we need now is Drina gobbing off about poor, spewy little Carly.'

'She won't,' I gabble, wrapping my fingers around the cardboard box in my pocket. 'She's up to her neck in it, like us.'

'No, she's not. They've got money, her folks. And sod all to do with the army. They could leave so easily, disappear, make it all go away for her if she squealed. Where are we going to go? Sleep in Victory Field? Like they won't find us there. They own the whole fucking town.'

'Can you believe she thought you were my sister?' I change the subject, even though just saying the word 'sister' makes me remember Ma scrabbling about for something to feed Kayleigh before I left this morning. Rach doesn't answer me.

'Rach...' I persist. In spite of everything I start to feel just a tiny bit warm inside, as I think about it. I always wanted a grown-up sister, especially now that I'm actually having to be one myself. Shop fronts clatter open around us as we turn into town.

'Wait here a sec,' she finally says as we stop outside Claire's, disappearing and reappearing in a jangle of bells with a plastic cup of water.

'Down the hatch,' she says, nudging the cup into my blazer. 'Come on.'

'Oh ... right.' I pull the crumpled box from my pocket. The cardboard comes away in my hand as I find the foil packet of pills inside.

'Now jog on, will you?' she says as I swallow, pushing the blister pack with its second pill back into my pocket for later. 'And make sure you don't lose those in detention. Stash them good. I'll speak to Jase. We can't use that clinic again, not now social services have cottoned on.'

She turns her back on my nod, disappearing behind the columns of earrings and bracelets twinkling at me just inside the door.

I swallow again as I peer into the dark at the back of the shop, pill like a lump in my throat as I look for her. But she's gone.

Marie ~ London ~ 2006

Inside the Scotland Yard press pen, the circus has already started. Battalions of tripods lined up behind the back row, microphone stands fighting over the podium up front, endless yards of transmission cables snaking all over the place. Usually I love this part, all process and detail smacking me round the face, *Come on people, let's go, charge!* No time to think about anything other than what needs to happen to get the information where it needs to be. But today, the whole thing would taste sour, if I didn't still have the dregs of bile in my mouth. They've done it, I think, hovering behind Jemima and doing the handshake dance, nodding and smiling at everyone massing into the room like a bloody flock of geese. We're all here, waiting for them to feed us breadcrumbs, hanging on their every word as if none of us have anything to say that's our own. Or are going to bloody bother trying, anyway.

Muttering my excuses to Jemima, I head to some seats in the back row, draping my coat on the back of a chair just below the army of tripods. Everything should feel a bit lighter now we're out of the rain and drying off a bit, but my clothes still feel heavy on my body. I keep expecting to see Dominic as the room thickens with people.

'The cavalry's arriving, I see,' Jemima says as she flops into the seat next to me. 'What a performance ... I need another coffee, obviously. Things like this only ever happen when I've not slept for two nights and had to watch the same hideous tapes at least eleventy-thousand times.'

'Stay there, I'll get them,' I say, jumping to my feet, sure I'll find Dominic in the crowd outside.

I push my way through the incoming traffic to the machine in the corridor, plastic cups dropping and filling without so much as a sound. All that hiss and fuss and sigh of Costa, I think. Maybe it's their fancy machines laughing at how stupid we all are. I join the line shuffling back into the room, scanning up and down for familiar faces.

'Cheers,' Jemima says, lifting and slurping as soon as I pass over a cup, squeezing back into my seat. 'This is such a circus. Apparently every news outfit in town is showing up...'

She fades as I twist around, still looking for Dominic.

'Shouldn't we save some more seats? He'll be here any minute now, surely?'

'He'll stay away if he knows what's good for him,' Jemima replies between gulps. 'He's his own worst enemy sometimes. Almost always too strung out to realise, but who could blame him, I guess. And now is definitely not the time to put a loose cannon in the room.' I stare at her immaculately woven head glistening under the lights lined up behind us. 'He needs to be careful, and he knows it. Better that he stays with the pack outside and listens in. Mary will pipe the audio of whatever's being said into his earpiece so he doesn't miss a word. We don't want him drawing attention to himself for all the wrong reasons. If he's in here, you can bet he will start yelling inappropriate questions.'

'Is that what you meant about a grudge? When you told him not to let it get in the way of the right decision?'

'I know what I said,' she interrupts, crunching her cup into her hand. 'You really don't get it, do you? Haven't you ever wondered why Dominic is so keen to show up every Met police failing he comes across? Or are you still green enough that you genuinely think no one in the news business has an agenda other than holding power to account?'

There's a crash and lots of swearing as a microphone stand falls off the podium, but I only have eyes for Jemima.

'But I thought—'

'His mum is in the police,' she says, cutting me off. 'Was in the police, I mean. She died in the line when he was twelve. He thinks they didn't do enough to protect her. It was a botched operation, from the little he's ever said about it. He'd never admit it colours his judgement – but it wouldn't take much for him to slip up when he's this upset. Especially when a git like Thomas is the one who might be ahead of him. Make a scene, cover himself in indignity, turn the story for all the wrong reasons...'

She trails off as my eyes wander to the cables snaked all over the stage, knotting and blurring into one big, black, smudgy mass. This new little nugget of information sits in my mind like a meteor just crashed in from outer space, blowing up everything I've ever assumed about Dominic. But before I can ask any more questions, hush descends as uniformed officers parade into the room.

I peer at them, lined up penguin-perfect with their chests puffed out in black and white. If I wasn't suddenly so confused I could pretend we were all in a cartoon.

'Here we go,' Jemima mutters as one officer leans forward to tap a microphone.

'Thanks for your patience,' he booms. 'The commissioner will be with you shortly.'

The commissioner? The entire crowd squawks with surprise, heads swivelling on every neck up ahead. And on cue, in she comes, pausing for the flashbulbs up front before walking herself to the single chair hidden behind the bundle of microphones.

Jemima curses, a low hiss into her collar. Unease prickles up my back as the room stills, like we're all birds on a branch, waiting out an incoming gale. If only I could actually fly away.

'Good afternoon,' the commissioner says, the piece of paper in her hand just visible above all the bobbles on the desk. 'Thank you all for being here on such an important day for the Metropolitan Police.'

I squint as she unfolds a pair of glasses on to her nose, everything about her so neat and precise that she could be a pencil drawing, a sketch I'm almost sure I've seen before; a page of a book I know I've read but can't quite remember, fluttering away almost as soon as I register it – peripheral but still unmistakable.

She pauses, pushing at her glasses with a fingertip. I hold my breath as the lip of the paper starts to tremble.

'Today marks five years since the conclusion of Operation Andromeda, and the successful conviction and incarceration of eleven offenders. These offenders were all mid-to-high-ranking military officers, found guilty of the most appalling of crimes, committed under the cover of Britain's most revered establishment.'

She pauses again, into a collectively held breath.

'At the time, we believed it was the culmination of years of painstaking investigative work. Hundreds of officers, thousands of hours, millions of pounds of taxpayers' money was spent on bringing the perpetrators of Britain's most prolific known paedophile ring to justice. These offenders systematically abused vulnerable teenage girls for their own sexual gratification. Secondarily, they brought the status of one of Britain's greatest institutions into vile disrepute. Their evil knew no bounds.'

'Spare us the history lesson, why don't you,' Jemima mutters under her breath.

My eyelid starts to twitch as the numbers clang around in my head. Eleven? Wasn't it thirteen? I snatch at the memory on the edge of my consciousness, so fleeting, it's gone.

'We now know that mistakes were made during Operation Andromeda. We now know that victims were failed, in the face of unimaginable depravity.'

She peers at us over the rim of her glasses, quieting even the snappers in their pit.

'After displaying such endless bravery in coming forward, and such incredible resilience over months of gruelling testimony, that is particularly unforgivable, a betrayal of the highest order. And I would like, on behalf of the entire Metropolitan Police Force, to apologise directly to them.'

She puts her paper down, holding her face aloft for the flashes and clicks erupting from every camera in the room.

'I want to pay tribute to the tremendous courage of some of these victims, whose harrowing testimony has brought new information to light.'

Her words slow, deliberate and precise, firing shot after perfect shot.

'I can confirm that as of today, we are reopening the case against General Minchin, and as such are launching a second phase to Operation Andromeda. All units in the South East Command have been mobilised and will report directly to me.'

Grenades this time, one after the other, bursting all around me.

'We believe there are several issues that need to be investigated and resolved if the law is to prevail. Only then will Britain be able to begin rebuilding trust in its military, and only then will the victims feel justice has truly been served. I would like to thank all of the officers involved in bringing this new evidence to light. And I reiterate my apologies to the victims of these horrendous crimes. We will not fail you again. I will not fail you, again.'

And with that, the atom bomb lands, room erupting as she stands, along with almost everyone else. I'm definitely the only person looking at the carpet, neat squares of its pattern puddling into a smudge. Wrapped in a mushroom cloud of pandemonium, it's only the clutch of Jemima's hand that bears me up and out down the hall, through the turnstiles and into the rain, hammering down again from the endless sky like the Earth is trying to finally scrub away a stubborn, ancient skin.

Carly ~ Warchester ~ 1997

The clock tower chimes ten as I hurry past, clanging round the narrow streets in the centre of town. Even during the week, on a random Wednesday morning in November, it's busy. Too many people with nothing to do, and a tiny, crowded town centre the only place to pass the time.

I elbow past the gaggle of women pushing buggies in a line just up the road from Claire's. You can always tell the army wives by the formation they walk in, but Ma can't even pretend to do that anymore. I fiddle with the pill packet in my pocket as I duck down through the subway at the edge of town. Either I sneak into school at first break and risk getting searched, or I go home and stash them with my Zippo and get a late detention. No choice really, is there?

I can hear Kayleigh's screams even before I get to the front door. I bolt upstairs to find her thrashing on the floor in piles of filth between the beds in our room, sweaty hair plastered round her head, face as pink as lipstick ... I try to pull her into my lap but she's hot as a bonfire, blue eyes rolling like marbles. Even I'm sweating trying to hold her, she's so hot, twisting and thrashing in my arms, spit turning into foam at the sides of her mouth...

Out of nowhere there's a shadow over us, a uniform filling the doorway. Ma's suddenly at my other side, steaming with booze, batting a filthy towel full of ice at Kayleigh's face. Even the smell of piss suddenly streaming from Kayleigh into the pit on the floor can't hide the smell of vodka, like Ma's wearing it on her skin. The uniform grabs at Kayleigh, standing, lifting and turning all at once towards someone else in the doorway. I know they're talking, their mouths are moving, but is it to me? Heads swivel as I stumble to

my feet, Ma slumping face down into the wet clothes on the floor.
I follow the uniforms down the stairs, at least I must've, because
now I'm in an ambulance, opposite Kayleigh, who's on a stretcher
in the middle, plastic mask clamped over her face. And suddenly
she's naked, purple blotches all over her body, bloated nappy
sitting at my feet like a dead white cat. They're rolling her over,
shoving at her other side, making her arch … Wait, what? A
sudden wet patch on my shirt, the smell of acid in my nose, a bag
appearing under my face as I retch into it. The scream of a siren
and a jolt as we start to move. Across from Kayleigh's pale, blotchy,
but finally still body, the uniform meets my eyes. Short hair, dark
eyes, pale, crumply face – I only realise it's a woman when she
starts to speak.

'You're her sister, are you?'

I nod, most of my face still inside the bag.

'And that's her mother back there, I take it? Your mother too?'

I nod again. Can't speak. Will I ever be able to speak again?
There's already so much I'm not allowed to say, and now…

'Does your sister have any allergies that you know of? Nuts,
eggs, penicillin? That kind of thing?'

The bag crinkles as I shake my head. She reaches out a hand to
touch Kayleigh's forehead, eyes narrowing at me.

'What's your name?'

I look down at Kayleigh. Her eyes are closed. She's breathing –
in-out, in-out – like the dip in her chest is also a paper bag.

'And hers?' she asks, hand hovering over Kayleigh's head.
'Number two going in now,' she yells. To me? To who? Resting
one hand on Kayleigh's hip, she pops a little white cartridge out
of a packet in her lap, like a toy bullet. I stare as she rolls Kayleigh
further forward on her side, lifting her top leg with one hand,
pushing the cartridge in between her legs with the other till I can't
see it anymore. Where can it have gone? Not where I think it has
… I retch again into the bag, eyes streaming as Kayleigh's little
body flops back on to the stretcher, limp and trembling.

'It's a suppository,' she says, using a heel to kick the empty packet under her seat. 'Just paracetamol ... Don't worry. We give it like that when we can't do it orally. She'll hardly feel it, and we need to bring her temperature down, it's dangerously high.'

I spit into the bag, gripping the edge of my seat as we lurch around a corner. A machine beeps somewhere. Has it been beeping all the time?

'You did well to call 999,' she says as sirens thud overhead. 'Your sister was having a febrile convulsion. They look worse than they are, but a temperature in the sky like that signals a dangerous infection somewhere. How long's she been ill?'

Another clatter, my feet flying into the air as we swerve. It's only then that I notice Kayleigh's been strapped down on the stretcher, so she hardly moves at all. I swallow bile. Who called 999? It can't have been Ma, but I know it wasn't me. It's the only thing I'm sure of.

'She'll get better faster if you talk to me,' Ambulance Woman says, raising her voice above the siren. 'Otherwise we just have to guess, and waste time ruling things out.'

She unfolds a massive piece of silver foil, laying it over Kayleigh like a blanket.

'It's thermal,' she says, as if I'd actually asked. 'Stops her getting too cold or too hot.'

More bile goes down as I look at my sister's head, plastic mask poking out of her foil wrappings like she's nothing more than a sausage roll. A screech and a jolt, and we stop, noise flooding into the back of the ambulance as the doors pop open, two other people grabbing the back of the stretcher.

'Female, three years old at a guess, febrile convulsion, stable,' the woman shouts as she follows the stretcher out, wheels clattering down the ramp. I stumble across the ambulance bay, trying to make sense out of the words flying back and forth over my foil-wrapped sister: seizure this, fever that, something about a rash? Every time I reach out to try and hold the stretcher it judders away from my hand, stupid silver foil blanket crackling in the wind like it's laughing at me.

'Sister here's the next of kin.' The woman jerks her head at me as the hospital doors swing open. 'Mother still at the scene...'

Nurses, doctors, paramedics all whirl in front of me as curtains whip closed around Kayleigh almost as soon as we're inside. And suddenly I'm alone, alone in this strange whirring lobby of a hospital, the only evidence of Kayleigh ever being here a bunch of shoes and a flash of silver foil moving around in the gap between the curtains and the floor of a cubicle. Everything starts to darken at the edges as I put out a hand to steady myself, except there's nothing to hold on to, nothing except air and more air, whooshing between my fingers as I clutch at it, falling backward into even more air until the scratchy edges of uniformed arms catch me from behind, folding my body into the seat of a chair, which cradles me like all of my bones have melted into skin, and there's nothing, nothing left inside me to turn me back into a whole person ever again.

Marie ~ London ~ 2006

'The commissioner!' Heads swivel as Dominic screams at us, hysteria amplified by the soaked neon-yellow waterproof clinging to his entire body. 'Apologised! For Andromeda! The commissioner herself...'

I unfold an umbrella over his head like a robot, the mass of cameras, cables and tripods around us a blur save for the sharp edges of New Scotland Yard's iconic sign revolving mercilessly over the commotion. Fat raindrops splat on its surface with every new question clanging around inside my head. Victims were failed ... Who? And how? We all know not everyone got caught. They never are, are they?

'She's got some front, that's for sure,' Jemima says, squaring up to him. 'It's her first term, she's making a point ... You are going to take that off, aren't you? You'll look like bloody Pac-Man on screen if you don't.'

Water cascades off his jacket as she yanks at it.

'No one has ever apologised for Andromeda before,' Dominic spits, pulling his coat open so hard the zipper flies off into a puddle. 'No institution, especially not the Metropolitan Police, apologises for anything. Ever.'

I look back at the line-up, a platoon of media spread out along the street, all repeating the press statement for the eightieth time. To reopen the case against that general, what must they have? And who must have given it to them? *Victims were failed.* I blink away the rain in my eyes, trying to zone out as the sign still circles mindlessly above the commotion.

'Well, they wanted every front page—'

Dominic swears so loudly that the reporter closest to us has to wave him away, even as she keeps talking into her camera.

'They've planned this for ages,' he says, eyes glittering as he straightens his tie, glaring down the barrel of Mary's camera readying opposite. 'They must have ... It's nothing to do with us, just a tidy little bonus that it's going to bury our trafficking story from here to the fucking moon. Screwed again by the Met ... and who knew it was the anniversary? As if anyone would mark five years since an operation that's long since been declared a total botch job.'

He prods at the earpiece in his ear, his thumbs-up to the camera at total odds with everything he's saying.

'So how would I know?' Jemima hisses, balling his soaking jacket under her arm. The umbrella slips from my hand as he grabs it, framing himself in front of the lens.

'It hardly matters now, does it? Move it, Jonas. And you, Marie, come on, I've got less than thirty seconds before they come to me.'

'Marie!' I jump as Jemima tugs on my coat, all eyebrows and fury, except I'm miles away in a rancid police cell in the dead-ends of Essex, wondering how many promises were broken, how much more there is to unravel, and what could possibly become of everyone when it does.

Jemima yanks me away just as Mary's light beams and Dominic's tone changes, smoothly recapping the press conference and all its revelations for the benefit of however many thousands of clueless people watching on the other end. Did any of them know before they turned on the telly that today was only ever going to be remembered as a truly historic moment for the nation, laden with symbolism and charged with emotion, as the Metropolitan Police commissioner herself reopened a multi-billion pound investigation into the British army, and took personal responsibility for its original failings, which left the country aghast with horror and the military on its knees?

'When's the next Essex train? Or any train that goes as far as

Warchester?' Jemima hisses at me, phone cocked between her shoulder and ear as Dominic keeps talking, spooling through charges amounting to a factory-line of abuse, as military in its efficiency as the organisation it lived to serve.

'I'll ... I'll check,' I whisper, fumbling for my phone. 'You mean you want to go straight from here?'

'Go where?' Suddenly Dominic's at my side again, yanking out his ear piece and reaching for his coat.

'Warchester,' Jemima says defensively. 'I assumed you'd want to head up straight away, work every angle you've got.'

'Oh, great idea,' he barks, trying and failing to zip himself back into his jacket. 'Let's all tip up to Warchester together, along with the rest of the travelling circus. Never mind that I had to stalk social services in Essex for months to get even the slightest tip ... No. All I need right now is to be left alone to work this. What you need to do is get all over Thomas. It's more than likely he's got hold of some officious prat at the Met who's been passed over for a promotion one too many times and decided to run their mouth. I need to know what he's got if we're to have any chance of being in front.'

My mind snaps back to Thomas. But before I can ask any more questions, Dominic's disappearing down the street and around the corner, the yellow smear of his jacket becoming smaller and smaller like he's a candle burning out.

'Marie?' I flinch as Jemima tugs at my arm again. 'Are you alright?'

I nod, watching the jabbering mass of reporters as I pull my phone out of my pocket.

'You may as well go back to the newsroom,' she mutters. 'It's fine if you want to go home, to be honest. I'll handle Thomas. Realistically, he's not going to tell *you* anything, and trafficking's on the shelf for the foreseeable, for sure. I'll call if I've got anything for you, OK?'

She's walking away before I can even nod again, yet another

grey raincoat splashing through the flood in a hurry. I float, just for a moment, on a cacophony of memory: Andromeda this, Andromeda that, Andromeda, Andromeda, Andromeda; fingers typing into my phone as if they belong to someone else, blue screen flashing the usual instruction almost immediately. Horns scream and tyres squeal as I step straight out in front of a moving taxi, climbing into the back before the swear words have left the front seat. This storm is so heavy the water's almost over my head.

'St James's Park, double time,' I shout, slamming the door behind me. No one in the newsroom will miss me for a few minutes. No one ever does. Much like no one missed Andromeda, the impossibly beautiful maiden chained to a rock and left to be eaten alive by the monster who desired her most of all. The Romans or Greeks, or whoever they were, got that bit right, at least.

Carly ~ Warchester ~ 1997

'Sister? How old is she?'

Words move over my head like the pricks of light dancing in my eyes.

'She's not said. She was chundering most of the way here...'

'I presume the mother's on her way?'

'God, I doubt it. She could barely stand for booze.'

'Ugh. Have social services got themselves involved yet?'

'Nope. Not here, anyway. You got it, or need me to wrangle someone in?'

'Don't worry. They're just finishing up with someone else down the corridor, as it goes.'

There's a snort. I blink open my eyes, head still rolling on my neck. The woman from the ambulance is in front of me with another woman wearing baggy blue pyjamas. Ambulance Woman looks down at me and smiles.

'Alright there?'

Nothing happens as I try to sit up. I close my eyes again as she propels me upright, neck pinching as I try to balance my head. It feels like it might sink into my body at any moment. When I finally look up, the pyjamas are gone, but Ambulance Woman is still cupping the back of my head.

'Let's try again, shall we? Alright?'

I think my neck actually creaks as I try to nod. My head stands by itself as she lets go, lacing her hands together in her lap as she flops into the chair next to me. Up ahead, there's silver foil all crumpled in a heap on the floor inside the curtains round Kayleigh.

I ask myself again: Who called the ambulance? And what's happening to my sister? It must have been Ma, except I know Ma can hardly stand up without falling down again. And Ambulance Woman saw all that. The pricks of light pop again as I start to grasp how hard it is going to be to hide even the smallest thing in here.

'So,' Ambulance Woman says, thumbs rolling round and round like she's winding thread. 'You going to tell anyone what's really gone on here?'

Round and round and round her thumbs go as we sit in silence. I keep swallowing. This time, I'm going to keep it all down.

'You're about to get asked a whole load of questions, by folks a whole lot more important than me. They'll be able to help you, and your sister. If you talk to them, that is. Otherwise they'll have to go digging ... and take all this out of your control. Is that what you want?'

The hospital bustles around us. Another big swallow as I watch a pair of shoes dancing on their own in the gap under the curtain.

'How's about I guess?' she says after a moment, thumbs starting to turn again. 'Let's see, now. If you're not sixteen yet, you can't be responsible for your sister. So, you'll both be made wards of the state, unless Mum or Dad show up. Is that what you want?'

I hold my breath.

'But if you're sixteen, you're an adult, aren't you? No reason you can't be responsible for your sister, instead of your mum or dad. Maybe you've got a relative who also takes care of you, who might show up instead...'

I take the tiniest sip of air, staring at the heap of silver foil in the distance.

'Course, being responsible for your sister will mean actually being responsible for her – staying with her in hospital, meeting social services, answering all their questions, all the fun stuff. Or getting your relative in here to do that. You won't be able to take her home otherwise.'

She pushes the tips of her thumbs together, hands shaped like a heart in her lap.

'So, then, big sister. Which is it?'

I slump as she turns to look at me. I didn't realise she was still holding me up straight.

'Can I have a drink?'

I lick my lips as I grip the edge of the seat. She passes me a plastic cup of water from a few more just waiting, full to the brim, on the table next to her. I feel sick again almost as soon as it's down, crunch the cup into my hand.

'Is she going to be OK?' I try not to look at her as I ask.

'Chances are, yes. Depends how bad her infection is, or anything else she might've accidentally swallowed besides alcohol. But she's in the right place now.'

'Can I see her?' I squeeze the plastic cup smaller in my hand.

'They'll come out in a sec,' she says, jerking her head towards the blue curtains.

'The doctors?'

'Doctors, nurses, yes. The police will also want to have a word, I should think.'

'Police? Why?'

'Well, you're minors, aren't you? School uniform and all that?'

She picks at a fingernail. I rub my eyes, remembering the clinic. Everyone wants to know how old I am, but no one actually gives a shit about it when they do, no matter what Rach says. And then an idea forms, the tiniest chance of a way out of here without having to answer any more questions.

I get to my feet just as the curtains swish open and a man comes out. His pyjamas are a different colour to everyone else's.

'Hiya, Flo,' he says, looking between us. 'You alright? Is this one of yours?'

'Yeah,' she says, staggering as she stands up. She's even taller than him. 'It was a house call. This here's her sister.'

'Is she going to be OK? Can I see her?'

'Hello,' he says, tucking the pen in his hand into his top pocket, pushing his glasses back on his nose. 'I'm Doctor Twena. And you are...?'

'Carly,' I say, flinching as my hand finds the leftover pills in my pocket. 'She's my sister. Kayleigh. She's three. I came in, and she was just flopping and screaming and burning and—'

'Yes,' he says, cutting me off. 'She was having a febrile convulsion. That means—'

'She put something up her bum,' I interrupt, pointing at Ambulance Woman in a fury. 'I saw her do it. Her.' I shake my finger. 'Twice. And then she stopped moving.'

'Yes,' he says again, smiling. 'It's a suppository. It's a common way of administering paracetamol in children, particularly if a seizure prevents us doing it orally.'

'She stuck it up her bum!' I shout, pushing and shoving at Ambulance Woman. 'She's only three. And you're telling me that's normal? She was twisting, flopping, screaming, spewing, and then suddenly she's just lying there, not even like she's asleep but like she's dead, like she's actually dead.'

I strain as hands close round my elbows, holding me still.

'If she's hurt her, I'll fucking kill her, I swear I will...'

There's a crunch as I stand on the blister pack that's fallen out of my pocket. Ambulance Woman bends to pick it up, handing it to the doctor before looking back at me.

'Those are mine,' I say, trying to reach for the packet, but my arms are pinned against my sides. 'I need them. They were in my pocket.'

I squirm against the person standing behind me as the doctor turns the packet over and over in his hand.

'You'll let me know how this one turns out?' Ambulance Woman says to someone over my head. Then she nods, turns and walks away, clumping off through the swinging doors and out into the open like this happens all the time.

'Carly, is it?' I twist round to see a policeman above me, hands still firm on my elbows.

'What do you care?' I say, straining against him. 'It's her you want. And you're just letting her get away.'

'I'm going to let go of you now,' he interrupts, 'but you won't get to see your sister if there's any more lip. OK?'

I squirm again. I can hardly leave Kayleigh alone ever again after this. I rub my elbows as he comes round to stand next to the doctor in front of me.

'We're going to go and see your sister now, Carly,' the doctor says, my pills still in his hand. 'And then we'll talk about what happens next, OK?'

'I ... I need those back,' I say, swaying a little as I remember why I needed them in the first place. 'Those pills. They're really important.' I shift from foot to foot as they both stare at me. 'Please? Please can I have them?'

The doctor turns the packet over and over and over in his hand before looking at me again. I stiffen as he leans towards me until I realise he's tucking them back into my pocket.

'Come,' he says, gently pulling on my elbow, guiding me towards Kayleigh's cubicle. I'm suddenly giddy as relief washes over me, hand closing round the packet at the same time as I finally catch a glimpse of Kayleigh, quiet, still and peaceful, all wrapped up in a soft knitted blanket like she's a doll, breathing the slow, regular rhythm that tickles my ear when I snuggle down next to her in the middle of the night, those precious moments somewhere between sunset and sunrise when it's just me and her and our dreams.

I drop my head on to the blue, padded mattress next to her face, cheek wet as my tears soak into the sheet. For just that second, we're Carly and Kayleigh again, together, warm and quiet in the velvet dark where nothing and no one can touch us, unless we want them to.

Marie ~ London ~ 2006

'I hope you've got an umbrella or something, love? Want to wait till this passes?' Neon-white teeth leer at me from the front seat as the taxi pulls over.

'You'll be lucky,' I snap back, pushing a pile of pound coins into his tray as I step back out into the flood, St James's Park lying soaked through the iron gate in front of me. Vibrations travel up my coat from the phone in my pocket ... Damn. I must already be late. I can never seem to move fast enough for anyone.

Inside the gate, the park is deserted, trees wilting under the weight of the storm, grass almost invisible as puddles pool together. I skate along the path towards the lake in its centre, rain so heavy I can barely see the fountain in the middle, much less the outline of Whitehall on the far side. Nothing except trees groaning with storm, branches creaking down towards the ground, like they want to break. I flinch as the fountain brainlessly spouts water on to a tiny duckling skittering into the reeds. For a moment, I hate myself all over again. And then as lightning pops, I see it. A lone figure moving deliberately towards the edge of the pond on the opposite side.

Hood up, head down, I start the walk around the lake, to the usual spot, each step heavier than the last, until another pair of boots splashes to a stop in front of me, the rest of the drenched park completely deserted. Even the elaborate and precise buildings of Whitehall's outer reaches are now completely fogged out.

I stare at his face, searching for clues. Tall, old, glasses. Hat. Everything about him is as grey and forgettable as shadow, apart from his army-straight back. We stand, speechless in the roar of the storm, waiting for someone to blink first. Except I can't see his eyes behind his glasses, all white and misty with condensation.

'Perseus,' he barks suddenly, jerking the umbrella in his hand towards a big weeping willow set a few yards back in the grass, away from the lake's edge. I squelch behind him, pushing my way through its drooping branches until we are both stood next to the trunk. I can't help but stroke its bark, fingering the slippery, dark grooves with my finger. This is a tree that has seen it all, but I know even a thousand-year-old willow canopy won't keep out this particular storm.

I rest my hand on the trunk, tracing a few more of its veins, sky growling with thunder. Some of them are wide enough to fit my whole fingertip.

'Perseus,' the man repeats, glasses practically sheet-white as he inclines his head towards me.

'Ah, but who am I?' As I say it, I stab my finger into a crack, as deep as it will go, pushing down hard on a notch inside the trunk, lightning flashing inside the canopy. It cuts both ways, our so-called arrangement. A secret isn't a secret unless both sides are keeping it.

'You're Athena,' he says, tilting his head down a fraction. 'How far are we compromised?'

I'm suddenly light-headed, fingertip pinching. I didn't realise I was holding my breath.

'There's an unidentified leak on Andromeda,' I say, prodding at the trunk. 'At least, I think there must be. I only found out about it just—'

'You think?' I jump as he interrupts, removing his glasses, one eye leering white and sightless while the other swivels towards me. 'I should not have to remind you that we do not communicate on a hunch. Who is leaking? And what is your plan?'

'I'll have it all locked down later,' I stammer, fingertip stinging as I pull it out. 'Just give me till the end of tomorrow. It won't take long. I couldn't have known it had anything to do with new information on Andromeda until the press conference was over.

Dominic is furious. He's home affairs editor. Every leak should have been coming to him—'

'Stop!' He cuts me off, mismatched eyes pointed like lasers. 'You know better than to lose discipline after all this. You cannot afford any more breaches of protocol!'

I gabble, teeth chattering as I shiver into my soaking clothes.

'I do know that whoever is leaking briefed one of our other reporters before the press conference. I just don't know who the source is yet, but I'm not long for finding out. I just thought it would be best to meet now so you had all the facts.'

'Enough,' he snaps as he replaces his glasses. Only now do I realize they were tinted all along. He holds up a hand and yet again all the questions I can never seem to ask die on my lips. We stand, frozen under the canopy until finally, he gives me a tiny nod.

'Who is the reporter?'

'Thomas Thorne. Small fry,' I say, letting out a sigh. He gives me another nod as he lowers his hand, straightening a glove one finger at a time. I blink at him.

'Aren't you going to tell me what the—'

'Pegasus,' he interrupts, bearing down on me all over again. 'You will say nothing to anyone without Pegasus. But be sure to wait for word, next time. You know the rules. You cannot afford to make any more mistakes. Remember that, if you cannot remember anything else.'

And with a flash of trailing willow, he's gone, disappearing into the storm like vapour, as if he was never here in the first place. Thousands of years of tree trunk prop me up as I look up at the canopy, green leaves turned black in the dark of the storm, threats colliding in my ears. This is how it's done, they said, way back, at that first whispered meeting; just after that first unexpected brush on the shoulder, a ghost's finger. You must know that by now, surely? After all, experienced journalists do, don't they? A tip here, a nod there ... perfectly normal stuff. And what goes around, comes around, doesn't it? One good turn deserves another?

Blood trickles from my fingertip as I push through willow, oblivious to everything except the emerging route in my mind, the only route I can possibly take from here. My feet move as if by themselves, but then they would, wouldn't they? I've planned for this since they took her away from me, since they told me to forget she was ever mine; every ticket, every obstacle, even analysing it out loud in those stupid meetings, just so I could keep thinking about it. *Victims were failed.* I speed up as the gate clangs behind me, weaving in and out of the growing crowds on the pavement – places to go, people to see, rain to get out of. Just a speck of her will be enough. That's all I need.

~~~

It's night by the time I get there, sliding silently out of my taxi on to the still-wet street, even though I don't look suspicious – just some girl in a raincoat getting out of a cab at night on a random residential road in the far suburbs. But still I shiver, tucking my head down inside my collar as I pad down the pavement, staying in the shadows. I'm not supposed to be here, never was, never will be. I'm the interloper in this world, not her.

The countryside night wraps round me, all velvet dark as I pass luxuriously spread houses, skate across driveways guarded by fat, pruned bushes, ducking below the odd lit window, amber patchwork on black.

I slow as I approach the parkland opening out at the end of the street. Dim outlines of play equipment, twisted statues in the moonlight. A bench. And ... sharp gasp as I stop.

Two figures. Ponytails, puffy jackets, cloud of smoke. Flash of patent shoe, pair of ankle socks.

My heart thumps like a fist in my chest. I knew she'd be here. She's basically a teenager, isn't she? A tinkle of laughter, a cackle of delight. Not even trying to hide it. I don't need a mirror to know I'm blushing, hard as blush can go, waves of the stuff coursing through my skin. I shuffle one more step forward, two, in spite of myself. Just so I can hear them. Just for a second.

'...So I said to her, Mum, I think I'm actually allergic to strawberries...'

Another hoot. I smile, cheeks stinging. Or is it my eyes?

'Mich, seriously! Strawberries are allergens, they make your eyes swell up and everything, and we eat them all the time, it's her favourite dessert. It's perfect ... look...'

They hunch, a blue screen flashing in the dark.

'Wow, you're right.'

'See? She looks like a cabbage-patch doll ... boxed as they come.'

A babbling stream of giggles. I inch closer.

'Let's roll another. We've got time, haven't we? They'll be asleep by the time we come in, anyway. No need to eat all her strawberries...'

Sniggers, rustling paper, suddenly pungent sweet smell. I tense.

'Where'd you get this?'

'From Adam. He practically gave it me for free.'

A flash of flame; more thick, sweet smell, curling across the air like a beckoning finger.

'He fancies you, that's why.'

'I know, silly. So why wouldn't I milk it? Do you want a blowback?'

The hiss of an inhale, a puff of smoke. Another step forward, irresistible finger.

'It's resin, he said. It may as well be pure oil. Straight off the boat from Morocco, apparently.'

'And we're all going on a summer holiday...'

Singing dissolving to snorts, jerking ponytails, waving hands. Just one more step.

'Did you see Kat at school today? She looked shocking.'

I stiffen. Kat?

'She's anorexic, she is. Totally. Ava told me she's been chucking up at break for months.'

'She must be, right? It's either that or doing those laps all the time, round and round and round, the running track's basically a mud bath. Like that guy, what's his name?' Clicks fingers.

'What are you on about?' Hiss, inhale, hiss.

'You know, that film...'

'Film? How much have you had?'

'Oh shut upppppp...'

Ponytails whirl as a can clatters away from my foot and two pale, tense faces are suddenly staring at me.

I freeze, just feet away. How did I get so close? They're as faceless, nameless and unfamiliar as the police officers on the podium, the crowds on the train, the leaves on the trees. The bricks holding up the houses, the bushes guarding the driveways. We've never met. How could I have thought we ever would have?

'Excuse me. I was looking for Katie.' I hear myself, loud, alien, the name like a fist in my mouth, harsh on my tongue, all sharp angles and corners. 'I thought ... Do you know her? This is where she lives.'

Silence, rippling with the breeze between us, a breath from the past with nothing to say.

'Come on, Chelle,' one murmurs, pulling her friend along as they brush past me, rustling up the street, disappearing down a driveway.

A door closes. A light goes out. And I feel the world just fall away, like vertigo, every meticulous step charted out in my mind folding in on itself as the night tightens round me, velvet zip closing.

There's nothing here for you, Marie. There never will be.

I push one foot forward, then another, then again. I think I hear someone call my name, somewhere beyond the night's sharp edge; so faint, it's gone.

Carly ~ Warchester ~ 1997

I wake with a start as the curtain squeaks along the rail, Doctor Twena framed in the gap. I don't even remember my eyes closing, but my neck feels like my head is way too heavy for it and there's a crust down my cheek from the corner of my mouth. The doctor smiles at me.

'You've slept. And for a while, too,' he says, pushing the curtain back. I squint at the figure next to him, short, blue jacket, peering at me like a mole. 'This is Nurse Govern,' he says, as they come into focus.

'Hello, Carly,' the woman says with half a smile. 'How are you feeling?'

I sit up, rubbing my back and neck. I must have literally collapsed in this chair. It can't have been for long though. The beeps are still beeping, Kayleigh's still sleeping, and I'm sure I met this woman only this morning, even though it may as well have been a million years ago.

'Nurse Govern works with social services,' he says. 'She's just going to have a quick chat while I check your sister over. I expect the rest of your family will be here soon, won't they?'

There's his eyebrows, popping above his glasses. Suddenly it's all scrapes and clatters as the nurse pulls a chair round to sit next to me. I start to panic. I can't hear the beeps anymore and Kayleigh's not moving.

'Everything's looking good, don't worry,' the doctor says as he leans over Kayleigh, pulling at a black loop of plastic around his neck.

'What are you doing with that?' I say, mouth furry with sleep.

He stops, eyebrows right over his glasses this time, like he's wearing doubles.

'It's a stethoscope,' he says, holding the curls of black plastic out to me, silver medal dangling from one end. 'We use it to check the patient is breathing correctly. I'm sure you've been to the doctor before with a bad cough or cold?'

He leans over Kayleigh with the silver medal in his hand.

'I'm going to rest it on her chest, that's all. I'll be able to listen to her heartbeat and establish whether she's got fluid in her lungs. We know she's got an infection, we just need to find the source of it.' He pulls the end of a tube out of one ear. 'Would you like to listen too?'

I jump as a plastic cup of water appears between us in the nurse's hand.

'Listen? How?' I say, taking the water without looking at her. If I pretend she's not here maybe she'll just disappear.

'I'll show you,' he says, medal hovering above Kayleigh. 'But I'm going to put this on her chest first, OK?'

'Won't you wake her up?' I say, crunching the plastic cup into my hand.

'No more than you will.' He nods at the cup splintering in my palm.

I glare as he eases the medal under Kayleigh's blanket and waits before moving it around a bit and waiting again. I don't know what he's waiting for, but the only thing that stirs are her eyelashes, fluttering against her cheek as she dreams. It was just a bad dream, I'll say when she wakes up. Just a bad dream. They're the only ones I have, and I'm OK.

'Here,' he says, leaning over her body to pass me the ends of the tube. 'Put them in your ears. You'll be able to hear her heart.'

The buds on the tube feel warm in my fingers as I plug them into my ears, a low thump suddenly flooding through my head. If I didn't know better, I'd say I was the one dreaming, but I've never had a dream like this before. I'm struck dumb by the sound of my sister's heartbeat, pure, strong and regular, ringing around my head like nothing else I've ever heard. Doctor Twena smiles as he presses the medal down into Kayleigh's chest, connecting me with the deepest insides of her soul. I press down on the buds inside my ears. I never want to let go of this tube.

'Do I sound like that?' I say, between thuds, voice foggy like I'm underwater.

'Probably,' he says, lifting the medal off her chest and passing it to me. 'Here, have a go yourself. Press it slightly to the left, below your collarbone.'

I panic, my ears dead as the connection between us breaks.

'Put it back,' I say. 'Can you put it back? Please?' I don't need to listen to my heart to know it's racing. Thuds stream back into my ears as he nudges it under Kayleigh's blanket, warming me from the inside out. *Clear as a bell*, I think he says, nodding and smiling to himself. Or to me? His eyebrows poke out again as he beckons for his tube back.

'I doubt it's a chest infection,' he says, my ears popping as I pull out the buds. 'We'll have a check inside her ears when she wakes up, as that can be a bit more uncomfortable.' He reaches out for his medal, wrapping the rest of the tube around his neck, out of my reach.

'I'll be back soon. It won't do you any harm to rest again too.' He nods at the nurse before disappearing behind the curtain.

'Here,' she says as she waves a tissue under my nose.

I sit, brushing away her arm as I stuff my hands under my legs, memories of the clinic this morning clattering back into my head like dominoes. What is she doing here? And how did she find me? There's a scrunch and squeak as she fidgets in her chair.

'It's terrifying, isn't it?' she says. 'When they are so small. All that flopping and shaking ... awful, really. It must have given you such a fright. But children are far more robust than you think. I expect the rest of your family will be here soon too?'

I dig my nails into the plastic chair. The minutes tick along with the beeping machines as she fiddles with some papers in her lap, just sitting there next to me like it's exactly where anyone, including me, would expect her to be.

'It's about time for your second pill,' she murmurs, pen paused above her papers. 'Have you got it with you? Or would you like me to get you some more?'

I glare at the floor as I pull my pills from my pocket, popping out the final one.

'Would you like some more water?'

I swallow without looking at her, chucking the empty packet under Kayleigh's cot, eyes starting to water as the pill lodges in my throat. Finally she gets up, stuffing her papers into the bag at her feet.

'I'll be back to check on you two again soon,' she says. 'Try and get some more rest. I'm sure this has been an ordeal for you.'

'Like I even know what that means...' I mumble, counting the perfect tiny squares of wool on Kayleigh's blanket until the curtain squeaks again.

My cheek rubs my leg as I drop my head on to my knees. It's only when I notice my leg is wet that I realise I've been crying the whole time.

Marie ~ London ~ 2006

'Hey!' Jemima pokes her head into the kitchen as I clang change into the drinks machine. 'Wow, you look like hell.'

'I couldn't sleep,' I say, running a hand through my still-wet hair. At least I managed a shower, a change of clothes, new armour. My midnight escapade to the leafy lanes of nowhere may as well never have happened. And people do far worse turnarounds in news-rooms all the time. Round here, it's normal. Standard.

'How about you? Have you heard from Dominic? Or any more from Thomas?' I shove the rest of my change into my pocket, blinking away faceless man as I finger the phone underneath.

'Nope,' she says, stabbing at the coffee machine. 'I think he just went home in the end, drowned his sorrows. Having to stomach a massive investigation being shanked into the long grass plus the idea Thomas is ahead of him is at least a two-bottle night. Olivia read him the riot act about pulling himself together. No doubt we'll hear it all again shortly when she gets going at the morning meeting.' She jerks her head up at the clock on the wall. 'Come on.'

I stumble behind her to the conference room, more tension in every step. A flood of details, whisperingly close. Almost the entire staff is churning inside the room as we slide in along the back glass wall, Olivia already vamping and gesturing up front. Behind her, a bank of monitors all flash the same information, as if their various logos and colours will disguise the fact the words are ident-ical. *Apology for Andromeda* is plastered along the bottom of each screen, yellow, blue, black, red, I think there's even purple some-where along the far wall. I snort into my drink as I spot one claiming *Exclusive*. It couldn't be any more obvious that this information is everyone's property. Except, of course, the only piece that I need.

'Good morning, everyone,' Olivia barks, clapping her hands. 'Let's get right to it, shall we? We've a busy day ahead. Thomas – talk us through the immediate priorities.'

I brace myself against the wall as he joins her up front, suit pressed like cardboard. Here it comes. Surely he'll spill his source, or as good as? In front of a crowd like this, he won't be able to help himself.

'We're making sure live reporters are available day and night outside Scotland Yard. We'll present all our programmes from there. You'll receive crew sheets and shift times in due course but please, prepare for twelve-hour rotations.'

He looks down at the papers in her hand as the room ripples with sighs. I bite back the start of a smile as I clench the icy can in my hand. I'm the only person ever pleased about overnights.

'First and foremost is the new commissioner's apology,' he continues. 'No one in authority has ever apologised so directly for Operation Andromeda before. Sure, there has been broad acknowledgement of the mistakes that were made originally, but it is truly historic for such a senior officer to take personal responsibility for it—'

'She's put herself on the line,' Olivia interrupts, waving her hands. 'She's made it her professional Everest, whether she meant to or not. And we will be holding her accountable, absolutely. I think we need a distinct profile piece on her. Who is Commissioner Anne Jaqlin? Tell the viewer her background, her career progression, why she went into the police force, what we know about her intentions as commissioner...'

I sketch the commissioner in my mind as I listen, all fine pencil strokes, black on white.

'Absolutely,' Thomas says, nodding and scribbling. 'Great idea ... brilliant. We're already putting together a background piece on

Operation Andromeda itself. To really remind the audience what this is all about. It's been five years since the last phase of the investigation concluded and the captain was finally convicted. What happened and why? It's almost written—'

'We need to drill into the mistakes that we know about,' Olivia interrupts again. 'We need to interrogate the laughable defence claim that it was partly down to the pressure of spending cuts. As if the restructuring of the military could ever excuse deviant behaviour such as this. I don't want to put the audience through another profile of Captain Robert Leigh Parish though. Every single news network will put together a rogue's gallery of convictions. What about those the Met admitted were beyond their reach? And why?'

Victims were failed. I squirm against the glass wall.

'Oh, we'll put all that in, definitely.' Thomas shuffles his papers as he replies. 'Of course, we'll bring you the script to read first.'

'This is about Gillard Minchin,' Olivia says, glaring at him. 'Pure and simple. That's why they've reopened the inquiry. It's about Minchin. A four-star general, recipient of every award in the book, accused of the most appalling of crimes. Why did the case against him, specifically, collapse? Why was he untouchable? Was Parish the proverbial sacrificial lamb? And what new information has come to light that has enabled the CPS to reopen the case now? Who are we calling on that?'

'Every military source we've got,' a voice pipes up from somewhere in the mob. I watch Thomas stiffen, self-consciously smoothing his perfect hair. Surely the military can't be where he's got his tip? There are only a handful of people who could have anything to spill to anyone. The idea they'd blab to a nobody like Thomas is as ridiculous as the idea they'd break ranks in the first place. My neck pinches as I strain to see who else is talking.

'We should have the army's chief of staff at the time on the phone within the hour, we're hoping for a junior Home Office minister as soon as they've sorted out their spokespeople, and we've got our own army of legal analysts who are already picking over the historic allegations.'

My head swivels between them. Thomas is hiding his eyes in his papers.

'Have you spoken to our own lawyers about this?' Olivia barks. 'That is critical ... Critical! We need to be 110 percent sure on what we can and can't discuss given there are new legal proceedings under way. I want a document circulated with clear, concise guidance on that within the hour.'

'Actually, Olivia, I thought a separate profile piece on General Minchin would also be a good idea,' Thomas says, clearing his throat. 'As you said, he was a decorated general, believed to have been at the heart of the most sensitive UK intelligence operations, and I've got some information that suggests—'

'We should discuss that with qualified guests,' Olivia says, dismissing him with a flick of bouncy hair. 'That's a far more interesting conversation to have with experienced military historians, or better still, military personnel. How do you propose we turn that into television? Have you ever seen moving pictures of Gil Minchin on military operations? In fact, have you ever seen anything other than his army-issue mugshots? No, I thought not.'

My hand clenches the phone in my pocket as Thomas crumples into another hair flick. Whatever he's got, this crowd isn't going to hear another word after that.

'Excuse me, Olivia,' Jemima pipes up beside me. 'What is your thinking for the investigative teams? There are obviously a lot of lines to pursue.'

'Extraordinarily, we hadn't got to that yet,' Olivia says, frowning at Thomas. 'Suffice to say, investigations are our most important focal point outside of covering the news developments per se. Of course, Dominic will be the face of these as home affairs editor, given this is an investigation led by the Metropolitan Police commissioner herself.' She flicks her hair at Thomas again. 'But I want you, Jemima, to liaise with Thomas in the first instance on leads.

You've both got plenty of them, as I understand it, and I will ensure researchers and producers are freed up to help whenever you need them. There are too many angles for one team to handle alone, and every news network in the country, no matter how big or small, is chasing all of them.'

I crumple my empty can into my hand as nods and murmurs ripple through the room.

'And let me be absolutely clear,' she continues, hands on hips as she surveys the crowd in front of her. 'I want no stone unturned in this investigation. I want every leak to come to us. If someone so much as farts about what really happened in Warchester, I want it on tape, and on Nine News. It is all hands to the pump on Andromeda from here on in. There is no other story in town for the foreseeable future. We are to swarm all over this. I want buzz worthy of a wasps' nest. I want an all-out, full-on, swarm.'

She pauses as heads nod and grunt at her, as if referring to them as insects is exactly what they'd expected her to say.

'Now, are there any other questions?'

No one even nods this time. I'm pretty sure the room would be totally silent if it wasn't for the endless looping commentary humming from the screens behind her.

'Let's get to it, then. Thanks everyone. We'll meet again as a newsroom later this afternoon. Watch your emails please. Gabe will send out details.'

I jump as my phone buzzes against my leg, swept into the crowd as it turns and funnels through the door in a jabbering mass. At least wasps swarm when they're angry, I think.

Carly ~ Warchester ~ 1997

I twist curls of phone cord round my finger, pulling them tighter and tighter until the tip goes white as the tone blares into my ear. I know Jase won't answer himself but surely someone else will at some point? This is the army, after all. Forewarned is forearmed. And it's not like I've got any other family to call. How else will I get us both out of here? Ma doesn't count, even halfway to sober. This lot wouldn't let us leave with her even if she was clean. Not after what they saw.

'Any luck?' Doctor Twena hovers next to me. I trace the silver number buttons with my white fingertip. I know this number like it's a tattoo on my arm but never call it.

'He's probably on exercise,' I say, stabbing at the phone as I try again. It's as if my fingers know what putting the numbers together will mean, slipping and sliding all over the place.

'On exercise?'

My finger pinches as I pull the cord tighter. I'm sure I've heard them say that before.

'He's in the army. They do it all the time, don't they? Exercise, training, the whole bit.'

'Indeed,' he says, leaning on to the wall next to me. 'Perhaps there's someone else you could call? Have you left a message?'

I ignore him, turning away as the ringing tone starts again. They won't let me out of here without you, I'll say. There's less questions this way. I'll beg, even. I can't just leave her here, can I? It could be even worse—

'Block 16, Second Lieutenant Black.' I jump as the phone barks into my ear. 'Hello?'

'Hi,' I choke out, warm blood rushing into my fingertip as I yank it out of the cord and press it into my other ear. 'I ... I need to speak to Jason—'

The phone interrupts me: 'Block 16, Second Lieutenant Black!' I poke into my ear as hard as I can to stop myself pulling the cord out of the unit. It would be so easy, I think. Just cut the call and he'll never know. But then...

'Sergeant Jason Gates,' I say, louder. 'I need to speak to Sergeant Gates.'

I jump as there's a burst of static, looping the cord back around my wrist till it stings.

'Jase? Is that you?'

'Block 16, Sergeant Gates,' he says, low and clear.

I flinch. Even with the hospital crashing around us I know how furious he is.

'It's Kayleigh,' I whisper, pulling hard on the phone cord. 'I got home from the clinic and found her having a fit or something. She was burning, screaming, foam coming out of her mouth.' I stop, gasping as I remember Kayleigh's small body all red and twisting, like a fish in boiling water. 'Jase? Are you still there?'

'Block 16, Sergeant Gates,' he mutters again.

'They won't let me take her home without you. I've tried everything, Jase, I swear. I've said I'm sixteen, that I'm grown-up, everything. But they saw the state of Ma when they came—'

'You should have sorted it without them,' he interrupts, hissing through the receiver. 'You actually called a fucking ambulance. What did you think would happen? They'd forget about Ma in a pissed-up heap and some schoolgirl in charge of a baby? You should have left her to sweat it out, or whatever it was. She'd have been OK.'

'I didn't! I swear, Jase, I didn't call them. Ma must have.'

He laughs.

'It must have been her,' I beg. 'I promise you, Jase. I'd never—'

'Do you think I believe this shit?' I jump as he shouts into my ear.

'Ma's drunk from the moment she wakes up to when she passes out again and everything in between, and you're telling me she called an ambulance because she actually noticed Kayleigh having a fit?'

'She did! No one else could have done it.' I brush away Doctor Twena's hand on my shoulder. 'And then I had to come with her, didn't I? I couldn't just leave her with them. You should have seen what they did to her in the ambulance—'

'Shut up,' he interrupts. 'I mean it. Shut up.'

I swallow, pulling the cord tight so my hand goes white.

'I'm sorry,' I mumble after a moment.

'You shouldn't have called me,' he says.

'But how else would I—'

'You know the rules. How many times do we have to go over it? No questions. No mess. You have no idea what we're up against – what I'm up against. You know I'm a sergeant now. We'll have to make it up.'

I start to cry.

'I can't leave,' he says. 'For fuck's sake, Carls, I can't even tell you what I was doing when you rang. How would I explain bailing, right here and right now? And the fact you're both in an actual hospital means there will be questions to answer just because of where you are—'

'But Jase—'

'Is she OK? Kayleigh? What's actually wrong with her?'

'I don't know. I reckon so but they won't even tell me anything proper because they say I'm too young.'

'So lie. What the hell is the matter with you? Do they want your passport? Birth certificate? Just say whatever you need to say to get her out.'

I finger the frayed badge on my school blazer as he fades for a moment, disappearing into a burst of static at the other end of the line.

'Carls, listen to me. Even if I show up in civvies it will get back to base. And then the questions will start – there'll be more loose ends to tie up. We can't have that. It will be worse for all of us, trust me. We can't have any questions. It's bad enough what happened at the clinic.'

'How do you even know about that?'

'How do you think I know?' I have to pull the phone away from my ear even though I know the doctor is still watching, his shadow hovering along the wall.

'Get her home without me, and without any more questions. Wait for a car accident to come in or something, then grab her and run. No one's going to bother chasing you if someone else is dying on the table. And then do as Rach tells you. I mean it. Just do as you're told. And don't call me again. You'll see me soon enough, and we'll talk then.'

My hand slips on the receiver as the line goes dead in my ear. I drop my head into my chest, arms limp by my sides, the blood rushing back into my hand making me feel giddy.

'Carly?' My head swims, cracks in the tiles on the floor moving like worms.

'Help me with her,' I hear the doctor say, arms looping around my sides, folding me into a nearby chair. A hand rakes my hair over my head as it lolls onto my chest.

'Come on, girl,' he says, patting my cheeks, pushing my head back on to my neck. I open my eyes to find him and the nurse staring down at me, heads cocked together in a heart shape. I drift for a moment. Maybe this is what having two parents would look like. Maybe...

'Did you get hold of your sister, love?'

The nurse's face hangs soft and pillowy over my head.

'There's a sister?' From this angle, the doctor's eyebrows are up in his hair.

'Yes,' she says. 'Rachel, isn't it?' I gaze up at her. 'Perhaps she's able to come help with Kayleigh. If your brother is stuck?'

The doctor gapes, looking back and forth between us. I clear my throat as Nurse Govern nods at me.

'She's ... she's been at work all day,' I say slowly. The nurse keeps nodding as I look between them. 'She works in a shop, I didn't think I'd be able to get hold of her. I'll try her now. She's ... she's seventeen...'

'Good,' she says, head wagging. 'And I'm sure she'll be straight over, won't she?'

She holds out a hand to help me up, like last time it's both warm and cool as it closes over mine.

The doctor sighs, hands on his hips as he looks at the floor.

'You'll let me know when she's here, will you?' he says as the nurse pulls me to my feet. I keep my hand in hers as we look at him.

'Of course,' she says, squeezing my hand. 'I'm sure she won't be long.'

I don't dare look back at him as she leads me over to the phone again.

'How did you find me?' I say as she passes me the receiver with her free hand, still holding on to my other one.

'We do regular ward rounds,' she says. 'It's part of the job, just as we regularly visit all of our local clinics. Doctors refer us patients with questionable injuries or illnesses so we can follow up in the community. Trust me, I was as surprised as you to see you again so soon.'

She cocks her head to the side, her hair lit up by the overhead strip lights.

'But why are you helping me?' I keep hold of her hand as I take the phone.

'It's my job, remember? We're just here to help you. That's all. We're here to make sure you don't have to go through it alone. You can tell us anything you need to, and we'll try to help you. It's as simple as that, really. There's nothing you can't say to us. You won't be in any trouble, I promise. I know it's hard to feel like you can trust people you hardly know. But I can assure you – all we're here to do, all I'm here to do, is help you. Look after you, when you feel like no one else is? Maybe you'd like to talk a little more, once you've spoken to Rachel.'

I drop her hand as I punch in Rach's number, but I can't drop her eyes, no matter how hard I try. They look straight through mine into my brain, like she knows exactly what she's searching for.

Marie ~ London ~ 2006

I jump out of the throng to wait for Jemima as we all squeeze out of the conference room. My adrenaline starts firing as I spot Thomas at her side. Public humiliation aside, he'll try to impress her, I'm sure of it, everyone does. He'll tell her everything if she handles it right.

My grip loosens around the phone in my pocket. Maybe Pegasus, that stupid winged horse, is actually about to get to fly? *You know the rules. You can't afford to make any more mistakes.* I fall in step beside them as discreetly as I can, walking through the newsroom towards the main desk.

'It's better than you think,' Jemima says, suddenly coy as Thomas rakes a hand through his perfect hair. 'You have to let Olivia get it out of her system at times like this. Just nod, smile, agree with whatever story she's come up with. Once she's blustered it all out you'll find she's actually focused and helpful.'

'What I can't tolerate is how unproductive it all is,' he says, with a sideways frown. 'Like I'm minded to come up with anything original after being publicly sacrificed at the altar of senior management.'

'It's a game,' Jemima continues smoothly. 'You know that. It has to be clear that she's the supreme leader, or else every correspondent will go round her. But she's probably given you a pass on that, hasn't she? What with your super-duper inside source?'

'Not exactly,' he replies, frowning directly at her this time. I fall back a step. 'It's about Nine beating everyone else, like it always is. She wants us ahead of the pack, and I'm halfway there. Simple as that, really.'

'Nice,' she says, nodding her head. 'I remember when working for Nine was enough to get you laughed out of press conferences. Look who's laughing now.'

'Oh, don't demean yourself, Jonas,' Thomas says, quickening his step. 'All this fishing's beneath you, isn't it? You've got plenty of your own leads to go on, from what I hear.'

'Easy tiger,' she says. 'Who's fishing? I'm as chuffed as you are if Nine's out front. That's all I want too. I just don't want to knock on doors if you're already halfway inside, do I? It makes us both look like tits.'

'Nice try,' he says, peeling away as we reach the edge of the news desk, frowning at me hovering just behind her. 'Icy Marie, is it? Give me a second, OK?'

'If you haven't already got an assignment for me, I thought I could work with Jemima,' I say before she can. 'We've been working together for a while.'

'Don't I know it,' he drawls, rolling his eyes. 'What sort of help do you need?' He tosses his hair towards Jemima as he asks. 'I assume it's more than just an intern? Even if she's flavour of the month.'

'A couple of politicos, if you can,' Jemima says, without skipping a beat. 'We know where we're going but could do with a researcher who also knows their way around Westminster. And Marie's an assistant producer, by the way.'

'Westminster, eh?' His eyebrows arch.

'Well, presumably that doesn't step on your toes?'

I hold my breath as they stare at each other.

'It's fine,' Thomas says after a moment, picking up the receiver on his desk. 'It's home affairs' back yard after all. You can toss balls around in there all you like.'

'Well, I'll be sure to let you know if anyone strays into our lane,' she replies. 'And if you can give politics a shove for me, that'd be great.'

I don't get a proper look at him as she turns, sweeping me with her into the sudden silence of an empty edit suite behind the desk. Eerie quiet descends as the door closes.

'He's such a git,' she mutters, hands flashing over the keyboard on the desk as she pulls up a video archive, clicking her way through snapshots of General Minchin. 'He's actually convinced he's as sharp as he thinks his suits are.'

I start to panic. Jemima never gives up a chase so quickly, especially if a rival reporter is involved. But noise floods into the room before I get a chance to ask, door opening again. I freeze against the padded wall.

'Hey,' Jemima says, without looking up. 'Sorry, I don't know your name...'

'Justin,' says a stiff frame in the doorway, all white shirt and black trousers. 'Thomas sent me. He said you needed some help from politics?'

Jemima ignores him, frowning as she opens another video file. I watch a flicker of irritation pass across the man's face, otherwise so smooth and clear, I wonder if he's ever had to shave. She swears as the frame freezes on General Minchin's army-issue close-up, tight face closed to all bar the teardrop-shaped birthmark high on his right cheekbone, marking him out as unforgettable. Also shaped like mainland Britain, apparently. In a certain light, I guess it is. Everything looks like something else in a certain light.

'Shall I come back?' Justin says, with a cough.

'Now I can tell you work for politics,' Jemima says, bearing down on him as she straightens up. 'Always looking for a way out.'

I wince as he laughs. I know she wasn't joking. The monitor is still full of the general.

'So what's your beat?' she snaps. 'Defence, foreign, treasury, what?'

'Home,' he says. 'I did my university placement there.'

'Interesting,' she says, as if it actually is. 'And did they teach discretion at university?'

He doesn't laugh this time. Minchin looks on as they stare at each other.

'What did you need from politics?' he says after a moment.

'I need contacts for as many defence ministry employees that you can muster,' she says, reaching for her phone now it's quiet. 'Preferably without asking too many questions to get them. I'm only interested in the period between 1995 and 2000. The higher ranking the better, obviously, but junior is good too. Just as many as you can pull together.'

'Aren't they a matter of public record?' I cringe as he questions her. 'If they're civilian contacts, rather than military?'

'Would I be asking if they were?'

'Jonas!' Dominic bellows from outside the door. I'm pretty sure Justin would crumple if he wasn't still holding on to the door-frame.

'What are you doing here? I thought you were headed to War-chester?' Jemima leans into the edit desk against the back wall. The general stares too, unblinking.

'Change of plan. You won't believe it when I tell you. I can barely believe it myself...' He trails off into a scowl as he spots Justin inside. 'What's this, a coalition of willing idiots? I don't think we've met.'

'What did you say your name was?' Jemima smiles sweetly at Mr Politics.

'Justin,' he says, trying to strain his way out of the tiny room without actually touching anyone. 'When do you need these contacts by?'

'Yesterday,' she snaps. 'So jog on, will you?'

Dominic twists sideways to let him out. I sag into the wall as quiet descends again. Still the general doesn't blink.

'Why are you fraternising with those suits from politics?' Dominic drapes his coat on the hook on the back of the door.

'Because we need grunt work, and fast. I'm trying to get us ahead on any leaks from the Ministry of Defence.' Jemima swivels her chair towards him before dropping into it. 'Thomas was pushing the military angle in the meeting only to take a royal pasting from Olivia, up at the front and everything. Even I almost felt sorry for him, but he's still not giving anything up. He must be properly nailed on to something.'

The foam walls amplify Dominic's laugh as he folds his arms across his chest, beaming. I feel the tiniest seed of hope germinate from somewhere inside the panic.

'Spill it, why don't you,' Jemima says as she stares up at him. 'You're even wearing a new suit. Where have you been? Or where are you going? Surely it's not for the benefit of Essex's finest?'

Dominic's gaze moves between us as he adjusts his tie. I let the foam cushion me as I lean into it, imagining my horse with wings. *We're about to fly away, baby.*

'I'm closer than I've ever been before,' he says, drumming his fingers on the desk. 'I'm so close I can literally taste it ... But I need to be certain that I'm not being played by the Home Office. Right now it feels like I might be, especially after showing them what we had on trafficking.'

'Really? Why?' I watch as Jemima's eyebrows raise at him.

'I've got inside the police on this, Jonas. Right inside. The problem is I barely needed to push the door before it opened, and then a few others swung open too. It's practically fallen into my lap—'

'Do you think Thomas is inside too?' I can't help but cut him off, heartbeat hammering.

'Forget about him,' he snaps. 'This is bigger than anything he'll ever get, no question. We don't need to worry about him anymore.'

'Talk to me, Dom, come on,' Jemima says as I crumple against the wall, foam edges suddenly unforgiving. 'You've obviously been talking up a storm all morning.'

I hold my breath as he straightens his already perfect tie. I know she's right. He's got something, but is it going to be what I need?

'It's starting to look like Jaqlin's after the Ministry of Defence. Their original big fish – that perverted captain – was nowhere near the tip of the shitty iceberg. The line is it would have compromised active intelligence if Operation Andromeda had gone any further back then. It wouldn't have been in the national interest, apparently – like the national interest is always the same as the public interest. So they are protecting someone, or something, and they are doing it deliberately. And it doesn't take much to work out what they were all still obsessing over at the time.'

Jemima whistles as he nods. The general's eyes flash sharp on the monitor.

'Exactly. Cold War nukes. The Brits could hardly take their eye off Russia's balls with the Americans breathing down everyone's necks. That intelligence operation was literally untouchable, it had to be. And it involved practically every unit in the country. Nothing was more important at the time, even as the government was busily shredding the rest of the military. Those spending cuts went the whole way through the nineties. Talk to anyone even remotely connected to defence and they describe that spending review as being like a nuclear bomb—'

'And that's where the case against Minchin comes in?' Jemima interrupts.

'Correct again, Jonas,' he says, reaching for the keyboard behind her, wiping out the general with the click of a mouse. 'But I have to prove it. It's all been too easy. Wait till you see this...' His hands flash across the keyboard as he pulls up a new file. 'I need a second source, even though this leak is iron-clad. You wouldn't believe it even if I told you. Madame Commissioner's got an agenda, for sure. It can't just be about all the money flooding back to defence instead of into her coffers, once they'd realised no one had the goods to have another go in the Gulf.'

A picture swims into focus on the screen, fuzzy and faded yet as unmistakable as the blood thundering in my ears. Time slows as I float, suspended, somewhere peripheral, somewhere even beyond the distance, pricks of light popping in my eyes with every shallow breath.

I think I hear myself cry out.

And then everything goes black.

Carly ~ Warchester ~ 1997

'I'm afraid I can't do that.' Doctor Twena stares up at Rach, who towers over him. She looks like an actual clown under the hospital strip lights, like she's painted her face with nail polish. It can't be proper makeup.

'I'm her sister, aren't I? I can take her home whenever I like.'

She scratches at new sores on her arm before putting her hands back on her hips. There's a cluster of us round the nurses' station now, blue pyjamas ballooning all over the place. I guess it makes better sense, now it's nearly midnight.

'She's not well enough to be discharged,' he says, waving the clipboard in his hand towards Kayleigh's cubicle. 'Her blood tests will take at least forty-eight hours, and it's only then that we can definitely rule out bacterial meningitis, not to mention clearing any potential alcohol poisoning.'

'Two days?' Rach shouts, glaring at me as well as him. I shrink into my blazer, slumping against the nurses' station. 'You're having a laugh, right? All this for a snotty nose?'

'Kayleigh has had a dangerous febrile convulsion,' he says, almost spitting as he talks. 'Her temperature was sky high, which is a sign of her body fighting a very serious infection. I can tell you, miss, that there isn't a snowball's chance in hell of her being discharged tonight, and her infection markers need to come down considerably for her to be ready to go home any time soon.'

'Like I give a toss what you say,' Rach mutters as she pushes past, marching towards Kayleigh's cubicle. There's a clatter as we all follow her, Doctor Twena gesturing with his clipboard.

'Don't fucking touch me,' she shouts as a policeman clumps

round the corner, blocking her path. I scuttle up behind her, plucking at her sleeve.

'Rach,' I whisper, shivering as my fingers brush cold skin. 'She was properly sick, seriously...'

'Shut your mouth,' she hisses as she bears round.

'Evening, Doc,' the policeman says. The doctor catches us up.

'Jonny,' he pants, 'I do appreciate you coming back in so late. Since the medical justification for keeping her sister in hospital doesn't seem to concern Rachel here, perhaps you could explain the criminal consequences of removing a patient from hospital without authorisation?'

Rach's arm feels like a stick in my hand. The policeman is a lot taller than her.

'You're her sister too, are you?' He looks her up and down. 'Got ID on you to prove it?'

'I'm her sister,' I gabble from behind her. 'We're all sisters.'

'Lovely,' he says, without looking at me. 'One big happy family, are we?'

'You can't arrest me,' Rach says, clenching her fist below my hand. 'I know my rights and all. You've got nothing on me.'

'True,' he says, fingering the handcuffs looped over his belt. 'Not yet, anyway. But if you take her out of here before the doc says she's ready, and she shows up again with who knows what wrong with her, then guess what happens next?'

Rach pulls her arm out of my hand as she stares at him.

'You'll need your ID for that bit too,' he says, smiling. 'Bit of a risk, wouldn't you say?'

'Can we just talk for a second?' I push myself between them.

'And that's the beauty of medical records, too,' he says, as if I'm not there. 'We'll know if you show up at Essex County instead, since they'll see everything from Warchester General.'

'Please?' I say, standing on tiptoes. 'We just need to talk for a minute.'

'Sure you can,' he says, taking a step back. 'You're sisters, aren't you? You can chat together all you like.' Rach keeps looking at him as I pull her away towards the wall.

'Not in here,' she hisses as she finally turns to me, speeding towards the entrance.

'One of us has to stay,' I say, putting out a hand to stop the swing door crashing into my face. 'Rach—'

'What the fuck is wrong with you, Carls!' she shouts into the wind as we step into the night air. 'Do you know how bad this is?'

'It'll get a lot worse if you end up in the slammer,' I say, heart racing so hard I think it might come out of my mouth.

Rach laughs, head pointing up at the moon overhead. I shiver as her lighter flares, purple lipstick almost black in the dark.

'What do we do?' I say, tears pricking my eyes. 'I think Jase'll kill me if there are any more questions. He said there would be questions just because of where we are. And there were two of them who saw the state of Ma, saw the state of everything...'

She doesn't answer, exhaling like she's a dragon.

'Maybe you should come back in the morning,' I continue, watching smoke curl and wisp around her head in the moonlight. 'Then she might be well enough for us to go without any grief, even if they come knocking afterwards. She might...' I trail off into the hiss of her cigarette. The forecourt is deserted.

'Please, Rach,' I say after a minute, reaching out to her. 'They never said we wouldn't be able to leave, did they? Just that I'm not old enough to take her myself. It's bad enough she ended up here in the first place—'

'And whose fault is that?' I jump as she interrupts, spitting on the tarmac between us.

'Ma called them, I swear she did,' I say. 'She must have. I would never...'

She laughs again.

'You didn't see her,' I say. 'I thought she was going to die. She was so hot that she might as well have been on fire inside—'

'We need her, Carls,' she cuts me off. 'We need her. Jason needs her, all of us need her. She's part of it too. Don't you get it?' Her cigarette crackles as she drags.

'Of course I get it!' I shout, tears streaming now. 'I'm the only one who really needs her. She's like the only good thing in my whole life. All this shit, everything I do is for her. I need her more than anything else.' I bury my face in my hands, stabbing my fingers into my eyes as I rub them. It's only when I blink that I notice the car parked diagonally across an empty ambulance bay next to us.

'Wait,' I say, sniffing as I stare at it. 'Is that...'

'Yeah,' she says, grinding her cigarette under her boot. 'I've got the papers and all.'

My head swivels between the car and her in disbelief. It looks like any car on any road in town, except she's got the keys.

'Rach,' I say, heart starting to race again. 'The police are actually waiting for you inside. You don't even have a licence. Do you honestly think you'll get away with it?'

'Doesn't matter,' she says, pulling out another cigarette. 'It's legit. Totally. Except maybe where I've parked it...' She trails off as her lighter flares.

I squint at the car. There's even the outline of one of those baby seats in the back.

'I don't understand,' I say. I don't understand anything that's happened today, I think.

'Well you don't have to, do you?' She reaches out to pull me into her arms. I slump against her, head spinning, feeling her ribs hard against my face, smell of smoke thick in every fibre of her clothes. 'Let's go get her, OK? They can't stop us, they know they can't. We'll wrap her up nice and warm in the back, get her some medicine from that all-night place on the way into town. And I know somewhere we can go get her looked at if she's a mess again. We won't have to come back here. I promise, Carls, OK?'

I feel her chin resting on the top of my head as her arms tighten around me.

'They're all just trying to scare us. They can't stop us taking her home if we want, and they know it. All that medical records crap ... total bollocks.'

'How do you know?' I say, muffled in her chest. 'They know everything at the clinic, don't they? Every time we go I get grief about the last time.'

She grips both my shoulders as she pushes me away, looking me in the face.

'That's because it's the same place isn't it? Same people, same place, same old story.'

'But what if she has another fit?' I blink at her. She looks mad, crazy even, the moon lighting her like a ghost, all white and black in the dark.

'She won't. She just won't ... And if she does, I know where we can fix it, promise.' I wince as her fingers pinch into my shoulders. I want to believe her so badly that I feel dizzy.

'I've got blankets and all,' she says, jerking her head in the direction of the car. 'I'll take you home, stay with you both tonight. Don't worry, OK? I'll sort it.'

'Stay? With us? You'll stay with us?'

She looks down for a moment.

'Yeah,' she says. 'Of course I will. I need you both too, don't I?'

Marie ~ London ~ 2006

Voices, a low hum, scraping at my conscious edge.

'...did she hit her head?'

'...shit, she must've ... that's blood isn't it?'

'...Marie? Marie ... Marie?'

Fingers paddle at my face, a hand snakes behind my head, another grips my shoulder.

'...roll her on to her side ... not her back...'

'...recovery position isn't it?'

'...leg needs to go up, wait...'

I open my eyes, try to blink, except one eye is mushed into the carpet.

'...splash some water on her face, here...'

I roll my head into the hand behind it, Dominic and Jemima's faces sludgy above me.

'...Marie? Steady on now girl...'

I blink and blink and blink. Their heads are cocked in a heart shape above my face.

'...no, no don't sit up, just hang on there, girl...'

I blink again. What am I doing on the floor?

'...put this under her head...'

The hand behind my head guides my face downwards as something is placed underneath.

'...it's coffee, look ... she's not bleeding, is she?'

The heart shape swims as fingers rake through my hair.

'...Marie? Wait, hang on, let me help you...'

I sit up, head thumping as I balance it on top of my neck. Dominic is squatting on one side, Jemima on the other. There's a chair wedged behind me against the desk. We're in an edit suite. Yes. Of course we are.

'Are you alright, girl?' Jemima frowns at me, hand gripping my shoulder.

Why are we in the edit suite? Something new, agonising, snags in my mind. I try to speak but only a croak comes out.

'You fainted,' she says. 'Hit your head on the way down...'

I flinch as Dominic rakes his fingers through my hair again.

'It's coffee,' he says again, rubbing his fingertips together. 'Here, look.' He shoves his fingers under Jemima's nose. They both turn and squint at me.

'Let's get her into a chair,' Dominic says. 'OK?' He smiles down at me. 'I'm going to lift you, OK? Just rest on my arm ... Come on...'

I summon every fibre of my body and try to move unaided but all that happens is goosepimples jump out on my skin. They fold me into the chair like a rag doll.

'Just sip it, OK?' Jemima hands me a plastic cup of water. 'Just in case...'

I will my arm to move but nothing happens. She places it on the desk behind me.

'What day is it?' Dominic stares at me.

'Do you even know what day it is?' Jemima tuts at him.

'What day is it?'

'Thursday,' I say, coughing. 'It's Thursday.'

He smiles as Jemima scowls. 'Very good,' he says. 'And what's my name?'

'Pillock,' Jemima says.

I wince as I raise an arm to rub my head. 'What happened?' There's an egg-sized lump under my fingers.

'You fainted,' Jemima says, reaching out to squeeze my arm. 'Clean on to the floor. Bang. Quite the statement.'

'Took my coffee with you, too,' Dominic adds. 'Fair enough, I suppose, since you buy me so much of the bloody stuff in the first place.'

I finger the egg on my head. My hair feels sticky, or is it my head? Something tugs deep inside again, merciless, insistent.

'I'm calling you a car, OK?' Jemima straightens, pulling out her phone. 'You are to go straight home. And if you're sick, you go straight to A&E. Ever had a concussion before?' She raises her eyebrows as I snort.

'I'm OK,' I say, smoothing my hair over the egg. 'Seriously, Jemima, I'm fine. It must've just got a bit hot in here...'

'Don't be absurd,' she says, lifting the phone to her ear. 'What's your address?'

'No, really,' I say, bracing myself on the arms of the chair as I try to stand.

'Forget it,' Dominic says, leaning over to flick a switch on the keyboard on the desk behind me. 'I can confirm, from bitter experience, that you don't stand a chance against Jonas on this one ... on any one, for that matter...'

My skin prickles as he fiddles with the equipment, memories clearing the fog in my head. The monitor. The picture. Andromeda. It's like so many of the dreams I wake up from, where I'm older and she's still a child. The idea it's just a dream flashes, so tempting and painful, I think I might pass out again. Except this time I can't let myself fall back to sleep.

'...asap,' Jemima says into her phone. 'Just come to the main door...'

Dominic straightens, smiling down at me.

'Bill will be here in fifteen minutes,' she says, tucking her phone back into her pocket. 'I left the destination open. You'll be OK to direct him, right?'

'I'm fine, honestly, guys,' I say, pushing myself upright. 'Just a funny turn, that's all.'

I rest on the wall so I can look at the screen without collapsing again, digging knuckles into my eyes. She's still young, in my head, and in the picture.

'Funny turn or not, you're going home,' Jemima says. 'If you feel better later, you can join the party tomorrow. But if you don't leave now, that's off too.'

The screen stares up at me, blank and empty.

'Who was that in the picture?' I say, leaning into foam.

'Eh?' Dominic says.

'That picture you loaded up just before,' I say. 'The little girl. Who was it?'

I cough as my voice cracks. I know who it was. The past laps at me like a drug, pulling me backward, downward.

'Here,' Jemima says, jerking my coat in front of me. 'Seriously, Marie. Put it on. I'll walk you out, let's go.'

'Who was it?' I say, louder this time. The soundproof walls bring my words back with the faintest of echoes. *Who was it. Who was it. Who was it.*

'I don't know,' Dominic says, leaning forward to tap at the keyboard. 'I'm not sure they all do, either. But they called her Baby Girl A.'

I brace against the wall as the picture flashes up again, scuffed and pixelated with age. I don't have to stare at it to know I could fill in the gaps, complete the outline, rebuild the soul from the inside out. Except I was never given the chance, was I? Neither was she.

'There's Girl A, and Baby Girl A, if you can believe that,' he continues. 'The list takes in half of the fucking alphabet. Girl A's evidence was at least in the public domain. But Baby Girl A wasn't – because she was Minchin's. So she, like everything else to do with him, was classified. That's their smoking gun. That's what my source says, at any rate.'

Something inside me collapses as I hear it, head dropping on my neck. I don't need to see her again to remember. There's nothing I'll ever be able to forget about this. All the years I've spent trying are suddenly worth less than dust.

'Come on.' Jemima takes hold of my elbow. 'Steady now, OK?' I shrink into my coat as she wraps it around me, moving me like a mannequin, out of the newsroom and into the lift, silence like a cloak as we glide to the ground floor.

'I'll check in later, I promise,' Jemima says as she leads me out to the waiting taxi. I nod dumbly as I fold myself into the back.

'Where to, love?'

I float for a moment as Bill calls from the front, acid reek of petrol, squeal of traffic, whip of cold air through the half-open window. That little girl – how she was in that picture – was known to almost no one. I understand that better than I understand what's left of myself. And yet, every time I try to examine the realisation pulling at the edges of my consciousness it threatens to overwhelm me. The series of events that must have led to Dominic ending up with a copy takes on the ugliest of dimensions, warping and shimmering into something so unfathomable it can't possibly be true. Except with every shallow breath, I know it must be.

There's only one reason he could have it.

And it's because I've only ever been lied to.

'Where to?' Bill's voice chimes again as I ask myself. Deep down I know I already have the answer but I won't believe it until I ask the question. I pull myself straight, summon everything that's left.

'Whitehall,' I croak, clearing my throat as the car accelerates away. 'Please, Bill. I just need to go straight to Whitehall.'

Carly ~ Warchester ~ 1997

I twirl around, fancy blue stud twinkling in my nose in the tiny mirror mounted on the jewellery stands near the back of the shop. Now the swelling's gone down it looks properly cool. Not so big so it looks like a spot, not too small so you can't see it at all. Just enough that it flashes in the light, like a real jewel. I smile at myself. In the right light, it even matches my eyes.

I run my hand down the pairs of earrings dangling from their black paper backing, hooked round the carousel in neat rows and columns. They'll make a charm out of anything these days. Surfboards, footballs, lollies, even broomsticks. I linger on a silver pair of bunny rabbits, mounted as studs rather than hanging from loops. It's either them or the teddy charms for Kayleigh's first pair, I think. Not that I'm letting Rach near her with that nail gun, mind you. Not after the hash she made of my ear.

The earrings rattle as the doors clang shut up front. I can hear Rach moving from the top to the bottom, turning keys and closing bolts, before the hum of the outer screen closing throws us into pitch-dark.

'Bollocks,' Rach mutters as she flicks on the lights. I twist my head this way and that. The blue spark in my nose is brighter under the strip lights than in daylight.

'What's up?' I say, poking at it with my finger. I still can't believe it's in there. She'd said no for so long that I thought I'd have to do it myself, and there's no way I could do that. Fair enough, she'd said, after all that drama at the hospital. You did good, she'd said. You always do good. Too bloody right, I'd said. It's because of me that everything is back to normal.

'Someone's been at the slides,' she says, tossing her hair off her face as she clumps over to me. 'Dunno how many times I have to show them how easy it is to nick stuff in here. There's no point making me assistant manager if I can't move things around.'

'Do you mean the hair bands?'

'Yeah,' she says, flicking more switches so only the lights at the back are left on. 'You can lift and stash in half a second. Handfuls-worth, easily. We need to put the bigger stuff up front.'

'Like what?' I finger the bunny earrings. I think these are the ones.

'All the bags, for starters. Those fancy rucksacks. And the thermoses too...'

'But then no one would come in, would they?'

'Eh? Why?' She stares at me as I poke my nose.

'Well who wants to buy those? I bet no one wants to nick them either...'

She shakes her head at me as I continue. 'You need stuff in the window people want, don't you? Else why would anyone bother coming inside?'

She turns to the carousels of earrings and necklaces, looping a thick, heavy chain around one of her fingers.

'Like those,' I say. 'See? They look ace, but try stuffing them in your pocket quickly.'

I jump as she swipes at the carousel, necklaces jangling as she spins it round and round.

'You finished?'

I nod, pulling my hair round my face to hide my blush. We head out, clicking off the rest of the lights on our way through the store-room at the back. A can of Coke hisses as she hands it to me, leaning on the small desk just inside the back door.

'Nice,' I say, sipping at the froth collecting in the lid. 'Do they bring these in specially?'

'For you,' she says, eyes narrowing as she looks at me – unless it's her makeup. She's been wearing a lot more lately. Black and thick around her eyes. Sometimes I can barely see them at all.

'Aren't you having one?'

She shakes her head. I sip at more fizz, bubbles popping against my teeth.

'Your Ma holding it together alright these days?' she says, boots clunking as she weaves her legs together.

'Depends what you call alright,' I say, tapping at the can. It makes different sounds however full it is. 'She's managing not to land us in it, if that's what you mean.'

'Social services have been round again, have they?'

'Yeah,' I say, gulping from my can. 'They're supposed to be coming twice a week since the hospital. I've been at school though. At least most of the time. Julie said she's depressed.'

'Julie?' she interrupts me. 'Who the fuck is Julie?'

'One of the social workers,' I splutter, bubbles sticking in my throat. I drank too fast. 'Remember? That nurse from the hospital. And the clinic. The one who thought you were my sister. She shows up with them sometimes ... What?'

Rach cracks her knuckles before smacking a hand on the desk.

'She says Ma can't take care of herself because she's depressed,' I continue, tensing my hand round the can. It's still nice and cold. 'Like she's so sad all the time that she doesn't even care if Kayleigh's wet herself, or if she's eaten nothing but beans from the tin all week, even if Jase has brought us better stuff.'

'She's been asking you questions and all?'

'A few,' I say, taking another swig. 'I know her game though, don't I? It's easy ... I just tell her what she wants to hear.'

'What about Kayleigh? Has she been OK?'

'You know she has,' I say, swallowing. 'She's still coughing like she's a dog or something, but that medicine you brought us is the business. She loves it too, can't get to the spoon fast enough. She sleeps better too, out like a light – bang. Nothing wakes her, not even the army jets. Where did you get it?' I drain the rest of my can.

'Doesn't matter,' she says, reaching for her coat hung on the back of the door. 'So long as it's still nice and tidy. Good job, girl. Not doing too badly, are we? Jobs, wheels, cash, the whole bloody lot.'

I snort as she fiddles with her zip. 'So what's up with tonight,' I say, crunching the can into my fist.

'Jase's back,' she says, bending for her bag. 'Just got the call, didn't I?'

'What's he doing, calling you?' I toss the can into the overflowing bin in the corner.

'You were at school.' She looks up. I pull my blazer around myself.

'So what's up with Jase?' I shake my head as she offers me a tab.

'Checking in, you know, the usual,' she says, squeezing through the outer door into the alley behind the row of shops. 'Look lively, will you?' She jangles the bunch of keys in her hand.

I push past her, wincing as puddle water flicks on to my bare legs. It's so narrow there's no choice about where to stand if I don't want to step on her feet. There's a clang and a rattle as the back door bolt finally closes. We pick our way up the alley towards the road.

'Jason wants to see Kayleigh,' she says, splashing as she clumps through puddles.

'He knows where to find her, doesn't he?' I say, shivering as water seeps into my shoes. I don't have those big chunky boots like her. Not yet, anyway. She looks all black and yellow in the light from the lamppost overhead as she waits for me to catch up.

'I told him we'd bring her in,' she says, lighter flaring as she sparks another tab. 'I know that's what he wants. Can't hurt, can it? Loads of army families do visits all the time. That's all this is. He said so, anyway. It's just a visit. That's all.'

I reach out to the lamppost as my legs go weak and tingly. I should have worn tights, I think, even though I know it wouldn't have made the tiniest bit of difference. Shivers move down my back as I fumble with the post. She won't look at me as she exhales, smoke funnelling between us.

Maybe this is the line between two worlds, I think, swaying on my feet. She's in the one where everything makes perfect sense. But over here, where I am, nothing about this makes sense at all. Time slows as I stare at her, looking down her nose at me like I'm a child on her elbow.

'He just wants us to bring her to the barracks, Carls. What's the big deal?'

I jump as she yanks her arm out of my hand. Was I tugging at it? She swears, eyes darting and hand shaking as she lifts her tab to her mouth.

'He's her brother too, isn't he? She's family. It's still warm and fuzzy even if she's got a different dad ... Nothing weird about that, is there?' She pulls harder on her tab. 'He said we owe them a visit, after everything that's happened. We owe them. Not the other way around.' Smoke pours from her nostrils as she purses her lips.

I gape at her, like we're the only people in a street full of crowds.

'They just got back,' she says, blinking hard. Could it be tears? I search her face. 'It was fucking awful, the worst yet, he said. It's times like this family really matters.'

I lean my whole body against the lamppost, lolling my forehead on to the ridges of cold steel. A bus clatters past, the posters plastered on either side screaming at me: *Your Army Needs You.*

'It won't hurt, Carls,' she says, somewhere outside of my ears. 'It won't hurt at all. They'll give her something, she won't feel a thing, won't know what's going on. She'll probably even just fall asleep. She likes that medicine, doesn't she? Where do you think I got it? You said it yourself, she's out like a light ... They just want to look at her. They won't touch her, just look. Won't touch. That's what he said. It won't mean anything to her. She might not ever remember it. She just has to sit there, doze, even fall asleep, whatever. It'll be easier for her than it is for us...'

For a moment I think I'm floating, like the cigarette smoke disappearing into the air.

'We have to, Carls.' Her voice furls around my head. 'It's the only way. We'd never find anyone else on the quiet. There'd be red flags all over the place. She trusts you, Carls. And him. It'll be like going somewhere with her brother and sister. We'll get her a present after-wards – hamburger, knickerbocker glory, the lot. That's all...'

Her voice seems to fade away as I rest my head on the post, lids drooping over my eyes, street chatter and hum rising and falling around me like radio waves, up and down, up and down.

It's just a bit of fun, they said. Something real, they said. We need you, Rach said, I've got no choice now, Jase said. And no one'll listen if you squeal, they all said.

Up and down, up and down, until suddenly, I'm the one in the world that makes sense, where I know these are promises that bring nightmares not dreams, where I know everything I'm doing is only so Kayleigh never has to. The world where she'll walk to school every morning in skirts that fit her, where she'll sleep, belly warm with dinner, every night, and where she won't even have to look to find her own four-leaf clover, and maybe she'll even find one for me too.

The world where I know I'm finally going to play to win, instead of lose.

Julie flashes into my mind as I straighten, frizzy hair like a halo around her head, an angel against the window.

'...Carls?'

I blink away the smoke of Rach's world as I look up at her, lamplight throwing twisted shadows all over her face, so warped I don't recognise her anymore.

Dangling from her hand, a pair of bunny earrings, all twinkly between her stained, yellow fingers. 'These are a good start, aren't they? I bet she'll love these.'

Part Three

Carly ~ Warchester ~ 1998

'You have to take her in,' I hiss, yanking at the hand cuffed to the table in front of me. 'Just pick her up and move her somewhere else. Why can't she go into a foster home? An orphanage? Or why can't I look after her. She could so easily just stay with me. There are babies all over the hostel, in practically every room ... How much more do you need to see for yourselves to get her out of there? Ma is completely incapable, other than give birth to her, she's never been able to do a single thing for her. You promised you'd protect her. That's the only reason I ever agreed to keep going over and over this...'

'It's going to get a lot worse if you keep doing that,' the policewoman drawls, nodding at my arm from across the table. I try not to wince as the cuff bites deeper into my skin, blood spotting the streaky tiles below. These are tiles that have seen it all before. Every last painful plea.

'Just take it off then ... I can hardly strangle the lot of you, can I?'

Metal rattles against the table as I shout, glaring at the rest of the officers in the room. This policewoman always comes with her own army. She's never bothered telling me her name, but they all call her ma'am, like she's the queen, except it's written all over her uniform that she's not. And every time she leaves the room they talk about her like she's anything but royal. All she wants is to be in charge.

'Try and calm down, love,' Julie murmurs next to me. 'You've done so well. So, so well. I can't help you if you keep physically lashing out at them. There's a protocol...'

'There's always a protocol,' I hiss at her, blinking back tears. 'This whole filthy town is built on protocol. That's why Kayleigh's still with Ma, and why she's still at risk, because apparently staying with her biological mother is more important than her biological mother being capable of anything other than getting roaring drunk.'

I kick at the table leg, shivering as my plastic chair squeaks, as if it's on wheels. I've been in and out of this sweaty room for months now, answering questions, ticking boxes, reliving every little detail, all so Captain Perv's wheelchair never, ever rolls again. And still Kayleigh's exposed. I can't understand it. I don't know what else I need to tell them.

'Couldn't we remove these?' Julie rests her hand on my shoulder. 'Carly isn't the criminal here. I think we established that months ago.'

'I am sorry, Carly,' the policewoman says, uniform creaking as she leans towards me. 'Julie's right, of course, there's protocol at work here, and if you keep raising your hand to my officers, these need to stay on.'

I thump my fist on the desk, shrugging Julie's hand off my shoulder. Like I'll ever pretend she's the queen just because they all do. I know her real name. I can read it on her chest.

'Could you bring me that Savlon, Phil?' the policewoman calls over my head. I can't help but relax my hand as she rubs cream into the scratches round my wrist.

'Does that feel any better?'

I shake my head, still staring at the floor. Now it's Julie's hand, finding its way on to my leg this time, warming up a patch on my revolting tracksuit. I don't even have my own clothes anymore, just police handouts. It was never supposed to take this long, once I'd told them everything. It's like they think they can make me remember other names and faces just by making me stew, as if I'm not doing my best to forget them all. I stiffen into a sudden clatter on the table, then a click as the policewoman finally releases my handcuffs.

'Don't make me regret that, OK?'

I pull my aching wrist into my lap without looking up. *Regrrairrrrt*. Scottish or Irish? A fly buzzes to death on the strip light overhead.

'I just don't understand why Kayleigh's still with Ma,' I say into my lap, tears spotting the grey fabric on my legs. 'What else do you need me to tell you to get her out of there? It's OK for you to keep asking me the same questions, but you never answer mine, do you? She was this close to being drugged up inside the barracks, and there's nothing standing between her and them, now I'm not there. Nothing.'

'Kayleigh's well protected, I can assure you,' the policewoman says. 'And that's in large part because of you, Carly. You're still a child yourself. You should never have had to look after her in the first place. You've been so incredibly brave coming forward with all this ... so, so brave...'

'But Ma can't look after herself!' I shout, looking up at her, a pair of glasses perched on her nose like someone's drawn them on to her face. 'She never could. That's how this all started. We had no other choice. But you still think it's OK to leave Kayleigh living with her.'

'Everyone you identified is behind bars, love,' she says. 'Everyone. The trials may not be over but they can't get to you, and they can't get to her.'

'You don't know that,' I sniff. 'You'll never know that. The whole of Warchester's the army. The place is basically built on squaddies. Army traffic even has its own lane in the road. There's no one round here without an army connection.'

'We visit with Kayleigh every week,' Julie says, squeezing my leg again. 'Your mum is having counselling. She has to report to the clinic herself twice a week and is very well supported. Kayleigh is thriving. Here, look...'

My eyes swim as she lays pictures out on the table. Kayleigh with her cuddlies. Kayleigh with her Aquarius charm. Kayleigh with her peachy cheeks, fuzzy white curls, butterfly eyelashes. I start to sob, burying my head in my hands. Every night on my slab of a bed, in my cell of a room in that pathetic excuse for a safe haven, shelter, refuge – none of the words they use fit what it really is: just another type of prison – all I ever wish for is that I could go back to lying next to her, even though I know what it would mean if I was still there.

Julie's arms slide round me, chair squeaking again as she rocks me. For some reason her chair is the only one that doesn't sound like it's on wheels.

'We're nearly there, Carly,' the policewoman says, papers rustling somewhere. 'So nearly there. We can't do it without you, remember that. You're helping us, and we're going to help you. And when this is all over, we'll protect you for the rest of your life. You can count on that. You can count on us...'

'Like I can count on anything,' I say into Julie's shoulder. 'I don't know who half of them were. Even Rach didn't.'

'You won't be seeing Rachel again for a very, very long time,' Julie murmurs into my ear. 'The case against her was straightforward. She was complicit, unlike you.'

'She was my friend,' I mutter, swallowing bile back down my throat as I pull away from her. 'She had to do it all too, but just because she's older than me she's going down for it? There's no protection on the table for her, just because of some random line in the sand deciding when we're all officially grown up? She was the best friend I ever had.'

'That's just it,' the policewoman says, shuffling the papers on the desk between us. 'No friend in the world grooms another friend for abuse. Without Rachel, this might never have happened to you. And there were others, Carly, you know that. Rachel was an accomplice in this entire sordid affair. It's that simple. She's a criminal. And with your testimony, she's going to pay for what she's done.'

'It just suits you better that way, doesn't it? It's a numbers game, and here's another win for you lot. Never mind that there are still so many losers left out there. You're locking up all the wrong people!'

'Rachel was an adult for almost the entire duration of—'

'Almost.' I pinch at the scratches round my wrist, make them bleed again. 'That's the point, isn't it. That's where your numbers game gets inconvenient. She wasn't sixteen when it all started...'

I trail off as Kayleigh's photos disappear under a booklet. Like two years make a difference. None of this adds up. And numbers always do, even if you don't want them to. I know that better than any of these grown-ups, who may as well be a thousand years older than both of us.

'Wait ... Can I keep one of those? Please?'

'Of course,' the policewoman says. 'They're for you.'

I shove her papers back towards her as I reach for the pictures.

'When do I get to see her again?' I trace the outline of her hair with a fingertip. 'I just want to see her once more before I disappear...'

'All in good time,' she says. 'We're protecting you both, Carly. We know what we're doing, you have to trust us on this one.'

I snort, fumbling with my precious photos, too late for a tear that's already warped a corner.

'Perhaps we can talk Carly through the next steps?' Julie says. 'That's why we're here today, isn't it? To go through her witness protection? Unless I've misunderstood.'

'Quite the stickler, aren't you?' the policewoman snaps at her.

I look at the floor, lose myself in the pictures I've found in all its cracks. There's Jesus on the cross, a clump of scratches on a tile at two o'clock. A cluster, like a perfect star, at eight o'clock. A whole chunk, a wonky triangle, is missing in action near eleven. And suddenly a booklet, thick and heavy on the table, unfamiliar words blocking out my star. *Me-mor-an-dum?* The letters disappear as she flips it open to lists, lists and more lists.

'As you can imagine, there's quite the pile of paperwork involved in a protection plan of this scale.' Her fingers drum on the lists in front of me. 'We need to make sure you get the new start you deserve. But we're almost there, Carly. Almost there. All I need for now is your signature, and—'

'Don't I get to read it?' I cut her off. 'I've never seen that booklet before. You're changing my name, changing my life, changing everything I've ever known...'

'There's nothing in here you don't already know,' she says, eyes narrowing to tiny slits behind her glasses. 'Ask away, go on, if you have any more questions. But I think you and I both know that you're a smart cookie, aren't you, Carly? I think you know that aspects of this plan could still change, of course, if you remember anything else between now and the end of the trial...'

Mugshots swim on the table in front of me. The same mugshots I've stared at a thousand times. A load of faces I never saw, and a few I'll never forget. A finger taps the same one it always taps.

'I told you, I never saw him. Ask Rach,' I mumble, searching for my star on the floor. Eight o'clock. And there's Jesus at two, dying all over again.

'Try to forget about Rachel. This isn't about her, it's about you, Carly, and about the rest of your life. Think about that. It's about the rest of your life, and everything it could be. Think again, now. Is anything coming to mind? Anything at all?'

I shove the papers at her without looking at them. There goes another fly, hissing as it buzzes out.

'Well, then.' There's the click of a pen and a scrabble of paper. 'There's still time, of course. If anything were to come to mind.'

'How much time?' I say, counting the points of the star. One. Two. Three. Four. Five. There's the little scratch that could be a sixth, except it isn't. 'You keep saying everything's nearly ready for me to go, and then out comes the line-up again.'

'Tomorrow,' she says. 'We're ready to move you out tomorrow. OK? It's all finally come together: where you'll work, where you'll live, all your new papers and documents. I told you, you're so nearly there...'

I look up, but instead of my triangle, I find her finger tapping a dotted line in the booklet.

'So that's it, then? After all this time, I just sign here and it's over?'

Julie nods as my head swivels between them. Too late, I realise I'm crumpling Kayleigh's face in my hand.

'That's right,' the policewoman says. 'Sign here, and it's over. At least, for now, anyway. No more hostel. No more hiding. No more reliving everything that's happened to you. You can bury Carly Marie Gates along with everyone else. You can bury her forever.'

She holds out a pen, pointing it at my chest like a weapon as we stare at each other.

'And we'll make sure no one ever finds her. You can be sure of that.'

I watch my hand as it stretches out like a ghost, like Carly is already dead, and traces out the loops and curls of C, M and G, the last doodle that her hand will ever draw.

Bye, Carly, who can map the stars in the sky without looking. Who likes to dance when no one's watching, to tell stories when no one's listening except her. Who loves to add, minus, times and divide, because numbers always give her a straight answer. The pen stabs as I remember her.

Bye, Carls. Your story's over. You never have to tell it again.

I decorate my signature with kisses, just one last line. I guess I loved her once, didn't I?

Marie ~ London ~ 2006

In real life, this journey, the one from the newsroom to the Ministry of Defence, takes all of five minutes; but in my life, this twisted wreck of a double life, this wretched excuse for a fresh start, new chance, second try – any of the mindless terms they came up with to try and disguise the fact it was nothing more than the last roll of a loaded dice – well, this journey may as well have taken a thousand years. The inside of that taxi has seen every frame of my pathetic existence, from birth to now and back again, except all I could see, and will ever be able to see, is Dominic's picture. The fact his police source has shown it to him can only mean one thing, and every blink makes it clearer, every rub of my eyes makes it sharper, every acid swallow makes it louder, like it's screaming the answer directly at me.

Go back, Carly rasps in my ear as I stumble through the entrance, fumbling for my press pass. They lied to us, she hisses, as I smooth my hair over the egg on the side of my head. Everything they said, everything they told us is a twisted mountain of lies! I jump as someone brushes past me, tutting. Did she say that out loud? Who did? I rub at my head, fingers stabbing at the child inside. Now it's Rach, sneering as she holds Carly's hand. Make it right, she purrs, as I join the back of the line through security. You're the only one that can make it right.

'Marie Grant, Nine News,' I chant under my breath as we shuffle forward. That's my name, isn't it? I count backward with every step forward, remembering when it changed, reprinting it on my bones. The security arch squeals up ahead as someone forgets about the phone still in their pocket. I'll never forget though, will I? How could I ever forget? Carly weeps, curled in school uniform, rocking in a ball just inside my eyelids.

'Gateway badge, miss,' a guard shouts as I approach the reception desk.

'I'm press,' I say, fingers trembling as I dangle my pass. 'I'm with Nine News...'

The guard catches up to me.

'Have you got a Gateway pass there?'

'I must have left it...' I fumble in my pocket.

'Do you have an appointment?' He fingers my press card without looking at it.

'Yes,' I say. It hardly matters that I don't.

'This is the lane for visitors,' he says, pointing.

I shrug his hand off my back as I move to the desk. The man behind the counter is on the phone but arches his eyebrows at me anyway.

'Shacklin,' I say, clearing my throat. As if I'd forget her name even though she never once bothered introducing herself. 'I'm here to see—'

'Could I see your Gateway badge?' He puts his hand over the receiver.

'I'm press,' I say, slipping my pass across the counter.

'There's nothing else on the slate for press today. What were you expecting?'

'I've got an appointment to see Shacklin. That's her name. Shacklin. If you could just tell me...'

He puts the phone down as if no one was ever on the other end.

'...which office she's in, I'll head on up.'

'There's no Shacklin in this building,' he says, computer screen throwing blue shadows on his face as he frowns at it. 'With a C? Or just a K?'

I kick the wall holding the counter up as realisation starts to dawn. Like anyone's name would ever be real in this twisted business. I scratch at my ear as the whispers start again.

'Can you try Pegasus? Is there anyone called Pegasus?' I grip the sill as I hiss.

'Pegasus? Like the horse?' His nose wrinkles as I glare back. 'You said you were press, right? Which outlet?'

A lump of hand appears on the counter next to me.

'Everything alright over here?'

I twitch as the guard's shadow falls over me. And then I shout, words tumbling from my mouth as Carly screams, deep inside my inner ear.

'Andromeda! Why don't you try that? Try anyone here that answers to Andromeda!'

Hands become vices around my upper arms as I twist and buck against the counter, another guard appearing to haul me into a small room next to the desk. At least I think there's two of them. I may as well be blind for all I can actually see. There's a thud as the door closes. And there aren't any windows. There never seem to be any windows.

'We've got a live one, boss,' the guard says into a red telephone mounted by the door as I squirm against the hands holding me down in a chair. 'With the press, apparently, saw the pass. No, no Gateway badge...'

'Do that again and it's bracelets,' barks a female voice behind me.

'You can't cuff me,' I shout, ramming her with my back. 'I haven't done anything.'

'Try me,' she hisses, digging her fingers into my shoulders.

'...Andromeda, she said. What? Yes, Andromeda...'

'Give it up, Baz,' the female guard drawls behind me. 'Just call Nine, that's where she reckons she works, isn't it? Then we can chalk her up as another nutter and get out of here.'

I stop straining as he glares at us, poking a finger into his ear.

'...Pegasus, or something. All sorts. Ranting and raving really ... What, now? Why?'

The whirl calms, suddenly, like we've all passed into the eye of a storm. Carly quiets as I sit, perfectly still. The guard tenses her grip on my shoulders.

'...Of course I will, if you think that's necessary ... Sorry, boss, didn't mean...' He pulls the phone away from his ear, blinking and staring at it before clicking it back into its red cradle.

'Baz? You lost it or what? It's gone five.'

He ignores her, hand still resting on the phone. I don't dare blink.

'Baz! We done or what?'

He turns, resting his eyes on me. Baz. For just that second I wonder what his real name is.

'See?' I say, wincing as fingers dig back into my neck. 'I told you, didn't I!'

'What's your name?' He steps towards me.

'Did they tell you to ask me that?'

We stare at each other.

'No,' he says, after a minute.

'Baz. What the fuck is this?' The female guard lets go of my shoulders.

'Don't fucking move,' he says to me, beckoning her over to the door. I wrap my arms around myself as they whisper in the corner, closing my eyes for just a moment to watch as Carly wipes her eyes. But then the floor shakes, my eyes start to water, and I find them both standing in front of me.

'You're coming with us,' the guard says. Baz.

'I am, am I? Where?'

'Upstairs,' he says. 'The boss wants a word. But no funny business, OK?'

'Who's the boss? Shacklin?'

'Just come with us,' he says, leaning forward to haul me upright. 'You've got an appointment, after all, haven't you?'

I tense as the woman's hand closes round my other arm.

'Yes,' I say, shaking myself between them. 'Do you do this to everyone who's got one?'

'You're a special case, apparently. Come on.'

We move as a unit across the lobby, Carly like a sprite at my shoulder, until we reach a set of lifts in the far wall.

'Steady on,' Baz mutters, pulling on my arm as my foot starts towards an open one full of people. Finally a set of doors yawns open, empty. We shuffle forward in silence, floating upward with a click and a chime. The female guard groans as there's another chime, except the doors are still closed in front of us. I stumble as I turn to see the back side of the lift opening into a dark passageway, facing another, smaller lift door.

'Down the rabbit hole, is it?' she grumbles, spinning me round. The second lift's much smaller and clunkier, jolting down rather than up, so deep we must be underground. We keep moving for so long I start to wonder if we're going sideways. I only know we've arrived when the doors open without warning after a particularly solid jolt.

'Where are we?' I ask, stepping out into a low-ceilinged, windowless corridor.

'Thought you had an appointment,' Baz mumbles, grabbing my arm, the female guard grumbling at my other side. I keep quiet as we walk and turn, searching the endless greyish walls and plastic floor for anything that might remind me how to get out again. Finally, we stop in front of a door at the end of the passage, which Baz opens with a thumbprint.

'In you go,' he says, pushing at the small of my back. I peer into the room, if you can even call it that. Dark, airless, no more than four feet square, another door set into the opposite wall.

'No way,' I say, bracing myself between them. I've been in enough of these to know what happens when they lock the door behind you. A whole lot of nothing for a whole lot of nothing longer. 'You tell Shacklin to open that other door and I'll go...'

The female guard sneers as Baz's hand closes round my arm.

'Bit late for all that now, isn't it?' she drawls as they lift and fling me across the threshold. I land in a heap as the door closes on their laughter, taking most of the light left in the room with it.

I sit, too stunned to do anything except blink. All I can make out in the half-light are the doors, embedded in the walls like the panels of lift doors, except I'm not moving and there aren't any buttons. One's behind me, where I came in. One in front of me, where I suppose I'll get out. Or will I go backward? I squint up at the ceiling. There is a small camera pointed directly at me.

'Who are you?' I jump as a voice echoes round the tiny room. There's a whirr as the camera suddenly swivels and glows red.

'Pegasus,' I say, staring up at it like an ember in the dark. 'Pegasus?' There's a click and the red light goes out.

'Pegasus,' I repeat, panic rising in my throat. 'You said. Pegasus. Pe-ga-sus.'

Nothing. My arms flap at the camera, up and down, up and down, like I'm a bird that can't fly.

'Who the fuck are you, then?' I shout, freezing as it suddenly flashes red again, rotating like the point of a laser.

The door ahead slides open, revealing the outline of a man with his back to me, hunched over a table against the far wall. I brace myself between the walls and blink into the brighter light. Apart from a low hum of equipment, I can see nothing else in the room.

'Aren't you going to come in?' He doesn't turn around.

Is there anyone else in there? I brace myself harder. Even though this room is only as big as my whole wingspan, I don't see any exits in the other one.

'I asked who you were,' I spit. 'Protocol's protocol, isn't it? Hardly worth insisting on it in the first place if you lot ditch it whenever it suits you.'

The walls slip a little under my hands as I force myself to stay upright. Finally he turns, blank and empty, dark hair and trousers, white shirt and face. He'd be a mannequin if he wasn't moving.

'Perseus,' he says, staring at me.

I search his face, his body. I've never seen him before.

'Where's Shacklin,' I say, arms pinching as they drop to my sides.

'Shacklin? Who's Shacklin?' He cocks his head, leaning back in his chair.

'I'm done talking to you lot. Perseus this, Athena that – all these random codewords are actually doing is hiding the lies rather than the truth. I need to see Shacklin. She owes me more than just answers and I'm not leaving till I get them...'

I trail off in spite of myself as he stands up.

'That's a shame, because there's no one here by that name,' he says. 'And yet, here you are, breaking all the rules, making a scene, drawing attention to yourself in all manner of damaging ways.'

He takes a step towards me. I start to panic again as I hit the wall trying to step away. The door must have closed.

'She promised me,' I say, scrabbling at the wall behind me. It doesn't feel like it could ever have been a door. 'You all promised. You all promised that Kayleigh would be kept safe. I thought ... I thought I could save her from everything that happened to me. She was supposed to have everything I didn't. That's the only reason I ever did any of it in the first place. You promised she wouldn't get hurt—'

'And you promised too, didn't you?' He cuts me off, shadow falling across my face as he comes closer. 'You promised you would keep answering our questions...'

'Yeah but you lied, didn't you?' I shout, shrinking against the wall as he comes closer still. 'You lied and lied and lied. They know. They've even got a photo.' I screw my eyes shut, trying to blot out the picture, in neon technicolour this time. 'The police are so far on to you that they're leaking actual mugshots to the press – the victims who were failed. The commissioner said it herself! And, guess what? Now I know too. I know what you did to her ... and to me. You let it happen. And you can't play me for a fool anymore.'

I stop as I open my eyes to see him sagging in front of me.

'A photo? Of whom?'

I laugh even though I think I might throw up. 'What, now you get to play dumb? Why else would I be here if I hadn't figured it out? Even you couldn't pick that little girl out of a line-up in the playground. They've got a photo only I would recognise...'

'Sit,' he spits, turning and stalking back to his desk to pick up a phone.

'No,' I say, tottering as I force myself to stand straight. 'You put me on to Shacklin. Then I'll sit.' I cower into the wall as he slams the phone back down.

'So tell me, Marie,' he growls, moving like a panther back across the room towards me. 'That's what we're calling you these days, isn't it? Tell me, do you know how easy it is to go from victim to accomplice? From child to adult, just with the flick of a switch? Miss Baines – Rach, that's what you called her, wasn't it? She was seventeen, you were fifteen. Which of you ended up in jail, and why? Don't you remember? Tell me, do you know how easy it is to blow up a person's new identity, especially when you created it in the first place, especially when so many members of an organised crime ring managed to escape without charge? And tell me, do you know how easy it is to move wards of the state, dependent on state protection, to brand-new surroundings and circumstances? To make them disappear without trace, if you want them to?' He clicks his fingers, so close now I can see every line in his face.

'You don't scare me,' I say, forcing myself to look into his eyes; black, like he could be blind. 'I don't even know you.'

'Ah, but I know you, don't I?' He's shouting now. 'I know everything about you. I know how precious this new life is, how hard you've worked to build it, how desperate you are to keep it intact, preserve its integrity, and yet how choked with guilt, how suffocated you feel for leaving others behind – others whom, without us, you would never see, never hear of again, and never know were being kept as safe as they could be.'

'That's the fucking point, isn't it!' I shout back at him. 'It turns out Kayleigh was never safe, and now the whole world is going to find out what you lot did to her in the name of the national interest.'

I flinch as he grabs my wrist, bending and squeezing my arm so unnaturally that I think it might snap.

'Oh, do be careful, Marie,' he says, inching my arm further and further away from its rightful position. 'You do want to see her again, don't you? Lest we make you an accomplice too. After all, it wasn't just Miss Baines who brought others in – you were always by her side, weren't you? What was it you said? Ah yes … "she's my best friend, we've got each other's backs, haven't we?" And it's Katie now, isn't it? Yes, that's right, I know exactly who, what and where she is…'

I pant as the pressure builds in my elbow, my other hand slipping and sliding against the wall behind me, bravado suffocated by pain, pain and more pain.

'This can never happen again,' he says, black, empty eyes bearing down on me. 'Do you understand? Never again can we tolerate a display as unhinged as this. Never.'

I feel drool trickle from the corner of my mouth as I gasp, agony radiating from my elbow.

'You will get to the bottom of the leak in the police, do you hear? And you will communicate by approved channels only.'

I cry out, bent double now – anything to minimise how far he can move my arm. He laughs, before spitting on to the floor.

'You are a tiny piece of this, Marie. Tiny – a speck, if you will. We could scrub you out without trace, like wiping dirt off a lens, like flicking lint off a sleeve, except we haven't, have we? You need us far more than we need you, far, far more.'

I crumple on to the floor as he releases my arm, which is throbbing so hard I can practically hear it.

'You will find the source,' he hisses, looming over me. 'And your accounts are suspended until you do. Everything you depend on to live? You won't get access to any of it until you've covered up this mess.'

My hand closes around my elbow as I squint up at him, blinded by pain, only to double back over as he kicks me square in the stomach. And instead of crunching into the wall I find myself flying backward into the dim light of the holding room, the wall or door or whatever it really was, having been opened somehow, somewhere, by someone. By him? I hawk on to the floor, blood tang-thick on my teeth.

'Let's use Medusa, next time, shall we?' he says silkily, peering down at me, hands behind his back. 'Far more appropriate, don't you think? I rather think Pegasus gave you the wrong idea. There's no flying away from this. Not then, not now, and not ever. You have others to thank for that, of course. But for now, always remember that we're the ones who can turn you to stone.' He clicks his fingers, one-two-three. 'Just. Like. That.'

I hawk again, hitting the door as it slides closed, plunging me back into the half-light. Yet even through the shadows, I can make out the faint gleam of a slug's trail inching down the door towards the floor, the unmistakable mark of a creature evolved only to chew through everything in its path.

But they always leave slime behind, I think, as memories collide in my mind. The slime sticks long after the slug has moved on.

And they've forgotten how hard that is to cover up.

Carly ~ London ~ 2001

Yet another jangle and clang as a tide more people sweep into Starbucks, puffs of stuffy city air wafting behind them like hot breath. Carly's never spent an English summer anywhere other than the flat, empty east before. Sure, it gets warm, but even the slightest bit of wind tears off the North Sea and barrels across the Fens without so much as a blade of grass in its way. But Marie, well, she's just finishing her second summer struggling to keep a toehold in a city where at least a hundred other feet are fighting over every leg-up. Here, choked between overcrowded buildings, overflowing buses and the swarms of people who live, work and party in London, even the slightest rise in temperature turns the air into fleece. And yet still they come in their hordes, to queue by these machines belching boiling steam, to slug hot milk as if it's ice water, to chatter and squawk over their latest fancy coffee like this is something the English have been doing for hundreds of years.

I shrink into the padded cushions of my chair in the back corner. The only reason I ever agreed to meet here is there are suddenly so many of these ridiculous places that you'd never find anyone unless you knew precisely, by exact street corner, which one they'd chosen to hide in. *Star-Bucks*, I think, turning the name over and over in my mind. It's not even a word, is it?

Up ahead, the door clangs again, a group of girls, all string vests and cut-offs, shimmying their way along the counter into a fresh funnel of steam. I crunch an empty plastic cup into my hand as I stand, squinting into the cloud. Even though the fog dulls the gloss on their hair and paint on their lips, it's no match for the frizz peeping up at the back of the line. And there, as the steam evaporates, is, most definitely and unmistakably, Julie.

The cup splinters into my hand as I sit back down, blood thumping through my head like I've stuffed it even further into the bloody oven. I know she's seen me. She's the one who told me where to sit.

'I almost didn't recognise you,' she says as she sits down in the chair opposite. 'Golly, the heat's unbearable, isn't it? It's not even August anymore.'

'That's good, right? You told me to cut my hair short...'

I trail off to clear my throat. I haven't spoken all day. Our meetings have got further and further apart, but she looks the same as always. I wonder if she ever cuts her own hair. It never seems to change, always the same-length circle of fuzz around her head. It's probably the most reassuring thing about her.

'Aha! I knew I had some somewhere.' She rummages in her bag, holding out a packet of polos. 'Try one, go on. You'll be amazed how cooling a strong mint can be.'

'I'm alright,' I say, frowning as the string-vest girls settle down across three tables next to us in a squawking cloud of perfume. 'Can we go for a walk, now you're here?'

'If that's what you'd like,' Julie says thickly through the polo in her mouth. 'It's no cooler outside though, to be honest. In fact, the traffic makes it worse.'

I stand even though she's still talking, glancing through the swing door up ahead.

'We're better off in here,' she says, looking up at me. 'Come on, love. Would you like a muffin? I might get myself a little something...'

I sit back down. She smiles at me.

'But I don't want a muffin, OK?'

'I know,' she says, wiping sweat off her forehead into her hair. 'You've done very well to get yourself here. That in itself is a real achievement. Every new day is an achievement. You need to remind yourself of that.'

She cocks her head. I look at the floor, streaked brown with spilled coffee.

'Would it help if I start with a home update?'

I nod, sweat beading on my cheeks. She pulls a thick, sealed envelope from her bag, pushing it across the table.

'I'm not going to lie to you it's been a tough few months settling with the new family. The confusion and trauma of moving around is still very much with her...'

I reach for the envelope, an escaping tear blotting on to the top as I picture Kayleigh packing up her pathetic selection of possessions into yet another plastic bag as she's bounced from family to family.

'... but I think she's over the worst of it now. We're very lucky that she's at an incredibly supportive school, and even though she's further away now, they are very keen to keep her there.'

I sniff, cradling the envelope in my lap.

'This couple are also a lot more familiar with foster care. Unlike the last,' she says. 'They've got two older children, so not only have the benefit of having raised them, but have also fostered a number of others in the past.'

'Are they girls or boys – the other children?' I swallow rising acid.

'Both, I think,' she says. 'They spoke very fondly of another girl who was with them for almost three years—'

'No, the older kids,' I cut her off, clutching my envelope. 'Their older kids. Are they girls or boys? Do they live there too?'

She cocks her head again as she looks at me. The string-vest girls toss their hair at each other.

'Girls,' she says after a moment. 'Two sisters. One's just finishing school, the other is at university. At least, I think she is. She doesn't live there anymore.'

I slouch back down into my chair. Now the string vests are laughing and laughing and laughing. Nothing's ever that funny.

'Tough as it is, I think you need to focus on yourself,' she says.

'Try to move on from obsessing over where she is and what she's doing. Like I said, every new day is an achievement for you, every single one. Just getting up, getting to work, feeding and clothing yourself is something to be proud of.'

I turn the envelope over and over in my lap. I wonder how many photos there'll be this time.

'You know it is, love,' she continues, reaching out to rest her hand on my arm. Warm, like always. Even in this heat, it's warm, not hot.

'You've got a job. You're earning your own money, making friends, living by yourself, building this new life, piece by piece. I know it's harder than I can even imagine, learning, adding, perfecting each piece, but one day you'll realise you've climbed to the top of the mountain and there's nowhere else to go but jump off and fly.'

More tears creep off the end of my nose on to the envelope.

'That's the problem,' I say, smearing them into the paper with my thumb. 'I'm stacking supermarket shelves. Hanging clothes that no one wants. Showing people where the bog roll is.'

'Running the warehouse is a few steps up from refilling the shelves, isn't it?' My hand goes slack as she squeezes my arm. 'Remember, it's one step at a time. Before you know it, you'll have taken ten, then twenty...'

'But they want me to move to day shifts,' I say, sniffing. 'Take up a management position, of all things. They need more people who can keep track of the numbers. I'm supposed to be happy about it. More money, responsibility ... someone who wants to work nights, they said...'

'Well, who does?' She takes her hand away.

'I don't mind, do I? It's quiet.'

'Your branch is the one by Piccadilly, is it? Right by the roundabout?'

'Circus,' I say. 'The one at Piccadilly Circus.'

She laughs. I can't help but smile a bit too. Imagine if

Warchester changed all of its roundabouts to circuses. The whole place would be a big top.

'It must be a right circus at 2.00 am,' she says, crunching into another polo. 'You'd be better off in the daytime, surely?'

I shake my head as Julie waves the tube at me again.

'Only if I cared about sleeping at night. It's alright, honestly. There are loads of offices open all night around there. In fact there are more offices than bars—'

'You should care about sleeping,' she interrupts. 'It's important. You can't lead a healthy life if you don't eat and sleep properly.'

'I sleep fine. Who cares if it's not at night?'

We scowl at each other. The string-vest girls crowd around something on the table.

'You're not eating much though, are you?'

I look at the floor again. 'I eat plenty. I should never have told you about—'

'You need to take care of yourself,' she interrupts before I have to say it out loud. 'No one else can do that for you. It's a step on the road, like any other step. But you have to take it if you want to keep moving forward.'

One of the string-vest girls jumps as I kick out under the table, hitting her chair leg.

'I don't blame you for dwelling on the past,' she says, reaching for my arm again. 'Or for doing what you need to do to keep it at bay. There's no one who could possibly understand what you've been through, how far away the other side really is. But all you can do is inch forward as best you can, one minute, one hour, one day at a time. The world's just going to keep turning. You can't stop it just because it's making you feel dizzy. Katie's in the best hands she could be.'

'Katie?' I stand, my chair crashing into the gaggle next to us.

'It's stuck,' she says, bending to pick up the envelope, which has slithered off my lap on to the floor. 'She practically came up with it herself, as I understand it, over time, as she learned to speak properly. And it made sense for her to have a fresh start too. After all, you're well and truly Marie now, aren't you?'

'Who knows,' I mumble, glaring at the string-vest girl pushing my chair upright towards me, disgust wafting off her like her perfume, sharp and tangy in the thick heat.

'Other people can only do so much,' Julie says, holding out the envelope as she stands. 'In the end, it comes down to you. There's nothing more unfair in the world, I know. But it has to come from you ... if it's ever going to really work. No one else can live your life for you, and this is your lot now. It's down to you to make something of it.' She slings her bag on to her shoulder.

'What, you're leaving already?' I say, pulling the envelope to my chest. 'That's a shorter lecture than usual, isn't it? We haven't even covered skipping counselling yet ... or how my BTC's going, or TBC or CBT or whatever it's called.'

'I've been as long as I can,' she says, gripping at the straps on her shoulder as she checks behind her. 'I can't afford to be missed, you know that. Technically, we haven't been in touch since the trial finished, have we? I'd never forgive myself if anyone recognised us and put two and two together. But I promise I won't lose touch. You can count on me to keep you informed, on Katie at least. I won't ever let you down on that.'

She leans forward, squeezing my arm again for a minute, before disappearing into another belch of steam as she walks out of the shop.

I stand, gulping great drafts of misty, stifling air; air that cloaks my whole world, even in the winter. If I follow her out, will I get to evaporate too, like she just did? But as I shove my chair into the string-vest girls, I notice the gleaming counter, bursting with cakes and biscuits, plump with promise.

Two muffins should do it. Plenty to bring it all back out.

Marie ~ London ~ 2006

The Thames churns below Westminster Bridge, swollen with storm – laughter and catcalls drifting off the black water as a party boat cuts a drunken path below. Is it laughing at me? I strain towards an edge of tinny music as its fairy lights twinkle. The night is high in the sky now, after-the-rain fresh, the amber glow of Central London's overworked electrics no match for the full moon, its luminous glow throwing ghost-shine over the peeling railings under my hands.

My head swivels at the crowds brushing past me, back and forth. Did I walk here? I must have ... but how did I burrow out of the ministry? And how long was I inside? There was a guard, a lift, a side door, a shove ... My fingers find the egg on the side of my head, ache pinching my elbow as I lift my arm. Now it's Rach that's laughing, clown paint striped around her eyes as I prod at my forehead. Worse still, it's Kayleigh, motionless and limp in silver foil wrappings on her hospital bed, machines beeping and wailing with warning either side.

You deserve it, Rach sneers, pulling on the cigarette in her mouth. You screwed us worse than any of them ever did, and now you're thinking about doing it all over again? I start to cough as her smoke rings pop, one-two-three, against the sides of my head. Petrol suddenly rotten in my nose; a horn, a squeal and a crunch, almost on top of me. A car, bonnet red and twisted, rammed up against the back of a taxi just ahead. More horns, more yells, more beeps and wails merging into a cloud of sound as anger and traffic pile up on the bridge in a matter of seconds. And still the water churns, bloated river whipping the banks holding it back. I turn

away from the commotion and start to walk, Carly a ghost at my
aching elbow, looking up for the moon as the shadow of Big Ben
passes over us. But all I get is the London Eye, blind to all it should
be able to see.

Shopfronts scud past with my thoughts – one step, another,
then another. Sooner or later, Marie will be the one with the fuller
story, the longer history; the one with a home, a job, a life, a real
existence. Except now I know how much of it is built on lies, and
who knows how many other promises were broken along the way?
What of Kayleigh, and all the promises made to her? I dig
knuckles into my eyes as Dominic's photo flashes up again, no
longer Kayleigh, now only ever Baby Girl A – all I have left is to
scream, bitter as the wind, right into a crowd giggling and stumbling next to me. That's the worst part of all. Now I know I've
been helping them. All this time, they've kept me on the wrong
side. All this time, I've been helping them hide the fact they broke
every promise they made to both of us.

Trafalgar Square opens up wide around me as I shake my head
till my neck throbs, but still I can't get it off. I have to let it go, let
her go, I don't know who she is anymore, even whether her name
is still Katie. Her many faces, real and imagined, warp and change
in front of me as I push forward, one step, then another. Teenagers
brush past, all bobble hats and fingerless gloves, hooting and
laughing … Could one be her? And how would I know if it was?
I've got no chance at life without keeping hold of Marie, without
keeping hold of myself. It's the only way I know how to belong,
how to tell other people's stories instead of my own. I search any
blonde-framed face I can see, grins freezing as they find me
haunted and staring, then turning away in disgust.

Chatter and bustle rises and falls as I keep walking, one step,
then another, Carly still hovering like a sprite on my shoulder.
Would we look the same to anyone who knew? Suddenly I'm sure
I can feel her white-blonde hair wisp below my short, dark crop.
I stumble as I pull at it, blinking the same watery blue eyes, tracing

a finger over my nose, remembering the freckles don't lie. The square leads to another traffic light, another corner, before I find pause to remind myself. At least I know what I have to do to bury it all. At least I still have one way left that never fails.

My stomach churns in anticipation as I turn the final corner. And finally I'm blinking into supermarket strip lights, where even at midnight it's as bright as noon. Carly's gone. There's nowhere for her to hide in here.

I'll take Dominic up to Warchester, I think, metal basket cool and solid between my fingers. He needs a second source, and that's the most obvious place to find one. No cameras, just us – a fishing trip, as Jemima always calls it. Except this time I'm the one doing the fishing, and I've got all the bait I could possibly need. He won't be able to help himself but talk. I speed up round the aisles as I shove things into my basket. Jumbo bag of crisps ... there. Salt and vinegar, always vinegar. Swiss rolls, plump with purple foil, beckon from a high shelf. I reach for one ... no, two; resolve hardening with every step. He has to go back to where it all began, and so do I. Everything has been a lie: my new life, Kayleigh's new start – how can I trust anyone on either side anymore? We both have to know what really happened. And I can't carry on without knowing it all. Back to the fridges ... Wait, where's the cheese? I shiver as I rifle through neat bricks of Cheddar. Getting to the source doesn't mean I have to pass it on. I can still decide. When all is said and done, I can still choose. Marie can choose. Carly's the one that never could.

I turn a corner, reach for some milk. Just to cool my insides down when I'm done.

This is where Marie finally figured it all out, I remind myself, giddy as I join the line to the tills. This is where she first met Jemima, loopy with sleeplessness on the overnight shift, permanently suspended in the half-light between dusk and dawn, bringing order to her own chaos by buying the same thing, at the same time, night after night after night. I shuffle forward, hunching behind the man in front, beer and smoke steaming off his over-coat. It's always the same before closing time. Everyone mad with something – grief, booze, drugs, you name it – but just enough of us to all stay invisible. My face twitches, the small start of a smile, before the picture flashes up again.

I unload my supplies, shoving the empty basket under the belt before wrapping my arms around myself, the seeds of control re-turning, just with the promise of my basket.

It will work. It always does. Only once everything's come up does it all finally go away.

Necessities in hand, I lift my face into the cool night air. I'll do it at the flat, I think. Carly's never there. She never was, after all. That place will always be Marie's.

Carly ~ London ~ 2001

I sneeze into my throat as I pause at the top of the path down to the house, lit golden by the rising morning sun. It looks like it usually does, like an exaggerated version of itself, extravagantly spread garden plump with landscaping and bejewelled with flowers, blooms bursting from every bush like flesh from a blouse. There are always flowers, even thistles in the dead of winter. This is a family that spends as much time ensuring all seasons are represented in their home as it spends ensuring everyone learns their times tables.

A shower of petals falls over my foot as I brush past the jasmine curling outside the front door. I sneeze again, wiping my eyes this time. With this year's autumn still heavily pregnant with summer, the flowers are as heady as cheap perfume.

'Look, I'm sorry, Marie, I really am, but Katie's just not well enough for visitors. I did try to call but it rang out...'

I flinch, as usual, at my new name, but she's too busy closing the door behind her almost as soon as she's opened it to notice, wrapping herself tight in her fluffy cardigan. Mrs Jolley, the mother of all foster carers, according to Julie. Very well equipped, she told me, as if enough money, space and siblings is all it ever takes.

'I was on the train,' I say, swaying on my feet, engraved brass nameplate on the wall to her side so polished and shiny it may as well be a loaded gun. This always happens when my visits fall right after a supermarket shift. Every inch of the journey, every twist of the train out of its Central London knot is too intoxicating to miss just for sleep. It's like a thread pulling me from the past into the future, except I know it will snap in the end. Everything does when the weight's as heavy as this.

'I really am sorry,' she repeats, leaning on the doorframe, like her fluffy cardigan and slippers can genuinely disguise the folded arms and set jaw. 'But she's been up sick all night and she's only just started to settle down. It's nothing serious – children do pick up everything going, don't they? But I'm not prepared to wake her – she needs to rest. Especially since your visits are so confusing for her as it is.'

She recoils as I steady myself on the doorframe, dislodging another shower of jasmine from the loops and curls around her perfect porch.

'We can find another time, OK? I promise we can. I'm happy for you to come back, when she's a bit better.'

'Your happiness doesn't really come into it, does it? You know you have to let me see her. They'll take her away from you if you don't...'

I trail off as I peer through the stained-glass window to her side, snatching fairy-like glimpses of neat hallway, cut flowers, bright children's trainers. Whose are they? Hers? Or do they belong to the sister? They should be mine ... I look away but catch the name-plate, practically laughing in my face at the very idea. The Jolleys. Even their name sounds like they should be from another planet. I stumble backward as she steps towards me, dislodging another shower of jasmine.

'Look, Marie, this is difficult for all of us, especially Katie. I'm sure that's all you care about, isn't it? She's not well – nothing critical, but she needs to rest, and much as I know how important these visits are, I also know I'm entitled to reschedule them if it's in her best interests. Which, I can assure you right now, it is.'

I stare at her, suddenly brick set and stout, sharpening the fluff on her cardigan. Marie and Katie. She's supposed to be talking about us, but these are girls I still don't know yet, no matter how hard I try.

'You're part of a life she doesn't remember,' she says, brushing petals from her hair. 'You must understand how hard that is for her, and surely even you can question what good it does reminding her of it all? If you want the best for her, that is. We've definitely turned a corner now, in terms of how she's settling down to life with us, but there's still a long way to go.'

'What corner has she turned? The one where she stops screaming in her sleep? Where she stops cutting herself just to feel pain? Where she washes her hands because the soap smells nice, instead of scrubbing until she bleeds?'

Even she can't answer back to that in time as the door cracks open behind her, breath lodging hard in my throat as wisps of white-blonde hair curl with the jasmine round the doorframe—

'Go back inside, sweetheart...' More wisps, whiter than a ghost, fringe the face that peers round the door. The shape of a heart, the colour of paper.

'Katie, darling. Come on now.' I freeze as Mrs Jolley bends to scoop up a ball of tiger-striped fluff rubbing round my leg. 'Here, go and take Peaches for a cuddle.'

The cat fixes me with a stare as she settles in skinny arms, elbows sharp as the bitten fingernails scratching behind its ears.

'Hello...' I whisper as I stare back. The face, still hollow and haunted, cloaked with more memory than any child should ever have. The hair, still patchy and thin from where it's been unknowingly pulled out in clumps during yet another nightmare. The eyes, pale and glassy apart from their rim of pink. The rest of the face mercifully covered by the cat's, unblinking and smug with the confidence of only the overfed.

'Peaches is tired, sweetheart. As are you. Come along now, I don't want you to catch a chill out here.'

A laugh, true and clear, escapes me, bidden simply by the sight of her, even if it's more painful than the sun bouncing back off the windows into my eyes. My sister, my baby sister. The half that makes me a whole, the only unbroken part left of me. The reason I put myself through it all, not just now, but from the start.

'This ... this is for you,' I say, fumbling with the comic I picked up at the station, cartoon-printed cellophane crackling round the plastic trinkets taped to the front. The child stares back at me, or is it the cat? I blink as I thrust it towards them. 'I'm sorry ... I'm sorry you have been sick. Maybe this will be fun for you ... for you to do sometime. There's colouring, stories, I think there might even be some stickers...'

I trail off as her new mother silently takes it from my out-stretched hand. White-blonde wisps burrow further into the cat as I sway with the jasmine, suddenly so dizzy with sleeplessness and pain that I think I might pass out.

'It's ... it's so nice to see you,' I choke out after another moment, more petals showering as I steady myself on the doorframe. 'Do you, do you think it would be OK if ... if I stroke Peaches? She ... she looks like a really lovely cat.'

My other hand reaches out as if by itself, twitching as it lands on a bed of impossibly silky fur. I hesitate for another moment before shuffling it backward and forward, the cat's pea-sized heart-beat thudding under my fingers. We stand, frozen in a pool of golden light as I fumble this way and that, fixated on the two sets of pink-rimmed eyes staring into mine. In another world I'd be seeing double, except I know better than my own which ones are hers. Eyes can never lie, no matter how hard they try.

'Come on now, Katie – you can take Peaches into bed with you. And your magazine. Just this once, OK? I won't tell if you won't...'

I snatch my hand away, fur suddenly like brush under my fingers. And with that, the thread snaps, sun piercing into my eyes as the cat jumps, a ball of fur disappearing into the bushes, taking with it any connection I'd had with the child quivering in front of me, enveloped this time by fluffy cardigan and plump, stern hands manhandling her back inside faster than I can draw another breath. As if promising to keep a secret could ever mean anything other than more lies.

'I'll be just another minute, OK, sweetheart?'

Mrs Jolley folds her arms across her chest again after closing the door behind her and leaning against it for good measure. It's only when I sniff that I realise tears are spilling out of my eyes, soundless, like water overflowing a glass.

'It will do none of us any good to keep going over this,' she says, peering over her shoulder into the hallway behind her, lit in a riot of clashing colour, sunlight playing a joke with stained glass. 'Not you, not Katie, not any of us. We need to break her pattern of destructive behaviour once and for all, and to do that, we need to remove anything that triggers her stress responses. Now I'm not saying that your visits are a trigger themselves, but she's not well, plain and simple, and I will not risk distressing her further by prolonging this one...'

I drop to my knees, cat curling round my leg again, a silken reminder of a connection broken much longer ago than today.

'You've had a moment together, as you wanted, and now I think you should leave before we risk upsetting her more.'

I croon at the cat, crumpling into my touch as I scratch round its neck, searching for anything else that might remind me of her now, rather than then.

'That's enough for now, Marie. I need you to leave, and quickly, please. She's not safe on her own inside.'

A car door chirps as it unlocks somewhere nearby, breeze rustling and singing through the bushes landscaping the path back up to the road; alien sounds, like the words she's still saying and I can't hear, much less understand. When Kayleigh was little, just looking at me would stop her crying, but now all it does is make her start?

'I promise I'll be in touch when she's ready, I really will. I know this is about you too, and we are supportive of that. But our priority is Katie, and I'm sure she's yours too, isn't she? I will make sure we carve out time when she's recovered and seems mentally robust enough to handle it without the consequences setting us all back too much...'

She recedes again as my eyes travel the lush, silken grass under the bay window. Maybe she'll just let me lie down here instead, just drift off blanketed by petals, just so I can be near her...

'OK? Marie?' The cat blinks as she coughs, looking at me expectantly. And I notice the thorny rose bush set squat and hefty next to the jasmine, dead flower heads snapped off into a neat pile around its base.

'Will you ... will you at least tell her how much I miss her?'

I cough as I say it, rather than let her hear the cracks in my voice; the cat suddenly gone, scooped from under my fingers back into the clutch of hers, as contented there as she was below my hand. That's the real problem with cats, I remember as I stand, turning and walking away in one fluid, swift movement. Soft and fluffy as they might be, they can never be trusted to remain loyal.

Only once I've made it back to the road do I hear her let herself back into the house. I don't have to look to know whatever remained of the jasmine has been scattered all over the porch by the slam of the door.

'This the Jolleys?' I jump as a postman shouts from across the road, arms laden with packages. 'Is this the Jolleys, love? I'm looking for Brambledown Cottage.'

'Yeah,' I mutter, sidestepping away from the gate as he catches up to me.

'Thanks, pet,' he says, pushing the gate open with his back. 'Makes a change from my usual route, all these driveways and gardens and whatnot. Just put some bloody numbers on the houses and we'd be sorted, wouldn't we?'

He pauses, his body holding the gate open.

'Or some mailboxes at the top so we don't spend all our time walking up and down ... You alright, pet?'

I nod and turn, hurrying away down the lane, breaking into a jog as I note the time. Country lanes become wider avenues and finally roads as I speed up, racing to the station, every thud of my heart wiping away the pain of the visit, stroke by stroke, breath by breath, gasp by gasp.

I reach the carriage just as the doors are closing, flinging myself into a seat. The train is deserted, that curious middle-of-the-day emptiness that only makes sense once you realise these towns were only built for people to sleep in. Something else Carly would never have known, much less understood. I have to find a way to belong, and Marie doesn't belong here. But maybe Katie will, one day, if I can just bring myself to leave her alone?

I let my eyes close as we slide out of the station, sleep washing over me with the rock and roll of the engine. My last thought before I fade out is the tinned peaches Jason used to bring us. When it had been a good week. Katie won't remember that if I never remind her.

Marie ~ London ~ 2006

'You still look awful,' Dominic says as I pass him his coffee, hot through the thin takeaway plastic. 'Did you rest, at least? Don't pretend you've slept.'

'It's the light. Even you look crap in it, trust me.'

I smooth my hair over the lump at the side of my head as he smiles up into Liverpool Street Station's cavernous ceiling. There are even birds flying overhead. I can pretend we're outside, if I can't pretend anything else.

'I'm starving. Have we got time for breakfast? I couldn't bring myself to even open the fridge this morning, let alone eat anything. I could have cultured penicillin in the salad last time I looked.'

'But you hate salad, so that's alright, isn't it? Why did you even buy it in the first place?' I peer behind him at the departure board as I try to engage in small talk.

'I like occasionally pretending I lead a normal life. If buying enough food to make myself a decent dinner on the off chance I'm ever home from work counts as normal, mind you.' He twists around to check the time just as the tannoy calls our train.

We weave our way through the rush-hour crowds to the platforms. At least everyone else here is also in a hurry.

'Are you serious?' I say as Dominic beckons me over to the first-class carriage. 'We can't get away with that, can we?'

'It's only a tenner extra,' he says, climbing in as the doors slide open. 'I don't get much out of this network so I'll take what I can get, thank you very much. And besides. I'm willing to bet you've never sat in first before, have you? Legally, anyway...' I can't stop my jaw hanging open as he winks at me. 'It's the least I can do after all that people smuggling you've willingly engaged in for my sake.'

I twist and turn, drinking it all in in spite of myself, as we move down the aisle to a table at the window. The carriage feels endless, one seat for every three in the other cars; cushions, plastic-wrapped snacks, even packets of tissues. I barely even notice as a woman with a buggy struggles in behind us, baby starting to cry almost immediately.

'It shouldn't be legal,' Dominic mutters, leaning towards me across the table. 'Don't you think? Babies in first? Outrageous. It's first for a reason isn't it? We're all here to work, or have more money than sense – and if it's the latter then there should be a separate carriage labelled "more money than sense".'

I drift off as he complains, watching the woman cuddle and soothe her baby, so bundled in layers of fancy striped blankets that she could easily be carrying a load of bedding if it weren't squawking and crying in her arms. She's hot, I think, craning my neck for a better look.

'Eh?' Dominic straightens, head swivelling back and forth. 'Who? Did I miss a supermodel boarding or something?'

'I ... I meant the baby ... It'll stop in a minute,' I stammer, looking out of the window at the train on the opposite platform. I didn't think I'd said anything.

'How do you know? What are you, the baby whisperer?'

I snap myself back to the task at hand as the train rolls out of the station, East London opening up around us, looming steelworks from its massive construction projects jutting as enormous and frozen as dinosaur skeletons. It would be so easy to forget where we're going now, the landscape is so alien. Especially with a view from first class. This train could be going anywhere but Warchester.

'The beauty of the Olympics, eh?' Dominic drawls from across the table. 'All that government tripe about a billion-pound shot in the arm for East London. The reality is the shires will languish in disrepair for years as a result. It's four years out and here they are, already pouring the fucking foundations...'

I let him rant, passing our tickets over to the inspector shuffling past us down the aisle. The more comfortable he is when we get down to business, the better.

'You're only valid to Warchester, miss,' the ticket inspector says as he punches the stubs. 'You'll have to buy yourselves new tickets if you want to continue on to Ipswich.'

'There's no danger of that,' Dominic trills from across the table. 'Can we expect the buffet car any time soon?'

'And there'll be a fine if you forget,' he says, scowling at him before moving along. The train bends its way north, sun suddenly dazzling through the windows, nature's own spotlight. I take a deep breath.

'I thought we could start in the city centre,' I say, training my eyes on the horizon rather than on Dominic as the landscape flattens out towards Essex. 'I'm going to guess folks will fall over themselves to talk about reopening the investigation after all this time. Warchester's built on the army, every street is named after a battlefield victory, there's practically a monument on every corner. Everyone will think they know something, or at least have an opinion—'

'Why would we bother with that?' He cuts me off. 'What's the point? We don't even have a camera with us.'

'You're not trying to film them though, are you? This is just about talking to the locals, softening up the ground, seeing who knows what and where that might take us. It's a small place.'

He laughs, strident over the baby's cries. I let blush spread over my cheeks. All the better he thinks I'm stupid. He'll feel the need to explain himself.

'I just thought—'

'Listen,' he says, spreading his hands on the table as he leans towards me. 'If you'd actually spent any time there, you'd know the place is covered in filth. The first sign you'll see out of the station is Welcome to Essex with the E and S scraped off. Walk for ten minutes, and you'll arrive on Butt Road, complete with adult emporium on the corner, no less. If Warchester's built on the army, then the army's built on sex.'

I close my eyes as the woman starts to cry over her baby's screams. It's the light, I tell myself. Look at the sun and you'll burn, Rach whispers into my ear. I prod her away, poking at my eyelids as Dominic curses in the background.

'Coffee,' I hear him say, trolley brushing past my leg. 'Black ... cheers. And could you get that young lady with the baby back there whatever she wants on me? Sounds like she could use it ... Here you go ... Thanks, boss...'

My eyes fly open into the jangle of loose change.

'What?' He frowns at me over the rim of his cup. 'Did you want something?'

I stare at him, dimly aware of a steaming cup of tea being handed towards the misery in the back corner, followed by a bag of crisps.

'Well?'

'No,' I say, blinking away sun spots. 'I just—'

'It sounded like it might help,' he interrupts. 'That's it. No more, no less. Shall we get back to your primary-school plan of action upon arrival?'

He smirks as I blush, for real this time.

'The only thing I need from this trip,' he says, looking out of the window, 'is corroboration that Minchin was being protected from the inside. Something that isn't from the police.'

I hold my breath as he pauses for a sip, landscape scudding past in a whirl to my right.

'And frankly, that's probably not going to come from anyone in Warchester unless I can get inside the barracks ... which is about as possible as teleporting myself there, as I told Jonas about eighty thousand times last night.'

'How do you know he was being protected?' I say, squinting at the slicks of wax bringing definition to his hair, one spike after another.

'Ah, now that would be telling, wouldn't it?' He folds his arms as he slouches into his seat. 'Except a version of it is leaking everywhere I bloody look. Jaqlin must be hell bent on sinking the Ministry of Defence over this. Every police gobshite in town is whispering in some hack's ear.'

'But if you've got a source in the police...' I trail off as he glares at me.

'Who said that? I never said that, did I?'

I shrink into my seat. As the trolley disappears through the doors at the back, I spot the young mother dabbing her eyes as steam clouds her face, head darting in our direction.

'The question is,' he continues after a moment, almost to himself, 'how do I get myself inside the barracks? And by inside, I mean into the past. Anyone there now will be useless unless there's a familial or regimental link of some sort.'

I turn to the window, watching meadows turn into sky then back into meadows again as my eyes drift up and down. The truth hovers like the sun's haze blurring the horizon.

'What about round Victory Field,' I say, imagining my words as the wisps of cloud floating across the otherwise clear sky. 'There must be community pubs round there. Army loyalists, sure, but that also means we might find someone connected inside.'

'You don't get that from Google Earth,' he says with a frown. 'Have you got anything else you want to tell me? All this from the venerable coffers of the *Deptford Gazette*? Or a field trip to the Essex coast for your geography exams?'

'I was on the copy desk,' I say, fiddling with the rim of the table. 'People misspell Warchester a lot. It sinks in after a while.' I feel his eyes on my head as I pluck at the lip of rubber fringing the window frame.

'I might yet get somewhere with social services,' he says after a moment. 'One lead's on the cusp of coming good, and loads more of them will have been involved—'

'You won't,' I interrupt, heart starting to race as I think about Julie. Anything not to bring her into this. She's only ever tried to do right by both of us, and put herself on the line countless times in the process. 'No one from there will talk. They'll be legally bound to the eyeballs, knotted up all over the place.'

'Oh please,' he says. 'Everyone blabs eventually. Everyone, unless they're guilty ... and actually, sometimes that doesn't even matter. Any legal obligations, if they even exist, are worth shit when we're dealing with grooming and abuse on such a grand scale ... Off somewhere, are you?'

'I need to use the bathroom,' I say, swaying as I stand. 'Sorry, won't be a sec...'

I stumble down the aisle through the doors at the end and lean against the tiny sink in the mercifully empty toilet cubicle, every thud of the train clicking another jagged piece of jigsaw into place in my head. Someone inside the police knows for sure what really happened, but Dominic still doesn't have enough to prove it. And I know how he can, but surely I'm not contemplating telling him without knowing the full story first? There have been too many lies for that, and Kayleigh ... I spit into the sink, heartbeat accelerating up my throat as someone knocks on the door.

'Please, my baby needs changing,' a voice stammers, a baby's screams fighting with the clatter of the train on its final push out of the station.

'I'm so sorry, I don't mean to be rude, but if you could just let us use...'

The words die in her throat as I push open the door.

'I'm so sorry,' she stammers again, squeezing the baby in her arms, its cheeks slushy-red with heat and fury. 'I didn't realise it was you ... and after you were so kind to buy me some tea...'

She dissolves, sagging in the doorway as she sobs. I am rooted to the spot as the carriage doors slide open behind her to reveal

Dominic, pausing for a moment before striding forth, wrapping a suited arm around her shoulders, crooning as he reaches for the baby, easing off its woolly hat, shedding two layers of its blankets, guiding her back towards the carriage with one arm while rocking and soothing the baby in the crook of his other. I watch the whole thing like a phantom. Is it a fragment of a dream? The doors slide open again as he walks her back to her seat, settling the now-contented baby in her arms like a doll.

'You were right,' he says as he walks back towards me, brushing fluff off his arm. 'The poor kid was boiling. Cooking, more like. She may as well have put her in the fucking microwave. Are you finished in there or what? I need a wazz. Come on...'

I open and close my mouth but nothing comes out. He snorts.

'I had a brother who was much younger than me – I still have, I should say, but he doesn't need me to wipe his arse any more...' He scowls at me, still rooted inside the cubicle. 'I helped a lot, once upon a time. I had to, anyway. Can we go now, please? Unless you want to stand around by the bogs, sniffing piss in the wind until we get there? There'll be enough of that later. If you won't trust me on anything else then at least trust me on that.'

I lift my face into the wind thudding through the open lobby window as he pushes past, willing it to smack some sense into my head. I don't know this version of Dominic. I don't think I ever have. But I sense myself, in contravention of every defence I have, starting to feel like there's the tiniest of chances I might be able to.

Carly ~ London ~ 2001

I'm halfway out of the supermarket storeroom, lever trolley in one hand, clipboard in the other, when I see it. Two skyscrapers, billowing impossible-looking amounts of smoke into a clear blue sky. I squint at the grainy television screen perched on the desk just inside the door, its acid-orange casing no match for the horror unfolding in black and white inside. A stack of papers fall all over the floor as I reach for the volume knob, jumping before I can turn it as one of the flaming towers collapses in clouds upon clouds of dust, like it was only ever made from sand to start with.

'Disgusting,' Darren mutters from behind me.

'What happened?' I say as the screen flickers. Suddenly the towers are back, belching smoke and ash into the sky.

'Just playing it again and again on a loop like that ... wankers,' he says. 'That's hundreds of dead people, right there. It's a fucking tomb.'

I stiffen as he moves to my side. Darren seems alright, but he's still just some guy who stacks supermarket shelves on the night-shift like me. So he's running from something.

'What is that – a film?' I freeze as the building collapses again, millions of tonnes of glass and steel disappearing quicker than I can blink.

'Where you been all day, under a rock? Thems the twin towers. The World Trade Center. In New York. Planes crashed into them...'

'Planes? Do you mean aeroplanes?'

'What other kind are there?'

There's another flash on screen and the towers are up again. I lean for the volume knob.

'Don't work,' Darren says. 'Never has. Least not since I've been here.'

I twiddle with the dial, twisting it back and forth. Down the building goes again.

'Was it an accident? The plane crash?'

He laughs. 'Course not,' he says. 'There were more planes n'all. One crashed in a field.'

'How do you know?'

He laughs again. 'Back on the hard stuff again today, were you?' he says, pushing past me. I brush down my arm where he touched me, staring at the screen. Now there are two people talking, with a map on the wall behind them.

'Appalling, isn't it,' Moe says, pausing next to me on his way into the storeroom. 'Just horrendous.'

'Sorry,' I say, grabbing the lever trolley I'd forgotten about. 'It won't take me long to sort out the soft drinks. Darren said the snacks need doing too, shall I pick that up?'

'The whole place is packed,' he says, gesturing back into the shop. 'I've never seen anything like it. It's as if no one can think about or talk about anything else, let alone go home to bed.'

'I could do the tea and coffee while I'm there, if that helps.'

He stares at me. 'Did you sleep today?'

'Some,' I lie, staring back. 'I had loads of stuff to do.'

I give the trolley a shake, its wheels rattling as the Jolleys' stupid shiny nameplate flashes in my head.

'I couldn't sleep either,' he says, running a finger under his eye. 'Every time I closed my eyes all I could think about were those people jumping from the windows. Can you imagine how desperate they must have felt? The whole building on fire behind them and nowhere else to go except deliberately plunge to their deaths. Just horrific.' He drops his head into his hands.

I turn back to the television. The towers are burning again.

'I can't believe they keep showing it,' he says, muffled into his uniform. 'Who would do such a thing? Just unbelievable.'

My breath freezes in my throat as a plane slams into the side of one of the towers, flames and smoke pouring out of the other side.

'It only took an hour for them to fall, or something like that, anyway. Billions of tonnes of steel and concrete just collapsing like they were matchsticks all along...'

'Was it just the Cokes that need doing?' I say, clearing my throat. 'Or shall I fill all the holes while I'm there?'

He looks up, propping himself against the desk. Maybe he'll stop talking about making me assistant manager now he's found me slacking by the telly like Darren.

'I might need you on the tills,' he says after a minute. 'So yes, I suppose. Do everything and then come out front.'

I head back out into the shop, replaying the slow-motion collapse of the towers with every blink into the bright strip lights. Finally, an image that makes sense to me. Every time my visits don't work out, I may as well be trying to rebuild a tower that has exploded into such tiny pieces they've disappeared into the air.

Except they never disappear completely. I can never forget about them, however tiny they are. Chatter floats towards me as I round the corner into the drinks aisle.

'How many should we get? That's way too much, surely?'

'Of Red Bull? Or just Coke?'

'Oh, Red Bull. No one's going to be sleeping for days now.'

'I'd get more than that, actually. We need at least three apiece.'

'When do the shifts change over?'

'Who knows. Like anyone's had even half a second to blink properly, let alone figure out the rota.'

I slide in next to the two women talking over multipacks of cans, peering into the gap where the Cokes should be. I'll need to make at least two trips to refill that shelf.

'Have you got any more of these out the back?' I jump as one of the women barks at me. 'We'll take all the Red Bull we can carry if you bring them out?'

I stare at her, neat and trim in dark office clothes. Is it the middle of the day after all?

'Come on, Jonas,' the other one says, tapping a foot as she rattles the basket in her arm. 'We haven't got all night.'

'I'm serious,' her friend says, looking at me. 'We have a newsroom army to keep awake for the next few days, months even. And it looks like we're not the only ones.'

She looks up and down the shelves of soft drinks, almost empty in places where various brands should be.

'Did you say you wanted Red Bull?' I ask, reading the ID badge looped round her neck.

'Gives you wings,' she says, smiling at me. I reread her badge. *Jemima Jonas, Nine News.* 'We'll need more than wings to get through this news cycle, but it'll give us a start at least.'

'Give it up, Jonas,' the other woman interrupts, yellow hair flying as she shakes her head. 'We're late enough as it is.'

'I'll bring them out to the tills,' I say, ducking and turning, chatter fading as I head back to the storeroom. News cycle? Is she on an overnight shift too? I balance sheets of cans as high as I can on to my trolley. But doing what? I clatter back up the aisle to the cash registers, searching the queues of people. It could be the lunchtime rush if it wasn't pitch-dark outside, air fizzing with banter and gossip.

'...left messages, loads of them...' someone says, dislodging a pile of magazines as he waves into the air. 'They all tried to call from the plane when they knew it was done for...'

'Unimaginable,' someone else replies behind him. Are they friends? She's wearing a ball gown and he's in gym clothes, bulging sports bag slung over his shoulder. At night?

'I mean, what would you say? If you could make just one call? I guess it's better than no warning at all ... or is it?'

'Where was that plane headed? Do they know?'

'It turned back to Washington, didn't it? They say they reckon it was going for the White House.'

'That's all speculation,' a voice shouts from somewhere. Jemima. I crane my neck. Can you even make phone calls on a plane? 'Rampant speculation. We'll never know for sure.'

'It was hardly supposed to crash in a field though, was it?'

I sneeze as ball-gown woman unwinds a feather boa from around her neck.

'Sure, it feels unlikely,' Jemima says, appearing behind me. 'But all the crew and passengers are dead. There will probably be more clues when they find the black box ... Ooooh, thanks, that's perfect!'

She beams at me, grabbing the handle of my trolley. How could a black box ever explain anything by itself?

'Could I borrow this? I promise we'll bring it straight back once we've dropped them all off. We won't be more than thirty mins...'

'Marie!' I jump as Moe repeatedly shouts to me from another till. 'Can you jump on? We can sort out the restock later.'

'Excellent,' Jemima says, as I hurry to the empty till station on my other side, abandoning my overloaded trolley next to her. 'Can we slide in here?' She's unloading sheets of cans on to the belt before I can even start it up, ignoring the ball gown moaning and complaining about queue-jumping. I start ringing up her purchases as fast as I can. There must be more than a hundred cans of Red Bull and at least thirty – wait, no, forty – jumbo bags of crisps.

'There is no way I am carrying all those,' her blonde friend says, sulking at the exit end of the aisle. I blush as Jemima rolls her eyes at me.

'Chill your boots, will you? We'll use the trolley. Marie, is it?' I gawp at her, clutching the bag of crisps I was about to scan. Is she still talking to me? 'Marie says we can borrow it so long as you return it straight away. You, that is, not me.'

I flush harder as she smiles at me again. I guess she can borrow

it. Why not? Moe will leave me out of this management conversation for sure if he finds out. I pass the last of the crisps across the
belt as they stack their supplies high in the basket, gasping as I
ring up the total. No one ever spends more than twenty quid in
here, overnight anyway.

'Jesus wept,' the blonde one says, eyeing the numbers blinking
on the screen. 'And you think we'll get away with that?'

'Of course we will,' Jemima says, fumbling with her bag and
pockets. 'Do you get how much work we're about to have to do?
Every source outside the newsroom is about to get cadged for even
the tiniest amount of intel. No one will care about a bloody drinks
bill.'

She passes me a bank card.

'I thought we didn't pay for info,' her friend mutters as I swipe,
head spinning.

'Of course we don't,' she says, winking at me as I pass her card
back. 'Not with cold, hard cash anyway ... Could I have a receipt
please?'

'Good job,' Moe says from somewhere behind me. I spin round,
heart sinking as I find him frowning at the loaded trolley waiting
at the end of the aisle. 'Wow. You girls must really be thirsty.'

'That's one way of putting it, I guess,' the blonde mutters, scowling at him.

'I know it looks absurd,' Jemima says, straightening and smiling
at Moe. 'But we've got a newsroom full of journalists to keep
awake for the foreseeable future. I hope you don't mind if we
borrow this trolley just to get the drinks down the road? I promise
we'll bring it straight back and if we don't, here's my card.'

I freeze as Moe beams back at her. Really?

'No problem,' he says, tucking her business card into the pocket
above his manager badge. 'It's a pleasure to meet you. And I'm
glad we can help, even if it's just to fuel the press.'

I jump as Jemima plucks her credit card from between my
fingers, winking at me before turning to thank him.

'Just return it before dawn, if you can,' he says as they clatter towards the doors. 'And good luck!'

He waves as they disappear into the night. I am rooted to my seat with shock. Having to explain away a stolen shopping trolley is worse than having to account for missing bottles of wine.

'Let's get the newspapers done, come on,' he says, turning back to me. 'Darren can handle the tills for now. Everyone will want a paper as soon as they can get their hands on one.'

I follow him dumbly back through the shop, then the storeroom, finally out the back into the alley where the delivery truck is already backing into place. There's not even a second to check whether the telly is still showing the burning towers.

'How come you let them borrow the trolley?' I say, blinking as my eyes adjust to the dark, the slow beeps of the reversing truck popping in my ears. 'Won't we get fined?'

'They'll bring it back,' he says, banging on the back of the truck as it gets as close as is safe to the open storeroom doors. 'They're journalists, not drunks. We don't need to worry about them nicking it. The worst they'll do is forget to bring it back till later. And besides, they'll be going through some pretty horrific stuff the next few weeks.'

He pauses, jumping on to the ledge at the back of the van to open the doors.

'Let's do these by hand so we get a few out quickly,' he says, passing me a stack of newspapers. 'Just put these ones out front to start with.'

I stare at the brick of papers in my arms, all bearing the same photo of the burning towers.

'Crack on, will you?' Moe frowns at me from inside the van, balancing another stack of newspapers on his bent knees.

'I don't understand,' I say, gaping at the picture screaming from the front of every paper. 'The planes crashed into the buildings? Both of them?'

'It was a terror attack,' he says, climbing down next to me with more papers. 'They did it deliberately. Two flew into the towers, another into the Pentagon. There was a fourth jet, but it crashed into a field. Who the hell knows where it was supposed to be going? There must be thousands dead. Thousands. Awful.'

'But why?' My eyes trace the loops and curls of flames and smoke, immortalised mid-rage against a sky so blue it looks like it's never seen a cloud before.

'Who knows,' Moe says, hurrying back inside with his papers. I have to trot to keep up. 'But it's all anyone will talk about for months. And the press, they'll have to hear every horrific detail, listen to every last desperate phone call made from those planes.'

I slow behind him, bright-lit shop dazzling as usual after the 2.00 am dark of the back alley. And it's then that it hits me. I haven't thought about anything else except the burning buildings since I first saw them an hour ago. Carly's gone, and Katie Jolley, up in those billowing clouds of horror, so choked with terror and despair it's impossible to imagine anything else.

I look down at my papers, electrified, tingles running up and down my back as I realise.

This is how I make them evaporate. With worse stories than mine. I know they're out there. I've just never thought to go looking for them.

Marie ~ Just outside Warchester ~ 2006

Dominic groans as the train jolts to a sudden stop in the middle of a field, the immediate absence of purring engine giving way to tuts and sighs as the same realisation dawns on the few others in the carriage. I squint out of the window at the meadows around us, grass whipping with the wind, catching the distant roar of the A12. There's no dip and roll to these fields. If we were still moving, we'd probably be no more than ten minutes out. Overhead, a loud pop ends the start of an announcement crackling from the speaker before it's even begun. I wobble as I stand, moving into the aisle.

'That's not exactly a good sign, is it? I'll go and see if I can find someone.'

Dominic swears as he gets up too, pushing past me out of the carriage.

'You've got to be kidding,' he snaps, scrabbling at the second set of doors ahead of us.

'Isn't there a button?' I say, straining to see round him. 'Sometimes you have to ... ow!' I shrink as he steps backward into me, looking up and round the doorframe.

'They're automatic. Aren't they? Those ones were...'

We turn back to the doors we just came through, flat and gleaming like a closed window. I step so close to them that my forehead almost touches the glass. Did I float through them?

'That's impossible,' I murmur, prodding the glass with my finger. 'Did you have to push a button on the other side?'

'Of course not. They just opened.' Dominic kicks the glass. Nothing.

'Try those again,' I say, twisting back round to the other set. We push at them, Dominic swearing as he runs his finger down the groove in the centre.

'This is absurd,' he shouts, punching the glass and pacing the two steps back to the other doors. And just like that, we're trapped in the lobby – exit door on either side, glass doors forming the rest of the box around us. And just like that, I realise I followed him without thinking twice about it.

I rest my head on the glass, staring at the bobble hat motionless on top of the seat in front of me. That was the warning and I missed it. That woman and her baby, immediately knocked out by his cocktail of kindness, attention and understanding. I should have known then. I should have remembered immunity can never be guaranteed.

'Try those again,' I say, twisting back round to the other set. This can't be happening ... trusting Dominic? I watch as he pushes at them, swearing, running his finger down the groove in the centre.

'The power must be out,' I say, drumming my fingers on the doors we came through. My heart beats with my fingers, one, two, three. I look down at my chest, half expecting to see a pulse ... Still my heart beats, steady and regular, rather than accelerating up my throat like vomit. I swallow reflexively. But there's nothing to swallow.

'It can't be. These ones only just opened, didn't they?'

I reach for the light switch resting by the window, flicking it up and down. One, two, three. Nothing. Yet my heart beats on, calm and smooth, even as Dominic's fingers brush my hand to stab at the switch.

'For the love of God,' he shouts, punching at the window. 'A fucking power cut?' He turns to the exit door, jabbing at the release button. 'Since when are these trains even electric?'

'The whole line must be out,' I say, feeling my way around the strange sensation of calm sweeping through my body. I'm trapped in a small glass box with an angry man, I tell myself, steeling for the panic that should wash over me. Except it doesn't. Nothing happens. I just stand, hand slipping from its brace against the wall. Dominic starts to shout, banging on the doors back into the first-class carriage.

'I don't understand,' I mutter. 'I don't understand...'

'Of course you don't understand,' Dominic yells, giving the doors another punch. 'Nothing makes sense about this, does it? They opened once, so they should open again, shouldn't they? ... Again and again and again ... but no, of course they don't.'

He slithers to the floor, rooting around in his pocket. I peer up ahead. No one's seen us, much less heard us. The carriage may as well be empty, except the red bobble hat still perched above the seat a few rows up. And all that's beyond the other doors is a long corridor with another closed door at the end.

'At least that's the driver's cabin.' I point into the carriage. 'It must be. Someone will be out of there soon enough.'

'What if all the bloody doors are stuck?' He glares up at me, switching on the phone in his lap. 'And why did you follow me, anyway? Now we're both stuck in here.'

'I thought...' I clear my throat. I don't know what I thought. I stare at my sketchy reflection in the glass, tapping a finger right over the bobble hat up ahead. I know she won't wake up. Still I tap. One, two, three. *Wake up, Ma.* I jerk upright as the memories invade.

'You won't fucking believe this,' Dominic shouts behind me. 'I appear to be trapped in a space big enough for a rat – no, a mouse – after who only knows what has gone wrong on this tin can of a train...'

I stumble as he kicks out on the floor, catching the back of my heel.

'No, Jonas, the train to the moon. Where else? Except we're currently stuck in a field somewhere in the wilds of Essex. Look, can you make some calls? I don't have any numbers with me. Hello?' I twist round as he throws his phone at the opposite wall. It bounces off the steel below the window on to the floor.

'Have you got yours?' he says, blinking desperately up at me. 'I refuse to believe you would do something so unbelievably clueless as to leave it on the table.'

'Of course not,' I say, passing him my phone even though I know it won't work. It never does out here.

'What kind of a useless network is this?' he groans as he stabs at the keyboard.

'Hang on, it might come back,' I say. 'Give it here, come on.' I know it won't. I slide to the floor, pulling my knees into my chest to avoid his. Silence descends as I fiddle pointlessly with my phone in between his sighs and groans.

'Aha,' he says after a minute, pulling a mangled packet of chewing gum from his pocket. 'It's the little things. Here you go, have one.'

He passes me the stub of a packet, a single tab of gum covered in crumpled foil.

'Thanks,' I say, turning the tab over and over in my fingers, his gum popping and cracking into the silence. My mind ticks, Carly hovering just around the corner of every mental alleyway.

'At least she's asleep,' he says, jerking his head towards the bobble hat. 'We could be stuck in here *and* have to listen to that baby squalling its face off.'

I tighten my arms around my legs, single tab of chewing gum hot in my hand.

'So tell me, Marie,' he drawls. 'Are you visiting Warchester for business or pleasure?'

I shiver, fiddling with my gum as Carly peers around a bend in my mind.

'You cold?' He frowns as I shake my head. His gum pops and cracks as he stares.

'So where do you want to start when we get there?' I say, shoving Carly back into the fog. 'Are you happy heading to Victory Field first?' But as soon the words are out I can see her outline in the distance, a heat haze on the horizon.

His eyes narrow as he looks back at me.

'That depends on how late we are. Who the hell knows how long we're going to be stuck here. We can hardly afford to fanny around for too long.'

'We won't,' I say. If I rest my cheek on my knees I can avoid his eyes ... there. 'I really think the pubs are the way to go. There's a ton of them, Britannia this, Gurkha that, all proud military bunting everywhere.'

'Gosh, Google Earth is the nuts, isn't it? Does it even show you the drunks slumped and ready to blab outside?'

'I told you,' I say. 'I was on the...'

'...copy desk,' he finishes. 'And I was the sugar plum fairy, once. Honest I was.' Another crack into the silence. The minutes tick by.

'So what's the deal with the police,' I mutter, shoulder prickling as Carly emerges, like a sprite, a thread of softest cloud. I lift my head, squashing her. Dominic's eyes blaze at me.

'You wouldn't believe how deep the rot is,' he says. 'The grooming was engineered from the very start. And it was much more widespread than the original inquiry ever uncovered. At least that's what I've got from one source. It starts and ends with that perverted captain...'

Carly unfurls around my head as I stare back at him. She's light, like the cloud of frizz round Julie's head. But she's out. I can't put her back in. Still my heart thuds; regular, trusting, unfamiliar.

'He was the mastermind behind Baby Girl A,' he continues. 'Her mum was an ex of his, in all sorts of trouble with booze and drugs. The definition of vulnerable, textbook. That's how they managed to get to a minor. It's almost always someone known to the victims, isn't it? Standard grooming, I suppose ... sick as it is to say so.'

Crack, crack, crack goes his gum. I twist round, looking over my shoulder. There's the bobble hat, motionless, peaceful, trusting.

'I don't understand,' I murmur as Carly whispers in my ear,

breath fogging the glass in front of me. He was killed in action, Pa, that loser, whoever he was, wasn't he? K.I.A, they said. What's that mean, I said. Money, Jason said. Spells Kia, Rach said. Like Mia. It's a girl's name.

'The question is,' Dominic mutters to himself behind me, 'how do I prove the evidence against Minchin was deliberately buried? The grooming ring itself isn't new.'

I breathe in, out, in, out on to the glass. That man, whoever he was, he's been dead for years. Deader than dead. He was never alive, as far as I ever cared. Even Jason couldn't remember his face if he saw it. Neither of us could.

'I don't understand,' I say again, resting my head on the glass. 'Which captain do you mean?' Robert Leigh Parish, Carly whispers into my ear. Robert. Leigh. Parish.

'Surely you went over that on the copy desk. He was the biggest of big fishes, if we're to believe everything we're told by anyone in authority. I mean, if people misspell Warchester so much...' Dominic trails off as I whip round, Carly roaring in my ear.

'You need to tell me,' I croak, 'what the captain did. Tell me...'

'I don't know,' he says. 'Don't know exactly, anyway. But they used him to get to the kids. Parish was the channel. It was likely via other family members, or some such. It almost always works out that way. And it probably helped that it's always harder to say no to anyone living with catastrophic injuries – handy, that. It wasn't enough to exploit vulnerable children, they had to go for people with disabilities too...' He trails off into a sigh before continuing. 'But none of those details will help us on this though, infuriating as it is. Because I need to be sure the police aren't setting me up on Minchin. And for that, I need a leak from somewhere else.'

'Tell me what you know about the captain,' I say again, even though I can't hear myself. Carly's screaming, screaming like she's on fire. 'I need to know everything.' I get to my feet.

'Don't bother,' he says as I bang on the doors. 'They can't hear us. We're all obviously locked in. We'll have to wait for a power surge or something.'

'Tell me!' I scream, standing on his legs as I stumble forward to the other doors. Or is it Carly? She's roaring now, hurling herself against the walls in my head, again and again. 'I just need someone to tell me the fucking truth. I thought that captain was just another one of the deviant tribe. And he's gone down for the rest of time now, hasn't he? There was enough evidence to convict him to the moon and back.'

I bang on the glass, using my head now, screwing my eyes shut. He'll never get out, they said. Neither will any of the others, they said, if you can identify them.

'Parish was definitely just another one of the deviants, but that's not the point, is it? Stop it, Marie, come on. Now is not the time to pass out again, OK?'

I shrug his hand off my shoulder as my head thumps. He must have stood up.

'Are you telling me he trafficked members of his own family?'

'That's the allegation, yes. That's how he got to Baby Girl A, and got Minchin his fix. Except that's not my story, is it? One thing Andromeda got right first was the grooming. The original inquiry at least figured out the main source of it. And now I'm being told the captain had some former association that he exploited via various family connections both inside and outside the barracks. Sure, I could keep going over the lurid details for Olivia, but that's not the point is it? The point is proving the state covered for Minchin specifically because there was too much to lose if it didn't.'

I slither to my knees, blood rushing to my head as it droops, lower and lower until my forehead hits the floor. In that moment, I wish for my neck to snap, for my head to just roll away from my body, for my memories to forever be detached from the rest of me, for the realisations thundering through my body like an electrical current to be shut off at source, just shut off as simply as flicking a switch, and then breaking the circuit so cleanly that it can never, ever be repaired. Except there my neck stays, and so too does my head. And so, too, does Carly, rippling out of the mist and settling down on to my skin like a layer of frost.

'... are you alright? Marie?' Carly hardens, Dominic's voice fades in and out of the screams in my head. Who's screaming? Is it me?

'Marie!' There's a clank somewhere above my head, one, two, three. 'Marie? Come on now, girl...' His face swims as I open my eyes, raising myself to sitting, feeling Carly like a coat around me.

'I swear to you, if you so much as come within a mile of the office after this, I'll change the locks to your flat while you're inside,' he says, sighing. 'Passing out twice in twenty-four hours is most definitely not OK...'

I blink at him. His face is grey.

'How many fingers am I holding up?' He gives me a thumbs-up. I can't smile. There's a sudden jolt and hum as the light flickers on overhead, doors gliding open as if they'd never been stuck. I've no choice but to steady myself as they fall away from me, Dominic leaping to his feet.

'Don't tell me you want to stay in here,' he says, stretching a hand towards me. 'Come on, get up...' He freezes as the speaker above our heads crackles to life.

'We apologise for the prolonged delay, ladies and gentlemen, but I'm afraid there's been an unprecedented power outage across the whole county, which knocked out the entire train...'

'You don't say,' Dominic shouts at the ceiling, beckoning for me to take his hand.

'We've been instructed to take this train back to London, where agents will meet you to help organise alternative arrangements to your final destination...'

'You are kidding me!' Now he's howling above the speaker, flinging his hands in the air. 'I can get around an active fucking war zone faster than this!'

Up ahead, the red bobble drops out of view below a head rest. She's woken up, I think. We've all woken up. I've woken up.

'...rest assured, you will be able to claim this journey back, if you've still got proof of purchase. Once again, we do apologise for all inconvenience as a result of this...'

'Inconvenience my arse!' Dominic grabs the headrest in front of him as the train starts to move, back down the track towards London. London, I think, its millions of buildings and towers and streets and parks crowding into my head. Where everyone's invisible. Where protecting yourself is as simple as crouching in one of its million hiding places.

'....agents will be passing up and down the train now with information about your onward options once we've returned safely to Liverpool Street.'

I get to my feet, rocking back and forth with the rumble of the engine.

'Can you believe this?' Dominic's eyes blaze at me. Out of the window, I can see the blank green fields of Essex lengthening as we speed up.

'Have you got reception yet? Check, would you? We can get a cab from Chelmsford...'

I laugh, a sudden, high burst of sound, mingling with the roar of the train. Carly shouts, so loud I'm sure everyone can hear her.

Dominic recoils, staring. I square up to him, Carly hanging like armour around me. You owe us, they'd said. Just put them off the scent, they'd said. National security depends on it, they'd said. It's in the national interest, they'd said.

And I decide. Marie decides. She knows Carly better than she knows herself. From now on, they can only ever be one and the same.

'The only place we need to go is Whitehall,' I say, gripping the headrest as we thunder down the track. 'But you need to promise me something, OK?'

'Did you bang your head again in there or something? What are you on about?'

I look up at him, swaying with the rhythm of the train, up at this version of Dominic I've finally figured out. The version that raised his baby brother when his mum died, the version that's got nearly all the answers because he's asked enough questions, the version that's as vulnerable, scared and betrayed as Carly. As me. The wild urgency I felt while we were trapped in the lobby has condensed into lucid, implacable fury.

'If I trust you, will you trust me?'

He nods as he steps towards me.

'I think...' I say, leaning forward so I can whisper. Can I even say it out loud? 'I think Captain Robert Leigh Parish was my dad.'

I rub my head as Carly screams, fire-alarm high. Somewhere down the aisle, the baby wakes up, and starts to cry again.

Carly ~ London ~ 2001

I peer at the cans of Red Bull, stacked as high as they'll go above the Cokes. If they weren't such an awkward shape I could get a load more of them into the space between the shelves ... damn. I trot up to the tills, leaving my trolley behind, loaded with the drinks I can't fit. I know they'll be in any time now. It's always straight off their break at 2.00 am, and who knows how many drinks they'll need tonight. The towers fell exactly one week ago, but they seem busier every time. I scan the tills, squinting into the dark beyond the entrance.

'The papers are here,' Moe calls to me from a few aisles down. 'Come out back, can you?'

I skip back down the aisle, arriving as Moe does, at the entrance to the storeroom. I've read so many newspapers, watched so much telly this week that I am actually starting to feel like the different person I'm supposed to be. Bit by bit, Carly's disappearing, as I crowd my head with horror stories. I've stared and stared at the picture of a man, plunging to the ground perfectly in line with one of the towers. The Falling Man, suspended in upside-down perfection. Who was he? Nobody knows anything for sure, except for the fact that he's dead. I've read every account of how the bodies sounded when they landed. How they may have even killed other people if they hit them before hitting the ground.

'It's a bit early for the papers, isn't it?' I flick a look at the telly on the desk. More maps of Afghanistan. I know what and where it is now. I could draw it.

'I split the suppliers,' Moe says, hurrying through the boxes to the back door. 'Some are printing earlier than others. So I figured staggering them would sell the most. Everyone's desperate ... We'll shift these in no time then send out another load at four.'

I shiver as I follow him out into the dark. It seems right that the temperature has dropped since everyone's decided the world will never be the same again. I jump into the back of the open truck before it's finished reversing, snatching just a second or two with the front pages by myself.

'Tora Bora? What's that?'

'Eh?' Moe looks up from the tarmac. He's already down and out with his stack.

'Tora Bora ... wait...' I reread the sentence. 'They are caves, apparently.' Caves? Where? Moe's already inside the storeroom as I look up.

'You can read it later, come on,' he shouts over his shoulder.

I jump down, trying to read as I walk. Tora Bora? I stumble as I crash into Darren walking back out to the truck.

'Sorry,' I say, clutching the papers to my chest as I flush. My head went straight into him.

'He's on crack again tonight, isn't he?' Darren scowls as he jerks his head in Moe's direction. 'Papers, Daz, papers, papers, papers. They cost fuck-all, don't they? So who fucking cares if they're selling out?'

I push past him into the shop. I don't want to miss Jemima. Moe's already heading back down the aisle towards me to get the rest.

'You can read one if you must,' he says, pausing as I walk past him. 'But on your break, OK? And only if there are enough left.'

I flush with thanks, hurrying up to the front of the shop, dumping my papers so I can rush back to the drinks. I'll find her there.

'Are these for me?' Jemima says, smiling at me as I round the corner of the aisle to find her next to my trolley, still stacked with the cans I'd left.

'Hi,' I say, catching up to her. 'Another busy night?'

'Always,' she says. 'What about you?'

I look at the floor. I hate that I'm still blushing.

'So are these for me?' She rattles the trolley.

'You can take those ones if you want.' I look up to find her frowning at her phone.

'Like I can just click my fingers and parachute a news crew into Tora Bora,' she mutters, stabbing at the tiny keyboard. 'It may as well have been on the moon before all this.'

'Where's Tora Bora?' I ask, before I can stop myself. Damn. My face must be purple now.

'Huh?' She doesn't look up.

'Nothing,' I say, fiddling with some cans on the shelf, as if they need tidying when in fact they're lined up like soldiers.

'Afghanistan,' she mumbles as she shoves her phone back into her pocket. 'It's in Afghanistan. On the border with Pakistan. There are loads of caves dug into the mountains. Like ratholes, except bigger. It's where the Americans think Bin Laden is.'

I blink at her, forgetting about my blush.

'Quite the news junkie, aren't you?' She smiles again. I literally have no idea what she is talking about.

'I just...' I look down again as she laughs, grabbing hold of the trolley.

'Well if you want to get into journalism, now's most definitely the time. There is enough work for an apprentice army. We just need warm bodies at the moment. If they come with a half-functioning brain too, that's a plus. Everyone is doing at least four jobs at once.'

'Do you want to take those drinks too?' I say, forcing my gaze up. 'It's fine if you do. I couldn't fit them in up there anyway...'

'I will, if that's OK,' she says, leaning on the trolley. She looks beyond knackered. 'It's a real help, you guys letting us borrow this. Every night I think we've got enough to last a few days but the pace is completely mental.'

'Are you always on the overnight shift?' I scuff at the ground rather than look at her.

'Not always. Hopefully soon I'll have done enough to move to days. Especially now it's so busy. But yeah, it's inevitably where everyone starts, usually after an internship or apprenticeship somewhere else. We all have to do our time.'

'I'll ring those up for you,' I say, hurrying alongside her as she starts to walk towards the tills. 'Is there anything else you need? You can leave these with me if you need to go back for other stuff.'

'Thanks,' she says as I slide in behind the cash register. 'I've got to rush back, actually. I shouldn't even be here, truth be told. I may as well be buried under a mountain of logistics.'

Panic rises in my chest as I start to scan her drinks. I've set my clock by her visits this last week. Every night, just gone 2.00 am. She'll come and I'll learn something else, something else so terrible that I can spend the whole rest of my night and day crowding my brain with it. What if she stops? Then what? The stuff everyone knows isn't enough for me. I need the inside track.

'I can imagine,' I say, even though I can't. I slow down, laboriously passing cans across the belt rather than just multiplying the lot, trying to stretch out every moment.

'You can do it too, you know,' she says, gazing somewhere into the dark beyond the doors ahead. 'Anyone can. The trick is to know when to listen and when to ask another question ... And to start right at the bottom and work your way up. And above all, to be curious. Always be curious...'

I clank the last of the drinks across the belt. How could I possibly do it too?

'Everyone has to start somewhere,' she continues, staring glassily into the night. She's slowing right down for someone supposed to be in a hurry.

'That's a hundred and eleven eighty,' I say, folding my hands in my lap. Even though it's only been a week, I've got used to the numbers.

'Sorry,' she says, digging around in her pocket. 'I was miles away. I'm so tired I barely know my own name. It's impossible to sleep during the day with everything changing so fast.'

'I can imagine,' I say again. At least this time I can, although the daytime is pretty much the only time I am able to actually sleep.

'Do you really want to be a journalist?' She frowns as she passes me her credit card. Did I say that? I barely know what she's talking about. 'You definitely ask a lot of questions ... and they aren't stupid ones, either.'

I fumble with her card, bending to pick it up almost as soon as I've dropped it.

'If you're serious, then get yourself an internship at a local paper. You need to do some hard yards on local stories. It's the best training there is. You wouldn't believe how many people show up with degrees in journalism and zero on-the-job experience. They couldn't chase a story if it bit them in the arse.'

I rip off her receipt, passing it over the belt.

'I would take an apprentice from the local rag over a university graduate any day of the week. See you tomorrow?'

I nod, gazing after her as she disappears into the dark. Maybe that's the way out, I think, watching as the doors open and close again and again in front of me until I realise I must have got up to follow her.

Marie ~ London ~ 2006

The train roars round us, swinging from side to side as it thunders back into London, as if all the energy it missed out on while the power was down is surging in bursts now it's back on. I swing with it, finally a rhythm that's in time with my brain, finally the sensation of power firing every cell in my body with the desire for justice and revenge. Carly's dancing, her wild spinning, marking out my mind's centre of gravity. And Dominic? He's frozen to the spot, brain whirring as loudly as the clattering engine. As too is mine – live-wired with information, with the certainty that finally, I hold all the cards. Finally, there's nothing they can say to bury me. I can prove everything, just by being myself ... and justice will follow, even if freedom never does. Dominic, and Nine, will make sure of that.

'Are you telling me you were part of this?'

He lurches towards me as the train veers west. I nod as all the answers suddenly stick in my throat, so much to say, finally, I don't know how to start. Behind my eyelids, Carly pauses, a ballerina on her tiptoes, peering at him.

'But how...' His words trail off into the air as he stares at me, then into the distance out of the porthole window.

'Marie...' he says to himself, before turning back to me. 'Is that even your real name?'

I look at the floor. We stand, wordlessly, swaying like trees in the wind.

'Yes,' I choke out after a moment. 'But it's my middle name. I've been using it since.'

'Since when?'

I swallow hard, propelling myself over the invisible line separating this phase of my life from the next, which is opening up in front of me faster than I can blink.

'Since I shopped him. Since ... Dom, I was the one who turned everyone in. It was me. I'm Girl A. At least, I used to be.'

Dominic whistles into the howl of the engine as Carly leaps into the air, suspended in a perfect star.

'But now you need to tell me everything,' I gabble, the words suddenly falling out of my mouth. 'Everything you've found out about that captain, that general, and what he did.'

'Wait a second,' he says. 'You're telling me you *think* Parish was your dad? You mean you don't know?'

'I never met him. He was long gone before I was even born. And then he died sometime after that. At least, they told us he died...'

'What do you mean? Who told you? When?'

'The army. It all happened when I was little. They showed up with his dues after he was killed in action someplace. At least that's what they said had happened. We never knew him.'

'Hang on, Marie. Just stop for a second—'

'Tell me everything,' I shout, punching at him, suddenly overcome by fury. 'You said it was a setup, engineered from the start. What do you mean? That we were picked off?'

'Who's we?' He grabs my fist, pulling me towards him. 'Help me, Marie. You can't just tell me you think Parish was your dad and expect me to put the rest together. Five minutes ago we were just two hacks working the Andromeda investigation!'

'She was my sister!' I screech as the tears start to fall. 'My sister ... my baby sister ... She was never supposed to get hurt...'

'Who? Who was your sister?'

I sob, sinking to the floor, clasping my knees as I rock with the train. My sister. I can't see anything else except her, warm, trusting and content in my arms. The only reason any of this ever happened.

'Marie...' I feel his arms fold round me. 'Do you mean Baby Girl A? Is that who you mean? She was your sister?'

I bury my head in my legs. This time nothing can stop the retch hurling up my throat. The train roars with me as we rock and roll, rock and roll, everything around me, inside and out, just screaming, screaming, screaming.

'OK,' Dominic says, somewhere over my head. 'How about we do this ... I'll ask you questions, all you have to do is nod or shake. OK?'

He starts as I look up, his face a curious mixture of horror, sympathy and shock.

'She was my sister,' I say, resolve hardening with every word. 'Kayleigh. She's Baby Girl A. Technically she's my half-sister but that never mattered to me. For a while it was only me, Ma and Jason, but the scroungers showed up soon as Ma started flashing her army cash. They paid her his military pension – at least that's what I was always told, anyway. I never knew anything about my dad, just that he died a soldier ... for all the good that ever did us.'

'They gave you his army pension, even though you never knew him?'

'Yes ... until Ma let one too many chancers in on the secret. By the time Kayleigh came along it was all gone. We didn't have a bean. She was so innocent and helpless ... I'd been taking care of myself forever, then I had to take care of her too. I didn't have any other choice.'

'Choice? What do you mean?'

'The army gave us everything we needed in return for ... well, you know. Jason was the one who sorted it all out, he'd joined up long before. We never had enough to eat, let alone clothes, or baby stuff. And Ma could hardly get off the sofa...'

'Are you telling me you were one of the original victims? You?'

I nod as he looks at me in worn horror.

'They wanted me to bring her in too, so I shopped them. I couldn't ... Who could? Kayleigh was the only reason I ever agreed to testify ... to try and keep her safe, to try and make sure she had everything I lost. It was like I got a second chance when she was born, like life just started up again right before my eyes. She was how I could make it all right ... I testified against them all, went over every last bit of detail, so she'd get looked after. At least I thought it was against them all...'

I trail off into the train's squeal as it leans into its final approach to London.

'They said we'd get a new start,' I say, rubbing bile from off my cheek on to my knee. 'Both of us were supposed to. They gave me a new name, money, flat, everything. Kayleigh went to a foster family, then another, and another ... and before long she didn't want to see me, or be reminded of anything to do with her past. And we were deliberately kept separate, so our new identities wouldn't be compromised. In the end, it was only because one of the social workers kept bringing me information when she shouldn't have that I ever knew how she was doing. I should have known there was more to it than just settling down ... I kept being told how she needed to break the link with her past but I knew, I knew she would never forget what we had, what I gave her, even if she was too young to physically remember it. It's been years since I've seen her. I don't even know who or where she is now ... only that it was all a pack of lies, from the word go—'

'Christ,' he interrupts, brow furrowed as he grips my shoulders, looking over his shoulder then back at me.

'So you need to tell me everything,' I say, finally lifting my head. 'Where did you get that photo? There's only one reason you could possibly have it now, after everything Jaqlin said at that press conference. What do you know about what happened to that little girl?'

'Let me just get this straight,' he says, eyes darting. 'You didn't know Parish was your dad when you—'

'No,' I say. 'I never knew him. Ma moved on to about a million other blokes after he died. Jason didn't know him either, I'm sure of it. Then again, he totally bought into the military – hook, line and sinker, like everyone else in Warchester.'

'Sergeant Jason Gates? He was your brother?'

My neck buckles as I try to nod. I remember Dominic will have read the case files. There was never any question that Jason would be spared a monumental jail term. He knew exactly what he was doing, even if he didn't understand what, or who he was doing it for.

'Just tell me, Dominic. Please...' I drop my head again, stop trying. 'What do you know about her, about Kayleigh? I need to know what really happened before I...'

'She's everything,' he says, words floating on the engine's song. 'She's the link ... I just haven't been able to believe it till now. She...'

He stops as I look up, and takes a deep breath.

'They brought her in for Minchin, I'm told. It didn't last long, but it definitely happened, probably in the gap between you turning yourself in and her being properly taken into care. It was all planned from the inside, from the word go. The abuse ring had been operating for years, long before you were brought in. I never knew about you specifically, but I've got two sources confirming the captain's link to Baby Girl ... sorry, to Kayleigh, and confirming that her mother was an ex of his, and that's how he managed to source her. Which means you're right. You were the other link in the chain. They set you up from the start, he was never really dead. You wouldn't believe what you can cover up in the name of intelligence...'

He stops again as I bang my forehead against my knees. Of course I can believe it. We're living proof of it. We're probably the only ones who will ever really believe it. It's unthinkable otherwise. Incomprehensible to anyone other than people like Dominic, who go looking for it.

'The allegation is it's been buried from the top down, because, at the time, Minchin and others were too involved in active intelligence operations. Parish also worked in those units. Were you ever told where your dad was deployed before he died? My bet is some off-grid Troubles operation infiltrating a nationalist community...'

I lose him as I remember how it was all Jason ever talked about. Intelligence. Like he was the only one who ever had any, or could possibly understand what it meant. Now it turns out neither of us could have even imagined it.

'... nothing can ever compromise defensive capability, especially not then, when the world was still obsessing over how many nuclear weapons the Russians really had. But now someone's inside operation has turned, and the Met has finally got enough to win it. The Andromeda failings are such an old score to settle – the CPS only managed eleven convictions in the first place by listing some of the victims as accomplices on the charge sheet just because of their age at the end—'

I think I say her name, but now Dominic's started, it's as if he'll never stop. Rachel, the closest thing to a mother I ever had. She was only ever a victim too.

'...I just haven't been sure, until now, that I wasn't being played – especially after our last story. And I've still got nothing to show that the state has been covering for Minchin all this time. I think that's been my problem: I haven't wanted to believe that the Met isn't covered in shit like it always is, always fucking has been...'

'I'm sorry about your mum,' I say, catching my breath as I see mute tears pouring from his eyes, his gaze fixed somewhere long back in the past. That's what happens when you've cried so much that you think it can't be possible to cry anymore. The tears just roll but nothing else happens, nothing at all. There's no sound. No release. Nothing except water.

'Yeah,' he mutters, dropping his head so his tears drip on to the toes of his shoes, close to mine now as he crouches down. 'I guess I'll always need convincing that the Met isn't at fault.'

We both stiffen as my phone starts to vibrate in my pocket,

sending tremors up my arms and into his hands on my shoulders. He sniffs as he gets to his feet, suddenly moving like an old man.

'Jonas,' he says, pulling his own phone from his pocket. 'She must have...' He stops, frowning down at the handset still in his hand. 'Wait – is that yours? Is she calling you? Or is it Olivia?'

I hug myself tighter, resting my chin on my knees as I look up at him. Shadows scud through the lobby as we speed through the tunnels on the final approach to Liverpool Street.

'No, it's not,' I say, squeezing myself so hard I think my ribs could crack, vibrations buzzing up and down the left side of my body from the brick in my pocket. 'But that's where we go after. Back to the newsroom, I mean. First, we have to go to Whitehall...'

'Whitehall?' He stares at me, hands frozen around his phone as I slide myself to standing, back against the wall.

'We need proof,' I say. 'And it needs to be admissible. It won't be enough for me to just tell my story. It doesn't matter what else you've got. They'll discredit me before the last word has gone on air, make you a laughing stock, not to mention blow up my entire life. And that is if we even get that far...'

'I don't understand,' he says as I dig around in my pocket. 'Proof of what?'

'I've been covering for them,' I say, dipping my voice as the train slows. 'Ever since they found out that I'd got myself a job in the news business. A tap here, a nod there ... the odd threat to my identity papers if I didn't. It seemed so harmless at the start, and I'd worked so hard. Finally, I had a piece of a life to cling to, keeping all the nightmares bubbling so low they didn't infect everything else. All they wanted was to know what was being talked about and that was it. Every time Andromeda poked at the headlines again, they wanted to know what new information did Nine have, and where was their investigation going. I had no reason to think it was much more than backscratching, like Jemima's always told me. And it was rare, until recently—'

I jump as Dominic's phone hits my foot, sliding into the gap where the train floor ends and the exit door begins, his hands still clasped round each other like it's still between them.

'All you need to do is come with me,' I say, bending to pick it up, pressing it back into his palm as he stares at me, tears dried to his face in streaks. 'I said you'd have to trust me, OK?'

'You're...' His words die in his throat as his bloodshot eyes search my face. 'You're working for them?'

'I guess I was...' I say, pulling my phone from my pocket, the word 'Medusa' flashing on its tiny blue screen. 'Once upon a time, anyway. Like I say, it seemed so reasonable at first. Remember, I had nothing until they set me up as Marie Grant. Literally everything I depend on to live was – well, still is – in their hands, not mine. When I started to resist, they made it about Kayleigh, even though I'd lost that trail years ago. She went into the bowels of the system and never came out, as if it wasn't bad enough what happened to her in the first place. But I'm not doing it anymore. And not ever again. Now, it's about us, and about Nine. We're going to bury them instead. They can't hide from what we've got ... There's enough to build a mountain over them. They'll never be able to climb out from underneath. And we won't even need the ball cam.'

And then, just then, as the train pulls into the station, I feel my face suddenly lift into a smile, my cheeks straining, eyes crinkling, energy firing around my body into the tips of my fingers, the ends of my toes. I've said everything, and I'm still Marie. Carly blows kisses to my head's inner audience, dancing and hugging herself with glee.

Carly ~ Deptford ~ 2002

'Morning, love,' Frank shouts.

I ignore him, skipping past his newspaper kiosk on Deptford High Street. It's one of those curiously warm winter days when, if you had to guess, you might say it was spring. There's even a green shoot or two around the place, as it's been so wet over Christmas. I can spot them even in the dark, in the half-light of a winter morning, when the sun doesn't come up until gone eight. Not that Christmas, or New Year for that matter, have even registered as far as I'm concerned.

Jemima was right. I found the *Gazette* by chance on the way home after who knows how many night shifts in a row, scrabbling for more papers to read. Even this tiny corner of South-East London was desperate for more hands on deck after those towers collapsed. No one could get enough of the news. Between that and the shop, my mind's been blurring and smudging everything. Even my dreams are out of focus, faded and fuzzy around the edges. Sometimes Carly even shows up in Tora Bora, which turns out to be just outside London, deep underneath Katie Jolley's house.

'Long night, was it?'

Frank's leer fades behind me as I scurry past and into the office. I can see Carly, just for a second, as I blink into the strip lights. I just have to blink again though, and she's gone.

'Hi,' I say to no one in particular, clearing my throat.

A few heads move, but that's it. I loop my coat over my arm, scanning the room for something to do. There's the low hum of typing, a few distant phone conversations, but otherwise it's quiet, little peaks and troughs of activity lapping through the air. Laurie's at the back, in the editor's office, a small room barely bigger than a cupboard, stuffed full of more paper than I've ever seen. Piles, stacks, columns of the stuff, they may as well be part of the walls. I know he's in there because even though I can't see him, the papers against the back wall are yellow. They go grey when the desk lamp's off.

I take a deep breath and step towards Andy, the sub at the end of the row. Sub. The word pops into my mind like I understand it, because now, I do. I'm learning a completely new language.

'Coffee?' I grip at the coat over my arm like it's a shield across my body.

'Mmmmm,' he says, frowning as he looks up, a finger of ash falling on to the desk from his cigarette. He doesn't know my name, but none of them really do, except Laurie.

'Can I bring you one too?' I arch my eyebrows at Kevin, two cubicles down.

'Cheers,' he grunts, eyes on the screen. I trot to the kitchen, a pokey little room next to the copiers on the side wall, not much more than a sink, fridge, microwave and a few wonky cupboards full of a bunch of chipped mugs. There's a single hook on the back of the door that no one ever uses, where I leave my coat. A full pot of stale-smelling coffee is still simmering on the pad underneath the filter. It must have been a long night here too, I think, filling two cups and setting a fresh round on the go before heading back out. Percolating, I think. *Per-co-lay-ting.* That's what they said it was doing when I asked.

'Ta,' Andy grunts, peering up at me from his computer as I hand him a steaming cup. 'Sorry, but I don't know your—'

'I'm just helping out,' I say, cutting him off before I have to answer. It still feels forced, no matter how hard I try to relax into saying it. 'Is there anything else I can help you with today?'

I force myself to hold his gaze as he frowns, itching at his hands. They are all flaky with something, probably to do with being junkie-thin. That's why I always ask him first. Junkies will never hurt anyone that feeds their habit, and Andy's was obvious from the off. Coffee and news.

'Are you the new apprentice?' He blows smoke over his shoulder.

'Not exactly,' I say, folding my arms. I wish I still had my coat. 'I'm hoping to be soon, though. So if there's anything you need help with, anything at all, I'd be glad to...'

'Balls,' he interrupts, leaning forward to duck his head below the top of his monitor. 'That fucking toe-rag...' Out of the corner of my eye I can see Kevin shrinking into his chair too.

'How much fucking longer do you need?' Laurie's shouts cut over the hum in the room before he's even standing next to us. I tense as he arrives at the copydesk, nervous energy sparking off him like a live circuit. 'Do you think I haven't even read the damn thing? I've signed it off ... and I'm the editor, not the fucking tea lady. And how many times do I have to tell you that you can't smoke in here, Andy. We're a millennium past 1988...'

'We're almost there, aren't we?' Andy says, coughing and peering down the line of cubicles at Kevin as he crumples a packet of cigarettes into his hand. Fury pricks my neck as I remember how Ma used to do that every time she tried to give up. They cost so much ... I shake my head violently so she disappears, right as Laurie smacks a hand on to the desk.

'Why the fuck are you waiting for design? This is our front page lead and you're fannying about with the sidebars?'

I step backward as he moves between the two of them, brushing past me like I'm part of the furniture. It's working ... at least I think it is.

'Not exactly,' Andy says, bracing against the desk to push himself out of his chair. 'As I already mentioned to Phil, I think the trial references, all the procedural stuff, is best off as a nib, but we'd need to make sure it was on the front page if so. That way we can also cover the other major trials starting this week, rather than detracting from the main interview.'

'Phil!' Laurie screams into the room. 'Get over here!'

Andy props himself against the desk, eyeing his chair. I wonder what nibs are as I watch Phil scurry across the newsroom, eyes darting like the swot who's just got detention.

'If I could just explain—'

'Wait,' Laurie snaps, as Phil arrives on the other side of the row of desks, wringing his hands. 'Phil? You're strutting about in my office for half an hour going over the bloody thing and don't think to mention it's not your shitty grammar that's holding us up but in fact a decent editorial suggestion?'

Andy crumples back into his chair, leather cushions wheezing along with him.

'He was practically rewriting whole chunks,' Phil says, scuffing a toe into the worn carpet. 'I couldn't help but feel he was bringing my editorial judgement into question. I thought—'

'All I said was,' Andy interrupts, 'that we could get rid of all the procedural details about the trial starting if we put the nibs on the front page too. That way your interview stands on its own, as it should ... We're his local paper. It should be all about Damilola Taylor's grieving parents, and not what time and place the thugs are showing up in court to have the riot act read out...'

'That is an excellent idea,' Laurie interrupts, clapping a hand on Andy's shoulder. 'Spot on. Too right. Even if you had to take me round the houses eight times to make the point, as usual. And now I see why you were waiting for design.'

'Exactly,' Andy says wearily. 'I was going to bring you the whole layout, once Kevin had finished working out whether there was room for a full news-in-brief sidebar.'

'We'll make room,' Laurie says, squeezing Andy's shoulder. 'And think big, would you? We're not just writing this up for the venerable folk of South-East London. Readers the world over – if they're worth their salt, that is – should be coming to this kid's local press for the real story. We've got far more detail and insight than the nationals, because we live here. It's about us too. This blood was spilt on our streets. So bear that out, would you? There are black kids being murdered by racist yobs the Western world over and there's never enough being done about it. Make sure it's clear to any Tom, Dick or Harry reading in butt-fuck nowhere why they can and should be identifying with this too. This is a story that can speak to all of us. Damilola Taylor's death is as universal as ... oh, I don't fucking know. That's your job. Find out whose, rewrite the whole thing and then show it to me again.'

I flinch reflexively, thinking about Damilola Taylor. Another story I'd never heard before I got here. Now I know everything about his life, his family, how they'd moved here just three months before he was murdered. Lagos, Nigeria ... I can pick it out on a map just by pointing a finger. When I blink and see Kayleigh, I substitute his school photo, think about his family's grief instead. And now I know what nibs are too.

'It's like staring at the sun, isn't it?' Laurie snorts as Phil and Andy survey him with a mixture of exhaustion and bewilderment, then turns around to find me hanging on every word.

'What the hell are you still doing here?'

'I was going to help,' I say, ignoring the horror spreading across Andy's face. 'I could...' I cast around wildly for something, anything to suggest that might keep me in this conversation.

'Don't you ever sleep?' Laurie interrupts, stuffing his hands into his pockets as he squares up to me. 'How many times do I need to tell you this? No one in Deptford, at least no one who buys this paper, gives a toss about those towers anymore. I can't take you on in anything less than exceptional circumstances, and those were exceptional ... and all my grand editorial ambitions aside, we are back to our local London flavour on the staffing front now, like it or not. I can't conjure an apprenticeship from thin air, no matter how many coffees you make or print runs you help with. And more to the point, I can't be held responsible for you doing yourself a mischief on my premises because you insist on working all the hours God sends ... Oh, what the fuck is it now?'

I try not to smile as Laurie is forced to freeze his fury in his throat: someone else hurtling over with a volley of instant, urgent questions. Sidestepping all the fuss, I lean down to whisper to Andy, still deflated in his chair.

'So I'm guessing you will need new photos if this is going to be a whole front page layout?'

I scan his computer screen for clues, Damilola's school headshot wallpapering my mind.

'Well, yes...' he says, frowning up at me as he itches those hands again. 'But that's not—'

'Let me check if the picture desk have got anything new,' I say. 'And if not, I can always help with sitting outside the family house. I know you're trying to make sure someone's got an eye on it at all times. I bet you don't have enough people to go round the clock.'

He nods, pursing his lips. Is it to stop himself smiling? I try not to jig on the spot.

'Will you tell Laurie? Please?'

'Yeah,' he grunts, swivelling round to face his computer. 'But don't even think about coming back empty-handed, OK?'

I hug myself with my folded arms as I scuttle round the desk. It's happening, I think. I'm making myself indispensable. Soon enough, it won't matter who I am, only that they need who I've become. The sum of other people's stories instead of my own.

Marie.

Marie ~ London ~ 2006

'Talk to me, Marie,' Dominic hisses, hurrying through the crowds swarming in circles inside Liverpool Street Station. 'Just wait, Jesus...'

He grabs at my arm as we weave out of the clamour, barging past anyone in our way. My arm jerks out of its socket as he yanks me out of the tide of the commuters spilling on to the road, pulling us into a small layby beside the main entrance.

'Just stop, OK? Just for a second. We need to talk this through.'

'Plenty of time for that,' I say, thumbing my phone. 'But we've got to move now if I want to stay under the radar—'

'I need you to listen to me, OK?' he interrupts, grabbing my shoulders. 'If you really have been colluding all this time, then you are in massive, unthinkable danger right now. Massive. The implications of what we're about to do are ... Fuck, I can't even compute them myself and I've been up to the eyeballs, trying to untangle all of this before you came along.'

'You're all I need though, Dom. Don't you see? I'm the one who can prove the coverup and we know for sure now that the police side is clean. There's no one with better connections than you to leverage them when we need them. Calling 999 would be about as useful as sticking a bullseye on my back.'

'You're not hearing me,' he says, rounding on me. 'We're talking about the government here, the army, the whole fucking establishment.'

'None of that matters,' I shout, pushing at him. 'The rot runs far deeper than just me... it's just I'm probably one of the only ones left who can, beyond reasonable doubt, prove the whole lot. And I've got a national network microphone to do it with, haven't I?'

'That's the point. That's the fucking point. There's a reason they started to come after you again. It probably never occurred to anyone that you'd be smart enough to crowbar your way to the position you're in now. No one ever bothers to think about the victims beyond the fact they were victims. Christ, I'm surprised you're even still alive.'

'They couldn't stop me even if they wanted to,' I spit, shrugging into his hands. 'I'm too close to everything now, and you're right – they were always so focused on what I could do for them that they never considered how many cards I might end up holding myself. It's far too hard to disappear a news producer so close to someone like you ... to someone like Jemima...'

'Jesus, Marie!' I recoil as he leans forward, shouting into my face. 'People disappear all the time. Don't you get it? Look at Parish – the man you've just discovered was your actual father. You've even got different names. You and your brother grew up with no idea who he was to you, or what he's been to anyone else. His own family never once questioned how he was killed in action. How do you think that was possible? And what do you think went on to convince him that grooming members of his own flesh and blood was fundamental to issues of national security? This is a top-down coverup, because it has the potential to bring down half the government. Making you disappear without trace will be the least of it.'

'And that's why we need to get moving. We haven't got time to work out how they got away with it. It only matters now that they think they still have... they're expecting me, they left me under no illusion of that...' I finger the egg, still swollen on the side of my head. 'I'm on the clock every time there is a new Andromeda line. They expect to hear from me. That's the deal. All we need is some incriminating audio, and we're golden with everything else you've got. We can blow the whole thing wide open tonight.'

'All we need is some incriminating audio...' he repeats, dumbly. 'How exactly are we going to pull that off? And what do you think you'll be able to do with yourself after we tell the world about it? You'll hardly sally off into the sunset.'

'I don't care,' I say, rubbing a kaleidoscope of memory from my eyes as Dominic stares at me. 'I just know that this isn't justice. It never was. There are so many lies, I can hardly breathe through them. I can't just up and start again, they've got all my papers, and for Kayleigh...' I stop at the sound of her name, a punch in my throat. The fact that Robert Leigh Parish, that Captain Perv himself, has turned out to be the same loser whose danger money started all this in the first place has got nothing on the thought of what was still allowed to happen to my sister, even after I turned him in.

'So talk to me,' he says, jumping into the gap. 'You want to record them? How? How on earth will we get anything inside the ministry? Won't you be searched from the inside out?'

'You said it yourself, it's a top-down coverup. They're expecting me inside, there's a whole drill. Look, see?' I hold up my phone as it starts to buzz again in my hand. 'They never take this off me, as I need the codewords I get at the last minute. The sooner I get in, the sooner I'll be out.'

'And what if you don't come out? Then what? I charge in after you and get tasered immediately, thrown into the stocks?'

'You call all your police sources. You've said that the Met has what it needs to blow this case wide open and win it, you just wanted to be sure you weren't being played...'

Dominic laughs, suddenly, high and mad.

'You need to make it real if you're going to get away alive. I mean it, Marie. You could be walking straight into a setup. I'm reconsidering it even as I say this. We need backup, logistics, the whole nine yards ... You can't be walking into this meeting with just me and a fucking pen in my pocket.'

'No way,' I shout, whirling away back into the street as he tries to grab me. 'I'm nothing without blowing this wide open, and doing it right now. I'll die rather than not do it.'

'I'm not saying we don't,' he hisses, pulling on my arm. 'Just let me tell Olivia, plan it out properly, have a calm conversation with a tight group who can extract us if need be. It took weeks to perfect the trafficking undercover. Sure, I whined my head off, but do you think I wanted to get nailed to a chair with no recourse? You want to take on a state-sponsored coverup controlled by powerful people who want your silence above all else, just with me shivering behind the fucking door?'

'We don't have time, Dom, don't you see? Every minute that ticks by is another minute they could spend discrediting anything I could possibly do or say against them. They've already frozen all my accounts – suddenly I haven't got a penny to my name. It will be my flat next. They know I know about Kayleigh now...'

Again just saying her name blocks the rest.

'So let me make it real then,' he says, falling in step beside me. 'You've got to make them believe you're still on side, that you're no risk to the operation. You have to give them dynamite. You can't make this up on the fly.'

'I can handle it,' I say, speeding up as we weave through the crowds, away from the station. 'There's nothing left that I don't know about this case, nothing I don't still feel inside my bones, watch replaying in the dark every time the lights go out—'

'Yes, there is.' I jerk as Dominic grabs my bad elbow. 'Let me remind you of what you've said yourself. Versions of the truth are leaking all over the place, and it turns out you didn't know the half of it. The press conference proves that. The Met sprung it on everyone so it could control the narrative. It's been deliberately planned and orchestrated – how do you think I got a copy of a photo? I won't be the only one with it either.'

I freeze, pain radiating up my arm. He's right, of course he is. And I don't have the source Perseus and his mates are looking for,

I've got nothing to tell them they don't already know. In all our feverish conversation, Dominic hasn't once let it slip.

'Why should I trust you about things I know better than I know myself?'

'Because I know what it is to hide, Marie. I know what it is to bury parts of yourself so deep you think you'll never have to confront them, only to find them worming out no matter what—'

'No, you don't. You can't possibly—'

'Ask my ex-wife, then. Or that pathetic excuse for a man she's now chosen to live with. You could even try my son. How about that? When he's old enough to talk all he'll parrot is how Daddy is a filthy, deviant homosexual—'

'You're gay? As if that could possibly be a dirty little secret in this day and age. Are you honestly trying to compare—?'

'There is no world in which I would ever equate hurting the people you love the most by accepting an inescapable fact about your soul with exploitative, criminal behaviour of the most horrific kind.'

In the nanosecond our eyes meet I see the shadows of years of confusion and hurt before he can continue.

'But even now, in this allegedly progressive and accepting society of ours, I can't talk openly at work – not that everyone doesn't know, or even care particularly. I still have to do my job in places where the best outcome men who love other men can hope for is being thrown off a building. There are still far more people walking up and down on this pavement, right here and right now, who if asked, would say I should be stoned to death, rather than welcome me with open arms as I edge out of the fucking closet. What I'm saying, Marie, is that I know what it is to hide. I know what it does to your insides. We don't have to have been through identical circumstances to have empathy for each other – there are certain emotions that are universal. I know what it is to live in terror of accepting every last bit of yourself, and feeling that the only person from whom you could possibly expect unconditional love is dead, or as good as. But what I also know, from bitter experience, is the only way out of it is to learn how to trust again.'

I turn, looking at him like we're the only two people in the street, in the world, as if the crowds churning around us are just invisible currents of air.

'So who is it?' I watch his face contract as he licks his lips.

'You have to promise—'

'I'm not promising anything.'

'You have to promise to use it, Marie. Or else this ends here. I'm not telling you, and you're on your own. I mean it.' He bears down on me. 'It will be the first and only time I ever betray a source. And I'm doing it to save your life. That's the only reason I'd ever do it. Be under no illusions about how high this goes. I need to know you understand me.'

'Who is it?' The faintest edge of street noise laps at me, in, out, in, out.

'Do you understand? Promise me, Marie. No story is worth dying for.'

'It's not a story!' I screech, crowds scattering as my hands fly above my head. 'It's my life. It was hers! So many of ours. They stole everything in the name of duty, as if it was a sacrifice we were bound to make. That we should feel honoured having served, like them. This is all I've got left. And to think not everyone paid for it.' I retch and gag as the vomit rises again.

'Marie...' Suddenly Dominic is close, close as the breath I'm panting into my neck. 'You can't do this if you lose control now.'

'Just tell me,' I spit. 'Tell me.' I look up at him, eyes the blue heart of a flame, the same as hers, all I can ever see.

Time slows, sounds of the world still turning, glancing off us like we're suspended in a bubble about to pop. And then his voice, a whisper on the wind, so quiet, I hold my breath.

'It's Jaqlin, Marie. It's Jaqlin herself. She says she was one of the officers involved in the protection programmes for the witnesses in the original trial – a deep-cover operation. It's equivalent to treason to blow those identities, we've got the Official Secrets Act to thank for that. Once she became commissioner, she became one of only a handful of people with access to classified testimony that never passed trial – the Baby Girl A photos. And that's when she decided to go after it. The commissioner's my source. Olivia was right about it being her personal Everest. She's staking her life on it too. That's how I know this is real. Because you – you must be one of those she protected. And I had no way of knowing she was legit till...'

And just like that, the bubble pops, the final piece clicks, the world turns again, smoothly and relentlessly, just as it should. Her name was never Shacklin, just close enough to her real name that she'd remember it, make it feel natural. How could I ever have thought I'd known who any of them really were? It's your middle name, Julie said, right back at the start. *You'll remember it, it'll feel natural. It has to feel natural.*

I bang my head with my hands as Kayleigh screams and screams, rolling again and again in the dirt on the floor of our filthy room, foam at her mouth, blood rings round her eyes. The Scottish accent, the pencil-fine glasses. She's on the right side. Maybe she even knew I was there, in the room, when she told everyone she was reopening the investigation, because new information had come to light. She hadn't known until she was made commissioner. It's her score to settle, too.

'Marie? Marie!' Dominic shakes me. My eyes blurry, unfocused. 'You've got to tell them. They'll panic. They know she's powerful enough to blow it. Someone fucked up along the line when she was promoted, took their eye off the ball. That's why they've started to tap you so much recently. They're panicking. She's only been in post for a few months. They'll have known the leaks were real. It's not all on you ... Steady, that's it...'

I let him guide me over the kerb, to the edge of the street.

'So let's go over it, OK?' He props me upright between his hands. 'You name the source. That's all you need to make sure you do. We'll have to bet everything on the microphone in that handset. Give it some preamble so we've got enough on tape that they can't hide from. It doesn't mean we'll name her in the reporting, but it will get them to spill enough for admissible proof. And she's well protected. She's got her whole police force...'

'...who are worth shit, right?' My voice comes from nowhere as I look up at him.

'I guess I'll always find that part hard to take,' he mumbles as his head drops. 'But she's iron-clad. We know that now. You're only ever as good as your sources. And you're the real insider, the real source. You're the only one that knows everything ... But we can only prove it together.'

I fumble for my phone, checking its battery. Suddenly we're moving quickly again, light-footed, nimble.

'Test it,' he whispers as I switch on the microphone, edging closer to a couple arguing as they wait for a cab a few paces down the kerb. A minute later, audio of a tedious domestic crackles into my ear.

'We're on,' I mutter, frowning as I tuck away the phone. 'Unless Jemima keeps calling me while I'm doing it, that is.'

'Jonas,' he says suddenly, straightening and looking out into the road. 'Jonas...'

'You'll have to keep messaging her,' I say, tucking my phone back into my pocket. 'Let her know what's going on. I can't afford to tie up this line. If she or anyone tries to call while I'm recording ... These microphones aren't exactly high-tech.'

'Jonas,' he says again, staring into space.

'Let's go,' I say, waving for a taxi. 'Come on, Dom, seriously. We need to move.' I open the door before the cab's fully stopped, only aware he's following when he clambers in behind me.

'St James's Park,' I shout, closing the glass grille on the cabbie's nod as I turn back to Dominic. 'Are you getting hold of Jemima or what?'

'Leave her with me, OK?'

I search his face as the cab pulls away into the traffic, silence hanging between us. There's nothing left to say. I can almost hear our heartbeats thrumming round the car, like a set of drums finally in time with everything else.

Marie ~ Deptford ~ 2004

'You should apply,' Laurie barks, sending the pile of files balanced on the corner of his desk on to the floor as he slaps a sheaf of paper in front of me. I kneel down to tidy them up. My habit of doing whatever needs doing round here is so ingrained I don't know how not to do it, even after almost two years of proving myself to be more than just useful.

The *Gazette* is all that rolls me through every sleepless night. No sooner has a long day become a week than it's become another month of moving forward, building a new life from the pieces of other people's stories instead of my own. My name is in every edition, embedded in practically every story the paper can find. It's how I've made it my real name.

'Marie, I didn't call you in here for a fucking spring clean. Do you think I regularly get faxes from national news networks soliciting bright and shiny young things? Someone up top must have got seriously stuck into the good stuff.'

I pile a few files into a neat stack on the floor before sitting back down opposite him. The tiny office is so full it's almost caving in on itself, but the messier it is, the more comfortable Laurie seems. Feet on the desk, he leans back in his chair, nudging the files against the wall behind him as if he's daring them to fall over.

'I ask you, Marie, why not? I wouldn't have been able to get rid of you even if I put a security guard on the door, but months of begging later you've gone all coy?'

I glance at the fax in front of me, *Nine News* logo stamped red in the top corner.

'Years,' I mutter, reading off the top line: *To whom it may concern...*

'Eh? Days, months, years ... who cares? Opportunity knocks, Marie. Don't tell me you want to lock the door.'

'I don't know,' I mumble, fingering the papers. 'I like it here.'

'Oh, come on,' he interrupts, swinging his feet out of the way so he can plant his elbows on the desk instead. 'Really? You can't win if you don't play, Marie. Don't prepare, begin! You know that. It's an internship at a national news network ... our state broadcaster, no less. Hundreds of yuppies will apply, stuffed penguins in suits with trust funds so high up their backsides they can't walk straight. In fact, that might explain why they are faxing all the local press. There must be something in it. Or maybe they have finally got tired of plums in everyone's mouths.'

I shiver reflexively. Plums in their mouths?

'Think about it. If you had a mouthful of plums you would sound like them too...'

I start, and stare back at him, craggy face faded and yellow in the windowless lamplight like old newspaper. I didn't think I'd said anything.

'Fine, I'll apply. But only if you read this.' I nudge the papers in my hand over the fax on the desk.

Laurie grabs them even as he glares at me. 'What the hell is it?'

'They're reopening the Damilola Taylor investigation—'

'And you think you're the first to tell me?'

'No, I—'

'Shut up for a minute, will you?'

I bite back the start of a smile as he reads the page in front of him. I knew I just had to get him to the headline. It turns out there were blood spots all over the two thugs the police arrested at the time and then released without charge only days later. Blood spots so large that even now they can be seen with the naked eye. Vital scientific data that didn't even need a microscope to pick it up. It's reappeared as if by magic.

'You wrote this? All of it?' The page droops from his fingers, Laurie looking at me like I've just smacked him in the face with it.

'Well, it sounds more like a coverup than new forensic evidence to me.'

I jump as he laughs, hooting and cackling like a mad parrot.

'Jesus wept, girl. And you wonder why we're having this conversation ... Just go and apply for the damn internship, would you? You've got a portfolio a yard long. Far be it from me to suggest Damilola's murder was anything other than horrendous, but it certainly did you a favour.'

I shiver again, Jemima's voice chiming in my head. *Right place, right time.* I've spent so long finding myself in the wrong place it's hard to ever believe there is a right one. But that's Carly, I remind myself. Marie's been in the right place the whole time. She climbed up and out of the supermarket and into the *Deptford Gazette* with no help at all.

'Have you already got someone writing all this up? Can I work with them? Please?'

'No, you can't,' he says, another shower of paper falling behind him as he suddenly stands. 'You, my girl, are finally being let off the leash.'

'Where?' I say, clutching the fax as I follow him, skipping at the words 'off the leash'.

'That lazy, not to mention useless, excuse for a court reporter that I must have hired while under the influence of, oh, I don't fucking know what, appears to be in the throes of one hangover too many and has not shown up for at least the zillionth time in his career.'

'I'm going to court? Which one? Really?' I practically have to jog to keep up as Laurie wheels round the corner to the kitchen, reaching for my coat hung on the back of the door.

'You do know you don't have to keep this in here anymore?'

'I never know where I'll be sitting, do I?' I shrug it on, crumpling the fax into my pocket.

'I need you at the Old Bailey. They're tying up some fag-end on Operation Andromeda. A back-door event, but still...'

I brace myself in the doorframe, other hand tightening round the paper in my fist. I can see Laurie's still talking but I can't hear a word. All the wallpaper in my head, gluey and thick, may as well have been painted in watercolour, washing away in great blurry tides so Carly's grey face is all I can see. Laurie's raging now as he stalks out, hands waving in the air as he yells. I summon the towers, trying to cover every inch of her with billowing clouds of ash and smoke.

'...we have to cover whenever somebody so much as farts on Andromeda, don't we? You've got to act big to dream big ... no point behaving like a local paper if you're making a play to be regional, I told him. If they want me to expand across London then we have to scrap with the big dogs ... and do I really have to justify covering every inch of one of the biggest inquiries of the bloody century? Anyway. Have you got all that? You're sure you know what you're doing?'

I move my head into a nod before stumbling backward into the kitchen, pulling the door shut behind me just in time to retch into the sink, an uncontrollable scream straight from the pit of my stomach. Marie can handle this, I tell myself as the tap gushes, roaring over the cries inside my ears. This is her life now. She's a journalist, she did that all by herself. She knew Andromeda might come up at some point, even if she didn't want to admit it to herself. So she stacked shelves by night and ran paper by day, every week laying a new round of wallpaper, every crack filled diamond-tight. Marie's the one who found herself a place where there's always someone awake, working on something diverting, better still, something that might even move the needle one way or the other. She found somewhere where there are always other pots about to boil over. She did that. Marie did that.

I release the paper in my fist as I wipe my mouth. And then it hits me, as I smooth out the fax, all crinkled and stained, on the counter top next to the sink. It's been there all the time. I just didn't see it, or didn't compute it. There, along the bottom, is

Jemima Jonas, Nine News – signature loopy and curly with Ms and Js.

She's found me, I think, her name warping and blurring into a helix as a tear rolls off my nose. I think somehow I always knew she would, when I was ready. I don't even notice the brand-new mobile phone suddenly buzzing like a demented fly caught in my pocket.

Marie ~ London ~ 2006

I curse under my breath as we pull up by St James's Park. Dominic murmurs back at me.

'Tourists,' I mutter, eyes running over the meandering crowds. 'Damn the unseasonable fucking weather.'

'Don't think about it,' he replies as we get out of the cab, door slamming on the jangle of change in the tray. 'Look straight past them. Just focus on making your meeting. If you feel the phone vibrate once you're together, then that's your cue. It'll be the only call you get.'

'How can you possibly be sure of that? Jemima hasn't stopped calling since—'

'Since when? Not since we got into that cab she hasn't.'

The gate clangs as we slip into the park. I force myself to move ahead without a backward glance, one last check on the phone recording in my top pocket. We've run down the clock. The time left is for doing, not thinking. The lake shimmers in the distance, soaking in after-the-rain sun as I quickstep my way to the fountain, runners, idlers, travellers weaving like sprites in and out of my peripheral vision. Round the lake, fountain spray needle-sharp, fallen leaves like glass breaking under my feet. And then...

'Excuse me, Miss.' A hand pinches my elbow, too close to the injured spot not to have known. 'Have you seen a little girl playing alone anywhere near here? I've lost my daughter, Kayleigh...'

I jerk to a stop, paralysed with pain.

'Now move,' comes the order, his bulk butting up against me.

I crumple into the hand at my arm as I realise it's the barrel of a pistol, not another finger, that's digging into my ribs. We march as one along the path towards the giant willow tree, lit lush and extravagant by the glare of the sun. Anyone watching would think we were a couple locked in embrace, hip-to-hip. I dare not twist even a millimetre to look for Dominic.

'Who are you?' I pant as I walk, the gun bruising as it prods. Willow rustles across my face as we duck between the boughs. There's a sudden release as he drops my arm and turns, blank face and forgettable hair meaningless to anyone but me. I freeze, eyeing his hands in his pockets, one bulging with pistol, and take a deep, juddering breath. *It's now, Marie. Now! Don't prepare. Begin!*

'I asked you a question. Who are you?'

'Perseus,' he whispers, thin line of lips hardly moving, a swish between the boughs. Nothing else moves, not even the fronds draped around us.

'And me?'

'You're Medusa, of course.' His tone, suddenly bird-song light. 'The gorgon with her eyes of stone, her crown of snakes.'

I step towards him, straightening up. My phone lies idle but listening, just left of bullseye.

'I've got what you need,' I say, eyes running over his empty face, white, expressionless. 'But I want something from you.'

Shadow falls over me as he steps forward. I have to purse my lips to stop even a hint of anticipation in my expression. He's so close we'll be able to hear his breathing on tape. And finally his face starts to animate, the notion I could possibly try to threaten him too much to take.

'You owe us, sunshine,' he spits. 'Not the other way around. Did you forget how you made it so big in the first place?'

'I want my ID papers back, and I want them now. If you show me proof you've reset everything, unfrozen my bank accounts, the whole lot, then I'll tell you everything you need to know to bury this.'

My gaze flicks to his pocket. I don't believe it's just a fist making it bulge. I jump as he pulls out a small, two-way radio.

'Perseus,' he mutters into it, eyes not leaving mine. 'Contact made.'

'Papers,' I say, forcing myself to hold his stare. Dominic's close, I tell myself. Just two more minutes. That's all we need. And then it will be over.

'Copy,' he says to the radio, before returning it to his pocket. The seconds tick past in a rustle of willow.

'Pass me your phone and I'll give you proof,' he says. My heart starts to hammer so hard I think it might fall out of my pocket on its own.

'How's my phone going to prove anything?' I lick my lips as I stammer.

'You wanted proof. How else do you expect me to show you we've unfrozen your bank accounts under a willow tree?'

I stare back at him, one eyelid twitching more than the other.

'Like I have one of those fancy internet phones,' I gabble, trying to sound like panic isn't chasing blood out of my veins. 'I don't work at the ministry, remember?'

'Shut up!'

Air leaves my lungs as his hand closes round my throat, face so close I can see the hairs inside his nostrils, aggression seeping from every pore. My vision starts to darken, closing at the edges as I dangle from his hand, small vein pulsing at his temple until ... Thud. I buckle and cough as he drops me.

'They were right about you,' he hisses, rigid metal so taut against his pocket it's unmistakable. 'No regard for protocol. Abject in-discipline...' A glob of spit hits my hand as he hawks into my face. 'Now don't tempt me, Medusa. Indiscipline never goes unpun-ished where I come from, much less where you came from. Your papers will be the least of it if you don't give up your source, and give it up right now. I have my orders.' He taps a finger on his pocket. 'And indiscipline has never been a problem of mine.'

I struggle to my feet. *Stay close, Marie. You've got to stay close.* I smooth down the front of my coat as I straighten, mucus sticky on my hand, my phone lumpen above my heart. I step even closer as I say it.

'It's Jaqlin. It's the commissioner herself. Nine have got to her. And she's coming for you.'

A sharp intake of breath; a gasp so sharp the tape can't fail.

'You heard me,' I say, emboldened. 'And you know what comes next. Protocol's protocol, isn't it?'

His lip curls as he glares down at me, the real gorgon if ever I saw one.

'Hermes,' he hisses after a moment. 'You will say nothing without Hermes, you insubordinate little cunt. You'll get word. And you know to wait for it.'

And with another hawk, glancing off my cheek, he disappears through the willow, sun dazzling me blind as the boughs part.

Marie ~ London ~ 2005

'Who's she?' Dominic doesn't even look at me as he asks, he just stares at Jemima. Dominic Greene, home affairs editor, Nine News's bright and shiny new prospect, according to Laurie. A man on a mission to hold the Metropolitan police to account, with a couple of exclusives already in hand to prove it. Sure, he's been shooting into an open goal after the London bombings, but where television talent is concerned you can't have everything, apparently. If there's a functioning brain on top of looking good ... I shove away thoughts of the *Gazette* and its mess of broken desks, columns of yellow newspapers, chunky old computer monitors. If I can get comfortable there, then I can get comfortable here. The open-plan newsroom with its endless lines of workstations feels so wide around us that we could even be outside. I can't even see the walls at either end.

'This is Marie,' Jemima says again, turning to me with an encouraging smirk. 'And how have you enjoyed your internship so far? What have you been working on?'

I blink at her, jumping as someone barges past in a hurry. She knows exactly what I've been doing since I got here. There's been no opportunity to work on anything but the London attacks and their aftermath until now. She brought me in, did the interview and has been in charge of me ever since.'

'Golly, an intern?' Dominic barely throws me a second look as he brushes down a perfectly suited arm.

'I've really gone up in the world, haven't I? An intern instead of an actual qualified journalist with experience. Albeit an intern your producer has staked her reputation on. Sorry – Marie, is it?

Jonas here seems to think we are in need of someone to wipe our arses for us when, in fact, what I need is voluminous amounts of grunt work, and fast ... not to mention discreet—'

'What are you working on?' His eyes widen as I interrupt him. Here comes Laurie again. *Telly's nothing compared to print. Fairies, the lot of them. Half the time it's just about what they look like. Putting themselves in the frame. Oh, don't look at me like that just because I have a face for radio...*

'This is proper investigative work,' he snaps. 'Details don't come cheap ... Now, don't tell me, you studied detective work in journalism school? After getting a first at Cambridge, presumably? And you speak five languages? None of which are plain English?'

Jemima socks him, rolling her eyes at me. I flinch as someone else pushes past.

'I'm sorry about him. It'll pass, I can assure you. He's usually quite charming.'

'I studied grunt work, actually,' I say, staring straight at him. 'With a bit of discretion on the side. Hand it over.'

His eyes narrow as he stares back. Rangy and tall, salt-and-pepper hair aging him well past his baby face, he's too filled-out to be junkie-thin-reliable. But I don't have to trust him if Jemima's here too.

'Funny,' he drawls after a snort, turning back to her. 'So this is your grand plan for trawling the dark net? We simply exploit the unpaid assets? All our actual news producers – apart from your good self, that is – too knackered after our summer of terror attacks?'

I catch my breath.

'Funny yourself,' Jemima says, glaring at him. 'Those underground online chatrooms, my friend, are your preserve. Neither Marie nor I are going anywhere close to those deviant hubs until the groundwork is done and we're good and ready for undercover. But unless you want to spend the next month inside the Home Office's online data portal, pulling together human trafficking trends, locations and routes, past arrests, demographics—'

'OK, OK, OK, OK...' He holds up his hands to cut her off. 'Blind me with drudgery, why don't you—'

'I studied that as well,' I interrupt, even though I've never so much as heard of an online data portal. Portal? *Pen and paper, Marie. Good old-fashioned door-knocking. Nothing is worth the screen it's typed on the internet...*

'I'm surrounded by the funny today, apparently...' Dominic's expression freezes as he looks between us. 'Fine, then. Whatever you want, Jonas. Since this is a long-term project. And if it is just for statistics...'

'So tell us what you need,' Jemima says smoothly, throwing me a sidelong grin.

'Numbers,' he replies after a moment, brushing the other perfect arm. 'Details of all past and current police operations on human trafficking. Someone needs to interpret the graphs, figure out where the weak points are, where we might be able to find an in.'

'There are tonnes of reports.' Jemima turns to me. 'Some of them are thick as books. There are massive amounts of data available – the Met has to make it all a matter of public record. You need to go through every line, every page. They always bury the detail that matters. Identify the most common trafficking routes, locate the countries where the law is flimsy enough for trafficking kingpins to bypass without raising eyebrows. We're interested in where there could be a business at work, the industrial-level stuff.'

'Of what?' The question is out before I can stop it.

Dominic snorts, before stalking off, shoving his perfect hands into his perfect pockets. I stare after him as Jemima rounds on me.

'Do you want this internship to really count? I can't carry you, Marie. It's not enough to have just jumped in over the London bombings and got your hands as dirty as possible. That is absolute base-level stuff – massive breaking news story, all hands to the pump, learn on the job and if you fuck it up, you're out. That's where the bar is in places like this. But now I am handing you an in with a reporter at editor level, putting a proper research project directly into your hands, and you've stopped nodding and smiling before you've even started?'

'I don't understand,' I murmur, squinting into the distance after Dominic. The newsroom throbs around us, everyone trying to be the loudest in their corner.

'You can't shy away from the hard stuff. Just say yes, whatever, whenever, and then get it done, pronto. Don't ask questions! You'll have to find the answers yourself if you want to be taken seriously. He said human trafficking, didn't he? Do you need me to show you a picture? You should never need to be told twice...'

'Why would anyone go to the trouble of trafficking people across borders?' I know I'm asking myself, even though she thinks I'm asking her.

'I told you, no questions,' she hisses, buttoning up her jacket. 'Not even to me. Just make yourself useful, get it done, figure out what else needs doing, and then do that. No one's got time around here for questions that don't lead anywhere.'

She stalks off into the hum as I slide into a cubicle at the end of the news desk, adrenaline coursing as I fire up the computer. Like I will ever shy away from the hard stuff. It's all I live for. I just don't understand why anyone would bother trafficking people from hundreds of miles away. I guess it's what happens when you can't see past what's going on just past your nose.

I think about her, just for a second, just to test myself, conjuring her face, her toys, her smile, even her laugh. These girls' stories are different enough to mine, I don't need to read them to know that. But they haven't figured on someone like me coming for them, have they?

I smile as the computer flashes, like it's smiling right back at me. And then I swallow the acid and get to work.

Marie ~ London ~ 2006

The light refracts off the floor-length windows that form two of the four walls of Olivia's office, so bright that if I could just angle one of the panes a fraction, I could burn the point of a dart into the leather of her chair. Beyond the glass, the City of London shimmers in the late-afternoon sun, its hundreds of tall, glass-fronted buildings trembling with their multiple reflections of each other, shifting and changing with every frond of cloud that drifts across the sky, no thought to what its shadow does to the shapes below. There's so much glass in this part of London that every window's a mirror, except it's almost impossible to ever see clearly. Olivia's rasp brings me back into the room, a crucible of light between all these versions of truth reflected back at me.

'I don't understand,' she says, all bouncy hair as she shakes her head. 'She's an intern, Dominic, isn't she?'

'I'm an assistant producer,' I say, as much to myself as anyone else. This is where it ends, I think, shading my eyes. If my screams are keen enough, sharp enough, I can shatter the whole lot, all the glass, all the buildings, all the towers of lies built up around me, around all of us. And it will be Marie, not Carly, who emerges from the rubble.

'You just need to listen to the tape, Liv,' Dominic says, placing my phone reverently on the desk in front of her. 'It's the last piece of the puzzle. It's all we need.'

'Oh, for goodness sake settle down, Dom,' she barks, a billow of fabric and perfume. 'I know you're desperate for a breakthrough on Andromeda but this is the stuff of fantasy—'

She jumps as Dominic bangs his hands on the desk.

'She's in danger, Liv. Genuine danger. And we're sitting on an atom bomb of a story, which, by rights, should never have been out of the public domain. All this time we've been equating national interest with the public interest when in fact, it's anything but. She never even knew that captain was her dad. It's only because of our leak that she's put the pieces together.'

Memories scud through my mind like a kaleidoscope, whirling into a mosaic of broken pieces, beautiful from one direction, horrifying from the other. *It was all a setup,* Rach groans into my ear. *He tapped Jase for you just to get to her...* I shake the kaleidoscope again, shards of reasoning and explanation flying into the air.

'You do that again and I'll call security. I mean it, Dominic.' Olivia's voice cuts through the air alongside another shaft of setting sun. 'Just sit down and start from the beginning. I want every source, every single source, every development. Marie, you too. Marie?'

She flops back in her chair in a jangle and huff of jewellery, daring us to follow her lead. We both stay standing, motionless, quieting the room. Even the sunlight feels like it's pausing on its way towards the windows.

It's finally time, I think. The last time I'll ever have to tell this story.

'My name is Carly Marie Gates,' I say, clear voice flooring the young Carly in my head. 'Carly Marie Gates. I had an older brother, who you'll know from the Andromeda case files as Sergeant Jason Gates. We had a baby sister ... half-sister. And her name was Kayleigh.'

I pause as Olivia's expression freezes, a painted doll propped in a chair.

'We grew up in Warchester, in army accommodation right next to the garrison. We never had much. That's how it all started. And I thought ... I thought it had ended after the first trial concluded. That's when I started living as Marie Grant. I was given full witness protection in exchange for my testimony.'

I shade my eyes as the sun sparks between the clouds.

'Everything I've told you about the *Deptford Gazette* was true – all my references: Laurie Scott, Andy Carbrook, they're all legitimate. All I've ever done is try to prove myself, to try and bury all this in the past, start again. When I got my first real news media job at the *Gazette*, that's when they started to tap me. It was always small stuff – little things really, just telling them what I knew of any new Andromeda investigations. It felt harmless compared to everything I'd gone through. Sometimes I didn't hear from them for months. I could really believe I'd left it all behind. But everything changed when I got my internship here.'

Dominic's seat wheezes as he collapses into it. I clear my throat.

'I have never fed you any false information. Nothing like that. But I've been under a lot of pressure to get on top of all potential reporting on Andromeda. I haven't ... I haven't felt like I've had any choice, really. I'm nothing without Marie Grant ... less than nothing. And they hold the keys to all that, all my identity papers, my bank accounts, even the lease on my flat. It would be so easy for them to make Marie's life impossible—'

'So what changed?' Olivia interrupts, hardly moving her lips. 'If this story is to be believed, why would you, out of the blue, decide it's worth risking your life as Marie Grant? If it's as simple as tricking the news media? After all, we're all as stupid as each other, aren't we?'

My words freeze in my throat as I blink light out of my eyes, squinting at her. She doesn't believe me. Of course she doesn't. No one ever does, until...

'This.' Dominic pushes his phone towards her.

I keep blinking. I don't have to look down to know what picture's flashing up on the screen. 'This is what changed everything. This is their new evidence. This is a photo of Minchin's pet. They call her Baby Girl A. She was Marie's ... she was Carly's half-sister. This is a photo of Kayleigh.'

I force myself to stare as hard as I can bear into the light beaming through the window, dark spots blocking everything else out.

'They … they all promised me she'd be taken care of, in exchange for my original testimony. That's the only reason I did it, that I turned … I thought I was saving her, as much as myself and all the others. Over the years it became harder and harder to visit her, as she started living her new life. She forgot who I was, didn't want to remember. Every time she saw me it … it turned everything sour, set her back too much. But then, when I saw Dominic show Jemima her picture—'

'Jemima,' Olivia interrupts again, glaring at Dominic as the phone drops out of her hand. 'Why isn't she here? She doesn't know about all this?'

'No,' he says, arm brushing mine as he stands again. 'She doesn't. Given the gravity of it all, I brought it straight to you. The less links in the chain, the better. And we don't have much time.' He's suddenly forceful, ready to fight again. I straighten with him.

'I went back to them once I'd seen it,' I say, before Olivia's had a chance to argue. 'A big part of me wanted to believe it couldn't be true, but deep down I think I already knew it was … I'd overheard so much of what Dominic and Jemima had already found out. Dominic told me that Baby Girl A's mother had previously been involved with the captain – Captain Robert Leigh Parish. That he'd been using other family members to get to her. And that's when I figured out that he must have been our dad too. Jason and I never knew him. He died – or at least, we were told he had – before I was born. And that's…'

'…when you decided enough was enough.' Olivia finishes my sentence for me, a small smile playing round her mouth. There's something in her tone that's off, something I can't quite work out. A cloud throws shadow across her eyes, just long enough for me to know I'm right. And then it comes.

'So tell me, then, Marie. What could possibly have been so rotten as to motivate Parish to groom his own flesh and blood?

Have either of you paused to consider this for longer than a micro-second?'

'Of course we have!' Dominic shouts, practically vibrating next to me. 'And don't tell me you aren't already there yourself. We hear it all the time – from every general on every battlefield, no matter whose side they're on. Humankind can plumb the depths of in-humanity in the name of intelligence. Are you honestly expecting a history lesson on what went on in Northern Ireland, for starters? Christ, the Allies had to let thousands upon thousands be mass-acred just so the Nazis never worked out they'd cracked Enigma!'

'And where's Kayleigh now?' Olivia's laser-gaze moves to me. 'Surely you must still have some connection with her? If it was only ever about her in the first place, and not just what would happen to you? You must have fought tooth and nail to maintain some level of contact with her?'

'I don't know...' Suddenly all I can manage is to whisper through the overwhelming pain in my throat. 'I ... I don't know. I haven't known for years ... She's gone. I used to wonder, some-times, if ... if she ever really existed, and that maybe my brain was just playing the ultimate trick, making me imagine everything I could have been but never was. But then ... then I saw Dominic's picture. It's from then. It's from ... it's from a time only I would remember. And I can't ... Please, Olivia. Please don't make me abandon her all over again.'

'Just listen to the tape,' Dominic interrupts, turning up the volume on my handset still quiet in front of her before anyone can say anything else. My voice crackles into the room.

'Who are you?'

'Perseus,' hisses the reply, faint but clear. The face, blank as all the others, reappears in my head, the crunch of frosty leaves under my feet, the bare tree branches of St James's Park traced across the clear sky like pencil drawings. The slap of cold air on my face, the needle-point mist of the fountain, my voice, controlled, deliberate. 'And me?'

'Medusa,' the tape says. 'The gorgon with her eyes of stone, her crown of snakes.'

Olivia leans closer, head moving back into the light, shadow falling across her back. Fizz of static, snap of leaves as we start to move. My ribs pinch as they remember. The carpet, alien underfoot, no leaves, no grass, no mist in this glass-fronted cell. Olivia is hunched over the handset, tensed, ready to pounce, except does she know what she's pouncing on? I mouth the words as I hear them again, ragged thrums off my collar. Papers, indiscipline, protocol. Jaqlin. Hermes. Evidence crescendos round the room until Dominic leans over to turn it off.

'Who was that?' She looks up at me, still hunched over her desk. I can barely see her.

'I don't know. I never know. They just text and I jump. I've always been given a password beforehand.'

'And that's Hermes? The new password?' She snorts, hair flying as she shakes her head.

'Right,' I say, horror spreading like ice water through my body. 'It's always something to do with...' I trail off. She knows where it comes from. We all do. By now we all know everything. I'm suddenly so angry I think I've gone blind.

'I know it's a lot to take in,' Dominic chimes in, words stroking at the edges of my white-hot fury. 'But this proves it; it proves it all. Our investigation is iron-clad. I've got two police sources handing me their nuclear new evidence against Minchin. A top-level source saying he was protected because of active intelligence ops – even now, they say it would compromise national security. We all know how worried everyone still is about Russian nukes. And here we have a mole, right in front of us, that corroborates the whole, sick, sorry business.'

There's a crash as the office door flies open, sending the plant next to it, so tall it should be in the ground rather than a pot, flying forward into the room. Through the haze and sunspots I can make out Jemima shrugging and pushing at Gabe behind her, trying to restrain her without actually touching her too much. I can feel Dominic's sigh next to me as much as I can hear it.

'Settle down, Gabe,' Olivia barks from behind her desk, folding her arms and crossing her legs, tying herself into a perfect knot. 'I asked Jemima to join us. You weren't to know. My fault.'

Gabe's eyebrows arch so high that they're the only thing I can see before Jemima slams the door in his face, glaring at Dominic as she stands beside us. I gulp, a sudden draft of air filling my lungs, soaking my body, sunspots giving way to stars and twinkles in my eyes. She's all we need, I think, seizing at more air, every cell in my body guzzling. Olivia trusts her far more than Dominic. We're almost there, so nearly there I can taste it with every fresh, delicious breath.

'Sorry I'm late,' Jemima says, straightening her jacket.

'Not to worry,' Olivia says, tightening her arms around herself. 'I only just realised you hadn't been included originally.'

The air in the room thickens, shafts of light like knifepoints between us.

'Now, Dominic,' she continues, 'could you fill Jemima in on this latest reporting?'

Out of the corner of my eye, I see Dominic lean forward, tapping at my phone on the desk, his movements syrupy, as if time has slowed down round us, as if just here, in this tiny glass box in the clouds, time is grinding to a halt, not to start again until it knows the way forward, the exact beat between every minute, every hour, every day ahead. Proof crackles out of the handset.

'I don't understand,' Jemima says after a moment. Shadow falls over my face as she moves in front of me. 'Was that you, Marie? Who were you talking to?'

'You know it was,' barks Olivia from behind her. 'You've always known, haven't you, Jemima?'

I shiver, suddenly cold in the shade. The ice water is back, a wash of fear as I stumble backward, crumpling into the chair behind me. And suddenly here's Olivia, standing at my elbow in a cloud of perfume, silk sleeves brushing at my cheek.

'What ... what do you mean?' Jemima stammers, reaching behind her to brace herself against Olivia's desk. 'I've got no idea what you're talking about ... Perseus? Medusa? What is this?'

'What was it you said – "hang on, let me be absolutely sure"?' Olivia's bracelets chink against my arm; cold, rigid steel. 'We'd had hundreds of applicants – with degrees, languages, apprentice-ships. You name it, they'd had it. But then along you came, didn't you, Jemima? Our fast-rising management star, with a ... ah yes, that was it, an "out-of-the box suggestion", you called it. Someone different, you said. Grass-roots experience, work ethic second to none. Also recommended by a government contact of yours that we really needed to keep sweet. I remember it, clear as day...'

I stop mid-breath, gripping the arms of my chair, mind barrel-ling backward. Suddenly it's 2.00 am, pitch-dark outside, neon light inside, cans of cold Red Bull spilling out of my arms in to a cold, tinny supermarket trolley. The towers, the falling people, the hijacked planes. And Jemima. That's where I met her. I know it, clearer than I know my real name. That's where I met her.

'Help me, Dom,' Jemima gasps, eyes darting between us, huge and dark. 'What is that audio? What is all this?'

'She's Parish's daughter,' Dominic says, voice floating into the supermarket in my head, future and past colliding under the strip lights. 'Marie – she's the missing link in the chain. Baby Girl A ... she's her sister, Jonas. Her baby sister. She went into witness pro-tection after the first trial and once she got into the media, it was back-hander after back-hander, every time, a threat to blow her papers. She didn't know her sister had been abused, until now. Until we showed her...'

There's something in his tone I've heard somewhere before – it was with Beata, coaxing out her story, every last little drop, no matter how harsh.

'And you know that too, don't you, Jemima?'

I screw my eyes shut as Olivia's voice chimes into the overnight aisles, strip lights flickering on and off as Jemima frowns down at me. Can I borrow your trolley, she'd asked. Please? We've got a newsroom to keep going all night, she'd said. Hadn't she?

'You know, because you helped plant her here, didn't you?'

And in that moment, it is as if we're suspended in those few nanoseconds before a massive explosion, as if the bomb is taking its last deep breath before bursting, sucking all the air out of the space around it before it re-emerges as dust, as tiny shattered particles of everything it once was. I touch my face – one side, then the other. I'm still here, but am I? Jemima? I open my eyes.

'I didn't know...' she says, slumped now on the desk behind her, a paper cut-out of her former self. 'Of course I didn't ... I had no idea she was anything to do with Andromeda. They just told me—'

'Ah, but they told you, didn't they!' I jump as Dominic shouts next to me. 'Someone told you to hire her, right? Someone from state, someone from Defence or Home – and that's how you ended up as Miss Uber Producer, isn't it? All the contacts, all the connections, everything you needed to bag the story when it counted the most. You took a bung. You took a fucking bung.'

His chair crashes over in front of me, but I hear nothing. Nothing except my ragged breathing – in, out, in, out, little gasps, memories whirling in a cloud in front of me. Victory Field at midnight. Jason. Kayleigh. The ambulance, the hospital. The hostel, the supermarket.

'Security, please,' Olivia says, somewhere over my head. 'Ask them to send up two guards, if you don't mind. Thanks Gabe. No, everything's fine, don't worry...'

'I didn't know...' Jemima says again, pleading. 'Please, Liv. Do you think I'd have consented to bringing her in if I'd known? I just ... We've all done favours, haven't we? I thought the contacts would be good for business, and her references checked out. Scott said she was the best apprentice he'd ever had.'

Laurie. I propel myself upright, shaking, wincing as his shouts echo in my ears. 'Fuck me six ways to sundown,' he'd yelled, charging out of his office. 'You fucking got it, Marie. A *Deptford Gazette* apprentice. At Nine News. You've got friends in high places. Put that in your pipe and smoke it, why don't you?' My hand clenches as it remembers, ink-fresh fax rustling crisp between my fingers, a first-class ticket to another life.

'Did he know?' My voice drifts, alien and faraway. 'Did Laurie know?'

'No,' Jemima says, looking at me for the first time since she heard the tape. 'He didn't. I just called him because he was your referee. I checked everything.'

She turns to Olivia, still billowing fabric next to me. In that moment I just wish I could lie down in her clouds of perfumed silk, watch them ripple in curls of gleaming colour.

'Please, Liv. Please. I would never have colluded in something as big as this. I didn't know. You've got to believe me.'

Olivia's suddenly at my eye level, squatting down, cupping my face with a soft hand.

'How are you doing, Marie? Is it OK if I call you that?'

I stare at her, huge amber eyes, smudged sparkly shadow.

'I'm sorry I didn't believe you ... and I hope, in time, you'll understand why I have to question every last corner of this appalling tale. So many failed children ... I'm so, so sorry. You poor, poor soul. What an unconscionable mess this is. An unconscionable, unforgivable mess – a stain on the soul of our nation. We're going to do right by these victims, I can promise you that. We're going to do right by you. And by your sister.'

I lean into her hand. I feel like I might drown, even though there's no water, just waves of emotion surging over my head. She stays like that, crouched in her silken folds, even as the door opens somewhere behind us and two security guards clatter into the room, slamming the door behind them.

'Miss Guy ... we got an urgent call. Is everything alright up here?'

I slump further into her hand as she glances over my head.

'Thanks for coming up so fast,' she says, almost purring. 'I'll explain more fully in just a moment, but for now could you please stay with Miss Jonas at all times, while I sort something out?'

'Is she OK?' A boot strays into the corner of my eye, shadow falling over us as one of the guards steps towards me.

'She's going to be fine,' Dominic says, resting a hand on my shoulder. 'I got this, Liv, if you want to sort out Jonas.' I crumple as she stands, rapid-fire instructions ricocheting over my head, doors opening, keys jangling, phones ringing, a sudden cacophony of noise, the post-explosion roar of activity.

'Did you know too?' I murmur, laying my head on my knees. 'About Jemima?'

'Huh?' He crouches, hand still on my shoulder.

'Did you...?' I pause as my air runs out, gasping. Sometime over the last few minutes I've forgotten how to breathe.

'Calm down, girl. In, out, in, out, that's it. Nearly there...'

I sit up, just as Jemima is escorted into Olivia's private conference room, landline unplugged, mobile phone and computer confiscated.

'But what will happen to her?'

'She'll get fired, obviously.' Dominic brushes his shirt rather than look at me. 'She won't have known who you were. She's telling the truth about that. Liv knows that too. Someone in Jonas's position should know to have asked more questions, even if she liked the early answers. Olivia's got no choice other than to cut her off. They'll use everything against us when we break this. It's going to be hard enough to distance ourselves from the fact that Jonas opened the door in the first place – whoever her contact was, or still is, probably had plenty to do with the whole sick lot in the first place.'

'Did you—?'

'No,' he interrupts. 'Of course not. I couldn't have picked you out of a line-up before our trafficking investigation. But I knew this morning, on the train. When you told me who you really were. Because Jonas had told me, after she'd brought you on for trafficking, how you had come to her attention. The *Deptford Gazette* thing never smelled right to me. That's why I've left her out of the loop since we came back from Warchester. I had to be sure of what I suspected.'

I know even before I blink that tears are flooding down my cheeks. The idea that my job, Marie's job, the very core of her existence, is even a fraction less than all my own work is too much to bear. I built Marie, not them. It was me. All me.

'Jonas'll be OK,' he mutters, still fiddling with his shirt. 'There's worse corruption out there. And she's tough, with a ton of relevant experience. She was played though, good and hard. And she'll have to own that. There is no way Liv could keep her here once we go full bore with this, no way. It'll be one of their first comebacks, that we were part of the whole stitch-up.'

'You mean...' My hands fly to my face.

'Steady on,' he says, gripping both my shoulders. 'Breathe, come on. In, out, in, out ... That's better. And no, I don't mean anything. This is the bit where we win, Marie. We do. All that idealistic shit they pump you with at journalism school – bearing witness, giving voice to the voiceless, holding the powerful to account – it's actually true, believe it or not, even if it does make you feel like a total wanker when you say it out loud to anyone with half a brain cell. Sometimes it really does work: you tell the terrible stories, and someone has to do something about them. Like trafficking. Do you think we ask women like Beata to prostitute their experience just for our network's sake? This is what we do, at our best. And it's why people like us do it. It amplifies us. It literally brings us back to life, too.'

His eyes, suddenly on mine, flash almost as bright as the last merciless rays of sun firing over the rooftops in the west.

'Right then,' says Olivia, all swish and tinkle as she arrives next to us. 'Shall we get to work? It's just the small matter of blowing open the biggest known conspiracy in UK history and probably sinking senior members of government, after all. Shouldn't take too long, eh?'

She gazes down at me, eyes like honey.

'And I haven't forgotten about our other little girl, either. We're damn well going to air our trafficking story in short order too, I can promise you that. But for now, tell me, Marie, are you ready for this? We'll be with you all the way, don't you worry.'

And as I nod, Carly's gone, taking the third shadow with her, all violet-pink wisps drifting, warping and disappearing into the last rays of setting sun.

Marie ~ London ~ Six months later

There is a girl. She's sitting, wedged high in the public gallery, short, dark hair smoothed sleek as a cap on her head. Technically, the case should have been heard in Warchester, where the offences were committed. But only the Old Bailey, with her statue of Justice and sword of retribution brandished high over the heart of historic London, was deemed fit for the trial of the twenty-first century. The honeyed-oak panelling of Court One is varnished against offences of the worst kind: the Yorkshire Ripper, the Kray Twins, the Soham murders. A centuries-old patina that can stand up to this particular case.

Elbows prod and coat-tails flick as dozens of other spectators jostle and gesture around her, but she stays calm; serene, even. Even though the world knows her true story now, only a few could put a face to her real name. And so the crowd is curiously comforting, its collective outrage a warm blanket. Today, there's no other place she could possibly be.

It's the last day of the trial. Closing speeches, so she knows she'll hear what everyone said all over again. She knows it will still be a version of the facts, each lawyer will sum up the evidence according to their argument, fixed on winning their own case rather than telling the truth. But international pressure has finally come to bear. Even the partial suggestion that the pressure of a global intelligence operation might explain depravity of the worst kind has crumbled faster than the aftermath of an explosion. Whatever version of the facts the defence comes up with, nothing will suffice other than total condemnation. And the media have united, all competitive differences suspended like

dust in the air. Those divisions will return, of course – all's fair in love and ratings, except during a collective attack on their soul. A brazen attempt to manipulate the facts from within.

Objectivity is sacred. Truth is sacred. And together, they know their voice will be the loudest. They're the ones with the microphone, after all.

The court stills as the defendant enters the dock. She stiffens against the murmur of anticipation, letting her eyes travel over the hunch of age in the once army-straight back, the defeated slump in what were square shoulders, the contours of the balding head bowed to the floor. The once-untouchable General Gillard Minchin, finally as diminished and trembling as the shadows in her head. The once-proud birthmark, his physical stamp of the United Kingdom, now wrinkled and shrunken as history. The red robes of the justice on the bench are as vivid and sharp as the truth. And so to the prosecution QC, fingers tapping lightly on the folder in front of him as he readies for his final curtain. The whole closing speech is in there, but he won't refer to it. He won't need to. No one needs notes for this.

The words, when they start, land like cloudburst. She can't stop it, she knows that. Nothing can ever stop a storm; a case of unimaginable evil, predicated on a sickening argument that the state had no choice but to turn a blind eye, trading the sanctity of our judicial system and the objectivity of our press for the continued superiority of our defence forces. And at the heart of it all, betrayed children, betrayed by the worst of the so-called civilised society into which they had the misfortune to be born. Incontrovertible evidence, from the victims, the collaborators, the co-conspirators. Shame on us all. Absolute shame.

There's a collective breath as the prosecution rests, the bright block-colour jackets of the media fidgeting on the press bench below like primary school children at assembly. She smiles the briefest of smiles as she notes Dominic and Laurie jostling over the most central position of all, before remembering Jemima will

also be somewhere nearby. Disgraced or not, she'll need her own closure. She was a victim too. Only full possession of the facts makes for a true collaborator.

Just for that split second, she finds herself wondering if Ma's also listening. Whether she's come far enough that she wants to see the house of cards finally come down for herself. And she affords another moment to the man she now accepts was her father. Could he honestly have known who they were to him? Was his own flesh and blood worth so little in the case for national security at all costs? As the defence rises, the stiff curls of the barrister's wig leer sickly yellow in the daylight flooding in from the skylight overhead. But she's strangely heartened, remembering this is the only court with a glass ceiling, with a view of the sky. She no longer needs to fathom the answers to these questions. All she need do next is watch the birds as they fly away.

And so it begins again. The war that had to be won. The intelligence that could only be overseen by one general. The crowd fidgets and jeers, the idea that the untouchable British army might only have one general able enough as preposterous now as it was then. The sanctity of the defence forces. The lack of funds, of oversight, of understanding of the pressures of the battlefield. The overwhelming pressures of duty, of living to serve.

She drifts with the birds, eyes travelling over the screen reserved for the most violated of witnesses, where countless children will have had to sit. A sharp intake of breath as she wonders – could *she* be here today too? And would she recognise her if she were? Even she couldn't put a name to the face she once knew so well. But the tension leaves her as a bird loops a lazy curl in the sky. She remembers this is bringing Kayleigh her own closure, too.

She stands as the defence rests, edging her way through the crowd jammed into the gallery. She doesn't need to stay for the final word. She knows what it will be. It's the only possible word that's left: guilty. Years of lies absorbed in a single breath, a single pronouncement. But that's what everyone else is waiting for. That's

not what this is about for her. She feels it in every corner she turns, in every step she takes through the winding corridors of centuries-old justice. This is about finally turning the page. Finally being in charge of her own script, and beginning her own story, knowing nothing and no one has been abandoned as she takes yet another first step.

The clouds roil overhead as she pauses on the pavement outside, unbuttoning her collar to better feel the incoming breeze. Cables slap as television cameras ready, paving stones glimmer as lights flicker on, for the media storm is seconds away, clamouring to amplify the verdict the country needs to hear. A nearby kiosk bulges with newspapers, headlines screaming to her from another life, their pages flapping as the January wind whips into a gale, sky suddenly quilting to grey and black.

And so the crowds begin to gather, clustering for information, no one's interest idle, everyone's breath baited.

Except there is a girl. And the girl is me, the only one walking away with purpose, with everything I need to finally move on.

I smile as the clouds groan with relief, rain falling like tears. And I spot Julie, walking towards me with a thick envelope under her arm, frizzy hair unbowed by the shower. I pause as we meet, silently taking it from her outstretched hand. She doesn't need to tell me what it is. It's the only kind of information that ever comes in these envelopes.

'I knew I'd find you here,' she breathes, so soft I can barely hear her, except I don't need to. 'I just wanted to let you know. I've finally found her, too.'

My finger trembles as I peep inside the file, thick with photographs, crackling with promise. And I find hope, immortalised in the faint lines around the corners of water-blue eyes. The unmistakable mark of survival; the mark of a tentative, incoming smile.

Acknowledgements

For some it only takes a village. For me it took a veritable metropolis.

Thank you first and foremost to the most courageous of agents and formidable of publishers, Jon Wood and Karen Sullivan. You both took a chance on a debut author trying to handle the most harrowing of subject matters and never once turned away. I could not have imagined a better home for *The Source* than Orenda, a publishing house with a heart that dwarfs the entire industry. This book is forever in your debt.

To Fanny Blake, without whose introductions, encouragement and inestimable editorial input *The Source* would have languished forever as a Word document. Similarly to Rupert Wallis, Midge Gillies, Sarah Burton and the whole crew at Madingley Hall. Thank you for the guidance, the laughs, the late-night 'workshops' and, of course, all the new vocabulary. I owe the class of 2019 so much more than just a Masters in creative writing.

To Tony Maddox, Mike McCarthy, Geoff Hill, and the incomparable Deborah Rayner. Thank you for lifting me up and making the ceiling disappear, again and again. Laurie Scott and Olivia Guy are pale reflections of the differences you have all made to so many. To Nic Robertson, Nick Paton Walsh and Richard Quest, without whom I could never have dreamt up Dominic Greene. Just remember you can always blame his less attractive characteristics on each other. And to the rest of Team CNN, the ultimate tribe – the friends that became family, the stories that became history, the memories that became legend. The world needs journalists like you.

To my first readers – Ben Blake, Jonny Sultoon, Michelle Jacobs, Noa Bladon, Tim Lister, Jamie Crichton and Geoff Hill (again)

for all the invaluable feedback. Similarly to Louise Sutton, Jack Ford, Jo Spain and the team at Lime Pictures. You got behind the story like it was your own and enhanced it beyond measure.

To Ruth Field, the mentor to end all mentors. I will never know what I did to deserve the Grit Doctor herself on my side. Thank you for the warmest of friendships, the most deranged of laughs, the grittiest of gritty encouragement.

And to my cherished family: Mum, Dad, Ben, Oli, Liora, Guy and Trixie. I am nothing without your love, belief, encouragement, support, and forgiveness.

Lastly to the victims. I have visualised your pain, I have imagined your suffering. It still feels wrong that I have appropriated your experience when I should have tried to do something more material about it. But when the facts themselves are under attack, the medium of fiction is a powerful tool. I hope you can see it is all in pursuit of the truth. And I hope I have done it justice.